The Dreamer

By J.R. Zimmer

Book Six

Fisher/Lafayette Saga

Badlanders Press

The Dreamer

©2020 by Janette Walker

ISBN 9781737626930

Cover design by Janette Walker
With Daniela Brinkmeyer

Fisher/Lafayette Saga

If There Hadn't Been You

Now and Forever

Someone Like You

Spitfire

Something Magical

The Dreamer

Eagle's Wolf

Coming Home (Free Ebook when signing up for my newsletter at www.jrzimmer.com. Not available anywhere else.)

You can find J.R. Zimmer at:

Web site: www.jrzimmer.com

Facebook: www.facebook.com/jrzimmer.author
Email: jrzimmer17@yahoo.com

For every dreamer out there and yes,
that means you!

The Dreamer
by J.R. Zimmer

Chapter One

May 1991
North Dakota

"Damn," she said, glaring at the computer screen. She'd just had the perfect dialogue pop into her head, and it fizzled before she could type it out because of the untimely interruption of the doorbell ringing.

"Damn it." Issuing a heavy sigh, Anastasia pushed the chair away from the desk as the doorbell sounded twice more. Apparently, whoever was outside was determined and not going away.

Briefly, before rising, she contemplated murdering the person responsible for this unwanted disruption.

It had taken her over thirty days to painstakingly work out the plot for the story she was writing. And now, just as the whole thing had come together, complete with the amazing opening sentence she'd crafted, some blockhead disrupted her creative moment.

"Damn it to hell."

Usually, Anastasia looked forward to a visit; they happened so seldom. People in this small community were afraid of being caught in her tiny house should her ex-husband show up. So naturally, it thrilled her that someone gathered enough courage to stop by. She just wished the person's backbone hadn't arisen at this particular moment.

"I'm coming!" she called out as she made her way through the tiny living room of her two-bedroom house. The moment she unlocked and opened the front door, a smile quickly replaced the frown on her face. "Gale!" she exclaimed with a laugh, then teased. "Good thing it's you. Anyone else would have been dead about now."

1

Gale Martin let out a very unladylike snort as she carried her bulk through the open doorway. "Let me guess. You're daydreaming again." Stopping in the middle of the small living room, she turned to face the twenty-four-year-old. "Honestly, Stasia. When are you going to get your head out of the clouds and become a member of the real world?"

With a roll of sky-blue eyes, Anastasia closed the door and locked it. "We've had this conversation countless times," she reminded her best friend. "You know how important writing is for me." She eyed the short, plump woman suspiciously. "Are you having PMS?"

Gale's mouth dropped open upon hearing that unexpected question, regardless of the fact she should be used to Anastasia's strange humor by now. "All right," she sighed, knowing there was no point continuing the conversation regarding Anastasia's fantasizing, "you win. And no. I do not have PMS, thank you." She settled her bulk onto the nearby sofa and ignored the groaning sound it made as it fought to accommodate her size. "However, since you haven't denied it, I will assume you were writing some tale or other and forgot what day it is." Seeing the puzzled expression cross Anastasia's delicate features, she held out the thick catalog she carried into the house with her. "Shopping day. Remember? You were going to help me pick out some new clothes."

Gale loved Anastasia as though she were her own daughter. However, that did not prevent her from secretly wishing she could have the younger woman's figure and looks. Good Lord. Anastasia would be attractive in just about anything. Including a gunny sack with cow manure stuck to it, she concluded, feeling a prick of jealousy sweep through her. But then she reminded herself that Anastasia's beauty had not guaranteed her a life filled with sunshine and happiness.

It totally slipped Anastasia's mind. Crap. Shopping day. How had she forgotten she agreed to have Gale come over today to spend time together?

"I'm sorry, Gale," Anastasia apologized, feeling guilt make its way to her heart. She hadn't meant to forget her promise to the woman who

was ten years older than herself. Especially when the woman's husband had probably saved her life a little more than a year ago, and the bond between the Martins and herself was worth more than anything to her.

"I can leave," Gale prompted, knowing Anastasia's writing was a therapeutic hobby. It was something she'd always enjoyed doing. But after what Anastasia endured over a year ago, it became a relaxation and kept her focused. It allowed her to switch off her mind every now and again whenever she began thinking about her ex-husband and the monster he'd become.

"Don't be ridiculous!" Anastasia gasped. "You mean the world to me. You and Jeff should know that." She crossed her arms under her ample breasts. "It isn't as though I can't continue my writing later and," she narrowed her eyes, "I don't want you to ever think you're not welcome. Understand?"

She met the woman's eyes and caught Gale's nod. "Good," Anastasia said, then walked into the spare bedroom, converted into an office, and turned off her computer. Moments later, after stopping in the kitchen to allow her poodle back inside the house through the back door, she returned to the living room.

"Now," Anastasia said, her voice filled with confidence as she extracted the magazine from Gale's hand, "Let's see what's hot for the fall season."

Gale watched Anastasia gracefully slide into the black vinyl recliner, placed a short distance from the couch, and begin paging through the home shopping publication. Grace and beauty. Gale sighed. There should be a law against having both. "So, what are you writing this time? Something about the woes of being a hairstylist and having to work with John Q. Public? Or did you begin that novel you've been talking about writing?"

Without glancing up from the page she stopped on, Anastasia laughed. "Now, that's an idea. Maybe I should write a book about hairdresser blues."

She looked back to the magazine, slowly paging through the women's clothing section.

A brief silence followed before Anastasia looked back at Gale. Her eyes twinkled as she revealed, "I heard from Redbook." She wiggled her light brown subtle brows. "Of course," she sighed wishfully, "you wouldn't want to know what they had to say." She averted her attention back to the wish book before the smile she was holding at bay got the better of her. She knew Gale's scolding of her daydreaming did not reflect the woman's interest in her writing.

"Well, for pity's sake, Stasia. Don't keep me in suspense!"

Giggling, Anastasia met the woman's eager eyes. "I won!" she cried. No longer able to contain her delight, she moved from the chair to dance circles about the small room. "Can you believe it? After months of entering writing contests, I've won!" She doubted if anyone in the world had ever experienced the amount of joy as she had when she received the congratulation letter from the magazine. And the hundred-dollar check awarded to the first-place winner of their short story contest. "They're going to publish the story in next year's January issue!" Reclaiming her place in the recliner, her face beaming as though she were a child who just received a pony for Christmas, she continued on zealously. "See, Gale. I told you. One of these days, I'm going to make it big. One of these days, it's going to be goodbye New Salem; hello Hollywood." A content smile formed on her face as she leaned back in the chair. "Yep. One of these days, I can close that beauty salon of mine and do what I love most and, best of all, get paid for it!" Her eyes took on a dreamy, faraway look. "One day, I'll join the ranks as a best-selling romance author. Just wait and see."

"Oh, Stasia, I'm so proud of you! I can't wait to see the story in print. But honey, you know not everyone becomes a best-selling author."

Hurt replaced Anastasia's joy. "You don't think I can do it?" she asked, feeling as though someone threw cold water on her. She knew

the odds of a publishing house accepting her manuscript were astronomical, but that did not mean she had to give up her dream.

Gale softened her voice. "Listen, sweetie. I don't doubt for one minute you could be a best-selling author. You have the talent. Obviously, Redbook thinks so, too. But I just can't understand why you write stories of romance. Ever since Danny-" she broke off, shaking her head sadly. "You never act as though you want anything to do with men. You don't date. All you do is come home from work and lock yourself away in there," she pointed to Anastasia's office door, "and write. And the only man I've ever heard you talk about is that guy who happens to be almost every woman's impossible fantasy-"

"You should know by now that Danny is the reason I enjoy writing romances," Anastasia snapped, cutting Gale off. "Just because my ex-husband turned into a psychopath after his discharge from the Marines doesn't mean I have anything against men and romance." She sighed. "As far as dating, you know that's complicated. No guy in their right mind from around here would risk looking my way. Court orders or not, Danny still thinks I belong to him!" She bit her lip; forced back the tears. "For the time being, I'm stuck in this two-bit town. I can't change that instantly, but I am working on it. Writing romances keeps my hopes up. Can't you see that? Through them, I can escape Danny anytime and find a hero to take me away from here."

"I'm sorry, Stasia," Gale told her gently. "I didn't mean to upset you. Sometimes my mouth gets ahead of my brain."

"My stories keep me happy," Anastasia whispered. "And it helps to express my emotions through the characters I create. At least I no longer blame myself for Danny's choices. It was not my fault his personality changed once they released him from the military hospital, and they sent him home to me."

Gale stood up, reached out, and stroked Anastasia's arm to soothe her. "You did what you could for him, honey."

Anastasia nodded, then sighed. "I just wish I'd given up on him before he put me in the hospital."

Gale remained silent, as she didn't know what to say.

"At least during the short time Danny was in jail, the judge had no problem putting his signature on the divorce papers." Anastasia continued. "That was a silver lining since Danny was refusing the divorce."

Taking a deep breath, she pushed the unpleasant memory from her mind. Although Danny didn't seem to understand why she didn't want him around, it was in her past. Thankfully, his family convinced him to move to Minot. That, at least, put over a hundred miles between them. Unless he'd gotten drunk and came to New Salem. It was never a pleasant experience for the town, or her, when that happened.

"I'm going to continue to pray for you," Gale vowed. "I know the good Lord will bless you one day because of your suffering."

Though not religious herself, Anastasia thanked her, knowing Gale's faith demanded she beseech her god on someone's behalf. Besides, she was not opposed to the universe giving her a break for a change.

Anastasia waved her hand in the air as though trying to erase the conversation about her failed two-year marriage. "That's enough of that. Time to move forward, and besides, you're here to shop." She reclaimed the magazine from where she tossed it on the floor when she told Gale about her contest win. Flipping through the colorful pages, she stopped on the section containing men's fashions.

One page caught her eye, and she stopped on it when a silly idea formed in her mind unexpectedly. Pointing to the attractive male modeling a western shirt, she giggled and asked, "Think I could order him?"

Gale paled. "What?"

"You heard me. I think I'll just order that knight of mine from this here magazine."

Maybe she was joking.

Gale hoped she wasn't being serious. However, just in case, she tried to sidetrack her by saying, "Fine. You just go ahead and do that, young lady. I just didn't know you were fickle."

"Fickle?" Anastasia's brows drew together in her confusion.

"Yes. Fickle." Gale pointed to the calendar hanging on the wall next to the recliner. "All this time, since he's the only one you ever talk about, I thought you had your sights set on him."

Anastasia's eyes followed the direction of Gale's finger to the calendar on display. Her soft blue eyes met the unique cat green depths of the man whose likeness stared back at her from the image.

His name was Mason Lafayette. Actually, Mason Richard Fernando Antoine Albert Lafayette, to be precise though she could not remember when or how she'd found that out.

Regardless of it only being a photo, she sighed dreamily. The man definitely had an aura of sex appeal about him. It certainly drew her eye the first time she saw his image on the cover of a popular magazine that showcased the rich and famous last year.

Anastasia knew she would never forget the first time she saw him. She had been browsing at one of the bookstores in the Kirkwood Mall in Bismarck when she walked past the magazine rack. His handsome face was displayed on the cover for Hollywood Now!, and those uncanny green eyes of his, framed by masculine dark brows, drew her in. When she picked up the publication for a closer look, to determine whether she imagined the color of those eyes or if a photographer's trick caused them to appear like that, she felt as though she connected with him.

She knew if she told anyone that they would say she was being ridiculous. Or was crazy. Or both.

But she purchased the magazine, read the article, and wondered if there was more to Mason Lafayette than what the reporter revealed.

Not that she became obsessed over the man. She might have joined his fan club, but she limited the amount of information she read about him. She knew that articles were written to sell the publications and did not necessarily reflect who the man was deep within his soul.

Realizing Gale was staring at her, she broke the spell she'd fallen under when she'd looked at the calendar. "Yes, well…" she cleared her throat, feeling stupid for having just lusted over Mason's facsimile. "You're the one who said I need to face reality. Considering there are at least fifteen to twenty thousand women in the United States alone swooning over him, I doubt he would notice me. Which, mind you, is less likely to happen than a kangaroo trampling through my flower garden." Mason Lafayette in New Salem, North Dakota. Right. As if that could happen. "Now, here's a guy," she tapped the page of the shopping magazine with the back of her hand, "who isn't too bad. Granted, he's not Mason," not by a long shot, "But still…" She turned the pages until she found one of the two order blanks. "I'm going to do it," she declared, beaming.

"You're not!" Gale gasped, staring at Anastasia's Cheshire cat grin and knowing, from experience, that that particular grin said she would.

"Yes, I am," Anastasia confirmed without pause. Picking up the ink pen lying on the end table, she filled out the information the order form requested. Under the place marked description, she wrote, the guy on page eighty-five, and send him quick.

Looking up, she caught sight of the look of complete disbelief on Gale's round face and broke into a fit of laughter. "Oh, come on, Gale. It will be harmless fun! What's the worst that can happen? The company will just send back my check," I'll have to be sure to add the shipping and handling charges, she thought to herself and giggled. "Maybe they will add a note telling me they're out of stock. Or he's backordered!"

That possibility amused her more than Gale's stricken expression, and she broke into another round of laughter.

Gale found nothing amusing about this hair-brained idea, and she watched open mouthed as Anastasia moved to her office to retrieve her checkbook.

"I wonder," Anastasia pondered out loud as she returned to the living room- Gale was still sitting there, staring wide-eyed- "Do you think the four to six-week delivery will still apply? Since this is the end of May, there's a good chance he could be here before Christmas."

"You are being serious!" Gale blustered, coming out from her daze.

"Of course I am. Why not?" She wrote out the check, using the magazine's price for the shirt the man was modeling as the ballpark figure and ripped the check from the register. "Who knows?" she laughed, waving the check in front of a very ashen looking Gale, "I might have come up with a new merchandising idea for this company. "You've heard of find-a-friend. Why not, Male-Order-Guys?" She placed the check and form into the envelope and licked it shut.

"But... you can't..."

"Oh, Pooh!" Anastasia said, "Who's to say what will happen? If it works out, they just may thank me."

"You're more likely to get a free trip to the loony farm," Gale predicted.

Anastasia chuckled. "Where's your sense of adventure, my dear? Doesn't your bible say you have not because you ask not? Well, I'm just asking. No harm done. Besides, it will no doubt give those poor people in the order department something to chuckle over."

"I don't know about this." The doubt was plain in Gale's voice. "If I hadn't thought you had done some crazy things before, I do now. This has got to be one of the strangest stunts you've ever pulled."

"Stranger than the time I showed your six-year-old how to play walrus with straws at the café?"

Gale's eyes widened at the memory. "The place was packed! Twenty-five-year-old's do not go around putting straws between their lip and teeth as though they were tusks, cross their arms, and make seal sounds in the center of a public place!"

"Pattie liked it."

"Six-year-olds don't know any better! They don't know when an adult is crazy."

Patting the woman's arm, Anastasia grinned. "I'm not crazy, Gale. I'm a dreamer."

Chapter Two

Five weeks later
The end of June

Carol Gibson didn't knock. She never did.

She stood for a moment in the doorway connecting the two luxurious hotel suites, looking for the man she pretended to adore, and found him standing next to the enormous bed. Her eyes narrowed when she saw the suitcase. He was busy filling it with clothing. "What are you doing?" she asked tersely.

He didn't respond. What he was doing was so obvious the question didn't deserve an answer.

He reached for a pair of black silk-cotton trousers, folded them, and placed them with the other clothing already in the last of his third piece of luggage.

His silence should have told her he wasn't in the mood to talk. But no one ever accused Carol Gibson of knowing when to shut up. "I asked you a question," she snapped, closing the distance between them with quick steps. "What in the hell are you doing?!"

All right, he allowed. Perhaps she is dumber than I thought. "*Emballage*," he answered, bracing for the explosion his answer would bring.

It didn't come. Not right away, and only because Carol didn't speak French, and he hadn't realized he hadn't spoken English. As soon as the matter was cleared up, the blond-bomb exploded.

11

"Packing!" Carol screeched, grabbing his arm to still its labor. "What for? The plane does not leave until tomorrow, and I thought we could-"

"I am not taking the plane," he interrupted. His voice was tense. He tore his arm from her grip, grabbed the white silk shirt lying on the bed, and shoved it into the bag without caring that it would be quite wrinkled by the time it was unpacked.

He refused to look at her. If he did, he just might strangle her. He was that angry.

"But you have too!"

This time, he faced her.

Carol wished he hadn't. She had never seen him this furious, and the rigid set of his jaw told her his anger was directed at her. She just wasn't sure what had set him off. Unless he had found out about- No. He couldn't have. She was always discreet, knowing how insistent he was about remaining faithful to one another, regardless of the fact there was no love lost between them. The only thing they shared was sex, and although he was a superb lover, the only reason she was involved with him was to advance her career.

But if that icy stare was any sign, he was thinking about strangling her. Or worse. He was going to end their relationship, and it was too soon for that to happen. There was still so much more she wanted to get.

It was too bad she didn't love him. He was handsome. That was unde-niable. His face could cause the Greek gods to weep with jealousy. But she had her own goals, and being stuck with a man wanted by practically every woman in the country just wasn't for her. Especially when she wanted all the attention for herself. She absolutely loathed the fact that no one paid attention to her whenever she was with him.

"You have too," she repeated, softening her voice to a seductive purr as she reached out to trail a long red fingernail down the front of the dark green silk shirt covering his broad chest. She needed to cool his

anger, and playing on the man's sexual drive would do the trick. It always did.

Well, usually it did. It just didn't this time.

He knocked her hand away with one angry swipe. "I," he gritted, placing his palm over his chest, "do not have to do anything unless I want to, Carol."

He wished he hadn't looked at her. His anger increased tenfold. God. He was honestly beginning to hate beautiful women, and Carol Gibson was undoubtedly beautiful.

The fact he'd brought this on himself, asking her to be his lover, was irrelevant. He should have known she wouldn't be faithful to him. They never were. Not that he gave a damn about her or any of his previous lovers. He had a healthy sex drive and preferred staying with one person rather than risk contracting some disease. All he asked for in return was for them not to be with anyone else, and he did not believe his request was outrageous by any means. Especially when he helped advance their careers as part of the deal.

Carol stared. "But the promotion-"

"Ended this afternoon," he finished for her. "My television appearances are not scheduled to begin for another three weeks, and before they do, I am taking two weeks' downtime." He scowled. "And why in the hell am I telling you?!" He turned back to his packing. "That time does not include you, *pute*."

It wasn't an endearment.

"You're leaving me!" she exclaimed, eyes wide from shock as the reality of what he was doing hit her full force.

His green eyes raked over her captivating features. "Get out of my room, Carol." His voice was sharp as steel. "And do not let the door hit you in the-"

The slap to his face cut off the snide remark.

13

He rubbed his jaw briefly before saying off-handedly, "By the way. You are fired. Both as my lover and from Citnamor Books." He turned, closing the suitcase as though doing so signaled the end of this conversation.

"You bastard!" she spat, glaring. Then a smug smile spread across her face, twisting its beauty into a reflection of the person she was. Cold and cynical. "You cannot fire me, Mason," she told him sweetly, folding slender arms across her small breasts. He could dismiss her as his lover but, "I am Citnamor Books leading lady cover model."

Silence. He carried the bag to the door as though he wasn't aware she was still in the room.

"Did you hear what I said, Mason?" she asked with a voice filled with confidence. "No matter what, I'll always be around." That little reminder should take the starch right out of him.

It didn't.

In fact, when he stopped in mid-stride to glance at her over his shoulder, the grin on his ruggedly handsome face told her she would not like what he was about to say. And the way he casually brushed back that longer than his shoulders, black hair of his away from his face only confirmed her suspicion that he knew something she didn't.

"You are only Citnamor's leading lady as long as I say you are." He dropped the suitcase with a solid thud before turning to face her once more. "Remember, baby? I am their main man. I am the one in demand. My face and body are on those covers, selling their books ten times faster than they used to move. The women who buy them could not care less who was on the damn cover with me, although I am sure they would prefer it to be themselves." He returned the smug smile. Hers was fading rather quickly. "The contract I have with Citnamor Books gives me full say on who I work with." He thumped his chest with his hand. "It is my name everyone is chanting. It is me everyone wants. Therefore, Citnamor Books, because they do not want to risk losing me to some other

publishing house, has agreed to fire you at my request." He smiled, and it wasn't pretty.

She paled ghost white. Her mind was reeling as she frantically tried to think of a solution to this unexpected turn of events. "But Mason -I love you!"

Quick thinking. Just not overly original.

He laughed with mirth. "Oh, that is rich," he sneered, crossing the room with bold, powerful strides. His tall frame loomed over her, and the darkening of his green eyes warned her he was boiling mad now if he hadn't been before. "You do not love me, baby. You love my fame. You love my wealth and the fact I was foolish enough to convince Citnamor Books to sign you on as a model last year. But most of all, you love this," he touched his groin briefly.

He anticipated the second slap. He caught her wrist in a vice-like grip. Lowering his face within inches of hers, he asked innocently, "What is wrong, baby? Did I strike a nerve?" He released her so suddenly, she stumbled back of her own accord. "Do not bother denying it, Carol. I have the names of six men in this hotel who will attest to what you like."

Her already pale face just went whiter. "How- How did you know?"

His smile was all teeth. "I did not," he confessed, though was amused with the fact she condemned herself.

"Bastard!" she shrieked.

He grabbed her arm. "I believe you already said that." He pulled her toward the door leading to the hotel hallway, stopping only long enough to lock and re-close the connecting door from his side before continuing across the room. With one quick motion, he opened the main door and shoved her out. "*Au revor*, Carol."

The force he used to close the door shook the walls.

Let her worry about the fact she was now standing in the hotel's hall without a key to her room. Nor wearing anything more than a sheer slip.

He ignored the pounding and vile language coming through the door.

He could not believe how wonderful it felt to have thrown her out. He should have done it long ago, and he vowed that it was going to be a long, long time before he took up with anyone again. Once he did, he would make sure the woman was ugly enough that no other man would have her!

He grimmest. Well, maybe not that ugly.

Pushing himself away from the door, he moved to the phone setting alongside the bed on the nightstand. With a few weeks of free time on his hands, he was considering flying to Paris. He had not seen his parents and younger sister since Christmas almost seven months ago.

He would have preferred to make the visit a surprise, but his parents' work schedule was almost as hectic as his Not calling first would be foolhardy. There was always the possibility they weren't in Paris but at some location filming another of his mother's movies.

He smiled to himself as the overseas operator placed the call. Sharing his mother with all of France had not been easy as a young child. She was the country's most beloved actress. Any film both Rosalinda and Charles Lafayette had a hand in making was always a major success.

The overseas connection was completed, and after the phone rang four times, the Lafayette's butler picked up. Mason could not help but tease the old man. The butler had a fit if a phone sounded more than twice. "Heath, you old goat. You are slowing down. I can hardly believe you allowed that third ring."

"Monsieur Mason!" the old goat exclaimed, chuckling. "It is good to hear your voice! And do not tease. I do my best. They should give me better help than these lazy servants your parents hire! Perhaps I should quit. Then we shall see who laughs at whom."

"You have been saying that since before I was born," Mason laughed.

"Ah, but perhaps I mean it this time!"

Mason laughed at the outrageous claim. The old man was hot air without steam. "Is my family there?" he asked.

"*Non, monsieur*," Heath informed him sadly. "It is too bad, *oui*? our mother will be sad she missed your phone call. She misses her little boy."

Mason hid his disappointment for not finding his parents at home by chuckling. "Heath. You must stop calling me mother's little boy. I am twenty-six years old!"

"Ah, but to me, you will always be little."

"Is mother on location? I have some time off, and I was thinking about coming home."

"You did not receive your mother's letter?" Heath tisked. "The three of you. Always busy, busy. All the time, working. I am surprised you still know each other's names."

"What letter?" Mason asked, though not surprised he had not received it. Heath was right. Ever since his own career of becoming one of America's hottest male media personalities five years ago, staying in touch with his family had become next to impossible.

"Your parents and sister have gone to America!" Heath exclaimed. "They are visiting the Fishers in that godforsaken North Dakota, again. It is the annual Fisher/Lafayette reunion. This year it is taking place at the Fisher's summer home on the shores of Lake Sacajawea."

Mason sat down, heart pounding with excitement. The reunion! He had not been to one in years.

He couldn't believe his luck. This leg of the promotion, comprising of visiting bookstores and Malls to promote Citnamor Books romantic tales, had ended in Billings, Montana, North Dakota's next-door neighbor.

He'd made up his mind before the old butler told him the one thing that would have sent him down the road, no matter how far away he was.

"*Monsieur* Hunter, that demon, is expected to attend."

Mason sat up straight, disregarding Heath's comment about Hunter being a demon. The poor man had never forgiven Hunter, then ten years old, for tying him up, then suspending him from the roof of the Lafayette mansion. "Hunter! *Merci*, Heath."

He hung up without a goodbye, too thrilled with the thought of seeing his childhood best friend to bother with formalities. Something he'd been looking for recently was a diversion from his always hectic schedule, and Hunter Sundance Fisher was the perfect choice. The man was a born hellion. He had spent two years as a Navy SEAL before joining a secret task force headed up by a man all the Fisher children, as well as Mason and his sister, considered an uncle. The United States government used Task Force Ghost for troubleshooting acts of terrorism or other activities that required quiet but effective means of elimination.

Mason threw himself back onto the bed, arms spread out, as laughter erupted deep within his chest. To hell with Carol Gibson. To hell with the whole world's population of women, for that matter. He was going to have a glorious two weeks of not having to put up with every female he came in contact with swooning at his feet. Or pinching his ass and always, without question, wanting him for a quick fuck.

It sure as hell was going to feel marvelous to be treated like a human being instead of a piece of meat for a change.

Chapter Three

He should have taken the plane.

The Corvette was brand new.

Well, that's what the man at the car rental place claimed, and since Mason knew Corvette's, as he owned several, he knew this one was indeed this year's model.

Last night he decided to have a vacation away from his adoring public. What better way for a person to get total solitude than by driving over four hundred miles alone? He had thought the idea was perfect—no screaming women trying to tear at his shirt, pawing his body, and asking for autographs. Blissful peace. Something he hadn't had in ages. That was what prompted him to rent the vehicle. And since it was a brand-new Vette, there should be nothing wrong with it.

But there was. The fact that it was now sitting on the shoulder of North Dakota's Interstate 94 with black smoke hissing from its hood attested to that.

He should have taken the plane.

"I will kill the son-of-a-bitch," he vowed, hitting the dashboard with his fist; surprised the vinyl hadn't cracked from the impact.

His tall, six-foot two-inch frame emerged from the small red sports car. A passing motorist witnessed him use his index finger as a fake gun to shoot the disabled vehicle.

Sweeping his blue-black hair away from his forehead, he leaned against the door. Crossing his arms over his broad chest, he told himself not to give in to the childish urge to take out his frustration by jumping up and down on the blessed hood.

The scowl on his face was the only reason the next motorist kept on going down the highway instead of stopping to help him out of this pickle.

His head turned left; green eyes scanning the direction he came from. In his mind, several murder plots played out as he remembered the sales associate who rented him this useless piece of fiberglass.

"I will kill him," he repeated and turned his head to the right. There wasn't anything to see in that direction, except for the ominous black clouds slowly moving toward him from the south.

He was in the middle of nowhere. Soon to be drenched, give, or take an hour, and miles and miles of gentle rolling hills lay in both directions, with only the highway he was standing on to keep him company.

God alone knew where the next town was because he hadn't a clue. It had been years since he'd been to this state. Far too long for him to remember if there was any place between here and Bismarck where he could get service, had he a means of calling for help. Which he didn't. Which made his scowl deepen all the more.

Oui. He should have taken the plane.

Issuing a heavy sigh, he tore off his shirt, balled it up, and threw it into the vehicle. There may very well be storm clouds far in the distance, but the muggy heat on this July first day was almost suffocating.

Leaning back again on the car, a devilish grin formed on his handsome face as he decided to tell Hunter the dishonest car dealers' name. That would guarantee the crook's demise.

But first, he needed to get off this highway.

There was a lot to be said for cellular phones. The most important one being, never travel into unknown territory without installing one first.

Well. Unknown wasn't precisely the right word. He'd been to North Dakota countless times as a child, so the flat plains weren't new to him. It was the delay in reaching his destination, causing his impatience.

That, along with the fact he hadn't been in wide-open spaces alone with himself in far too long to remember.

Now, standing on this highway, long-forgotten memories began flashing through his mind.

He remembered with clarity the day he found out the man he'd believed was his father wasn't blood related. He remembered the heartache and the horror of discovering the truth about his conception. It was why he lived with the Fishers, here in this state, for a year. Away from France and the hounding press.

For a moment, Mason closed his eyes, remembering that day. The day of his fifteenth birthday. He celebrated with friends and lost his virginity to a woman in her thirties. She'd been a beautiful woman, and he'd hit puberty at age fourteen. For a year, his hormones kept his body in a constant state of arousal, so when the woman, one of the boy's mothers, pulled him into her bedroom, he'd been more than willing to drop his pants. It hadn't mattered to him how old the woman was. She'd wanted him, he'd wanted sex, and it had been glorious.

That night, when he arrived home after midnight and climbed the stairs leading to his bedroom, he heard his mother crying behind the closed door as he passed it. It was unusual for his mother to cry those heart-wrenching sobs, and they drew him to stand outside of the door and listen to the conversation coming from within.

"I cannot tell him!" Rosalinda exclaimed, her voice breaking. "It will devastate him!"

"I do not want to do it any more than you do!" He heard his father's voice exclaim. "But we have no choice! If there were any way to continue to deny the truth, I would do so! But Mason is maturing, and every day he looks more and more like Pierre."

Muffled sobs came through the door then, but Mason could not be sure if that was because perhaps his father was holding his mother and she was crying into his chest, or if the sudden beating of his own heart

caused a rush of pressure to his ears that dulled out everything around him.

"You know I never wanted this," his father said, and his voice too was choked with emotion.

His father. But not his father.

Before Mason realized it, he'd slammed open the door to confront them. His own tears were flowing down his face as he cried out, "Tell me you are only rehearsing a script!" he begged as he stood looking at the look of horror on their faces because he'd overheard them.

But it hadn't been a script for one of their movies. It was true, and as they sat him down and tried to gently explain whose son he was and how he'd been conceived, he died inside because of that knowledge.

God, after all these years, the ache lay under the surface. Over time, he was able to once again see Charles as the father he always believed him to be. But sometimes the hurt liked to taunt him.

But they faced the rumors that abounded about his parentage. And gave him a choice to face reporters with them or travel outside of the country to live with the Fisher's for a year while his broken heart would be far away from the gossips.

He chose to come here. To North Dakota and live on the Fisher's ranch south of Medora.

His mother waited until after he left the country to hold the press conference to announce that yes, the speculations were correct. Her husband had not fathered Mason, though she refused to acknowledge who the biological parent was. However, anyone who remembered Rosalinda's kidnapping could easily guess Mason's biological father was a known criminal.

A monster.

Until the press conference, only a handful of people knew the truth about Rosalinda's pregnancy. Two of those people being Colten and Jacqueline Fisher, Hunter's parents.

Mason did not want to have those painful thoughts play through his mind and forced himself to remember the good times he'd had that year while on the Fisher's ranch.

The friendship he had with Hunter grew stronger, though, to this day, it boggled everyone's mind how the two of them could be best friends when they were polar opposites. Where Hunter lacked patience, Mason could let things slide past him without care.

Except for now. At this moment. With the Corvette's radiator laughing at him as it hissed black smoke out from under the car's hood.

The sound of an approaching motor brought Mason's head to the left in time to watch a white Ford pickup slowing down, then come to a stop behind the crippled Vette.

Thank the gods, Mason thought as he pushed himself away from the car door, and walked toward the pickup as he allowed the painful past to roll away to where it belonged.

It was history.

Surprisingly, once he arrived back in France that year, the country embraced him and, to this day, did not talk about Mason not being Charles Lafayette's biological son.

Something that here in America was not readily known, although once in a while, some reporter interviewing him would try to question him about it. It rarely happened, however. Word got around in those early days of his career that Mason would stop the interview and walk off the set when asked about that part of his life.

He established unspoken ground rules with the media. If they wanted an interview with him, they'd refrain from asking questions about his conception.

"Need a tow, son?" the older man asked. Opening the door of the truck, the man stepped out onto the blacktop.

"*Oui!*" Mason grinned, his mood improving immensely now that it appeared as though he was going to get off this highway. He would no longer be alone with his memories. Extending his hand, he said, "I would appreciate it. *Merci.*"

One of the man's bushy gray brows rose. "You aren't from around these parts," he drawled, taking in the size of the younger man. "That's a rich accent you've got there, boy." He took the offered hand, giving it a firm shake. "What the devil is it?"

"French."

The man chuckled. "Well, if that don't beat all! Didn't think I'd ever see the day I would meet one of them foreigners." He elbowed Mason in the ribs. "Bet them women swoon over it." He winked.

Mason laughed. "*Oui!* They do." If the man knew how close to the truth that statement was, he would probably go into shock.

"Name's Henry." He reached into the truck box for a tow-chain. "Yours would be?"

"Lafayette. Mason Lafayette."

Henry snickered. "Any relation to that pirate fellow from days gone by? Jean Lafitte, weren't it?"

Mason had heard the joke more times than he cared to remember. However, he could never comprehend why people could not understand the difference between Lafayette, pronounced La - fee- et, and Lafitte, which was pronounced La-Feet.

"Not that I am aware of," Mason answered Henry's question. He had no interest in researching his biological father's family line to find out if he was or not.

"Well, Mr. Lafitte," Henry said, and Mason cringed at the mispronunciation of his last name, "I'll give you a tow to the nearest town. 'Fraid I can't go farther than that. But there's a garage there." His eyes looked up, and he scanned the slow-moving dark clouds. "Sure looks like we're in for a bad storm. Haven't seen clouds like that in over five years." He unraveled the tow chain as he walked to the front of the Corvette. "Could use the rain, though. We've been having a drought for going on three years."

Mason studied the sky for himself, again. He agreed the storm brewing could be threatening. But, if he was off this highway and had a roof over his head, he didn't give a damn how much it rained. As long as it wasn't on him.

Chapter Four

Struggling with the last of the salon chairs, the two women returned it to its rightful place.

Anastasia grunted as they set the heavy burden down. Straightening, she kneaded the sore muscles in her lower back, almost groaning at the stiffness she felt there. "Thanks for the help, Gale," she said, reaching out to pat her friend's arm. "The place looks presentable once again."

Gale was doing some massaging of her own, working out a kink in her shoulder. "You know, sweetie. I keep telling you. Sunday is the day of rest. Why can't we do this on Saturdays after you've closed down for the day?"

Laughing, Anastasia moved behind Gale and began rubbing the woman's stiff shoulders. "Because, after I've been standing on my feet for eight hours, I don't have the energy to clean this," She waved her arm, indicating the three-station salon.

Gale caught the motion in the large mirror they were standing in front of. "I suppose that's understandable," she sighed, moving away from Anastasia's gentle hands to straighten the bottles of gels, mousses, and hairspray setting on the white countertop.

Anastasia surveyed her salon with pride. She was thankful she hadn't lost it while recovering last year from Danny's attack.

She had named the salon Shear Delight.

It wasn't a big space. Not when compared to the salons in Bismarck, an hour east via the Interstate. But, for a town the size of New Salem, it was perfect.

Located in the Golden West Shopping Center, less than a fourth of a mile on the north end of a town containing a little over nine hundred residents, it had a large clientele. A lot of the New Salem's population,

and surrounding farmers and ranchers, patronized her salon. For that, Anastasia would always be grateful. It told her, in their way, they cared about her and her fight to make ends meet and put Danny behind her.

Surprisingly, this was one place Danny never bothered her. If he had, it might have left her without a clientele because no one wanted to be around if Danny showed up.

They were terrified of him, and she couldn't blame them for their unease when he was close by and on one of his drinking binges.

She'd long since given up trying to understand what changed the man she'd fallen in love with. He hadn't always been abusive. Once upon a time, he treated her like a queen. But after his medical discharge from the Marines, that slowly changed, and he began drinking. This was odd because Danny had never been a fan of liquor, keeping his consumption of it to a minimum.

They'd met five years earlier. Danny, home on leave, was hitting the bars with a few friends and having a good time playing pool for a while in one place, then moving on to another establishment for a game of darts.

It was in the fifth bar the jolly crew entered that Anastasia Miller encountered Danny Sharp for the first time. The six-foot-six handsome Marine literally swept her off her feet. Although he was stationed overseas, love blossomed through the endless letters they'd written one another. His proposal had come through the written word, and three years after meeting in a bar, they married. But the happiness ended abruptly when Danny almost lost his life in an explosion that happened while he was in Iraq.

His body had healed, but he'd changed. Horribly.

"Are you still cooking supper tonight?"

Gale's voice drew Anastasia's mind back to the present, and she was more than happy to be there. She didn't like remembering the happiness that was stolen from her. The memories were too painful. "Of course,"

she said, managing a laugh so Gale wouldn't know she had been walking down heartbreak memory lane. "That husband of yours has been after me for over two weeks to cook my famous spaghetti for him, and I wouldn't want to disappoint Jeff after having promised the man."

The sound of distant thunder brought both women's heads around to gaze out the large window in the front of the salon.

"I'll be," Gale declared, moving toward the window to look out at the darkening sky. "It looks as though we might get some rain."

Anastasia couldn't prevent the giggle. "Rain? Isn't that the stuff that's like a shower but comes down from the sky instead?" The hope of rain diminished with the closing of last year's continuing drought and this year's heatwave.

"I'm serious," Gale exclaimed, eyes wide. "Those clouds are bunching together, and it's getting dark."

Anastasia's smile turned to a frown as she moved to the window and witnessed Gale's statement for herself. "Does look rather nasty. Why don't you go on home? There isn't much more to do here. Besides, I'm going to stop by the gas station and visit with Eric for a little while before finding my own way home."

"Eric, eh?" Gale teased, raising a brow. "This relationship is getting interesting. You visit him every Sunday."

Anastasia grinned, going along with the joke. Eric Miller was her cousin, not to mention he'd just turned eighteen. Definitely no chance at romance from that direction. "Yes, Gale. I confess. We've got a thing going."

"I knew it!" Gale exclaimed as though she was shocked by the news.

Anastasia sighed dramatically. "What's a woman to do when a kid tells a good joke? He's after my heart that one is."

"Well, you can share the latest laughs during dinner tonight," Gale chuckled. "Right now, I'm going to heed your suggestion and go home."

She moved to the reception desk, retrieved her purse from the counter, and extracted the keys to her car. "You're not going to stay here much longer, are you?"

Anastasia shook her head. "Less than fifteen minutes, actually." She walked Gale to the door. "See you tonight."

* * *

Gazing through the window of the service station, scanning the area surrounding the building's location, Mason had the uncanny urge to say, "Yeehaw."

How could there possibly be so much of absolutely nothing? Although he visited North Dakota enough times in his youth to know the answer to that question. The state's entire population gathered together would fit into Paris and still have room for more people to join.

Less than half an hour ago, the man named Henry drove into this town -Mason had yet to witness a single house, but Henry unchained the Corvette outside this station anyway.

"Welcome to New Salem," had been Henry's departing words.

Welcome to nowhere is more like it, Mason concluded.

From what Mason could see of it, New Salem comprised of two service stations, directly across from one another, a small café, and a six-unit motel. Added to these was a two-story building less than a quarter of a mile to the south with the words Golden West Shopping Center attached to it.

Shopping Center?

Mason's eyes snapped back to the building, unable to believe he read the words correctly.

What in the hell does an invisible town need with a shopping center?

He shrugged the question off. It seemed just as ridiculous as the huge cow standing on top of the hill just west of this garage.

Cow?

That warranted a triple take.

Sure enough. There was a giant fiberglass cow displayed on the hill. It was facing out toward the highway as though it were guarding something. For the life of him, Mason could not imagine why anyone would place a cow on a hill to protect nothing.

Unless, he speculated, it attracts highway motorists to the motel, café, and laughable mall.

And why couldn't he recall seeing that in all his years of traveling between Medora and Bismarck when he'd visited this state?

Probably because he and Hunter always drove on the back roads whenever they'd ventured off the ranch together.

He decided to ask someone about the statue and glanced toward where his car was being looked at. The teenager looking under the hood didn't appear as though he could find the dipstick, even if it were to have a neon sign attached to it. "Hey," Mason called out to the mechanic and grimaced when the kid bumped his head on the Corvette's hood. The dozens of questions he had regarding the town flew out the window, and he opted for the one most important to him and it had nothing to do with the area. "Have you figured out what is wrong with my car?"

The teenager's shrug did nothing to reassure him the boy knew anything about car engines.

I should have asked about the damn cow instead, Mason thought. Maybe the kid would at least know that answer.

Mason reached for the payphone attached to the wall next to his left shoulder with a heavy sigh. The only thing he had to keep himself from going insane was to make phone calls. He already tried the Fisher's lake home when he discovered this phone, but he hadn't connected with any of them so far. In desperation, he called the F&L, hoping one of the Fisher's would be there. Since their ranch was also a tourist location

that offered trail rides into the Badlands, he assumed he could have reached one of them there. But no. Their housekeeper, Sara, whom he'd known all of his life, informed him the ranch was being overseen by one of the seasoned summer employees. She expected none of the Fishers back until that coming Friday.

Unbelievable.

Out of sheer boredom, he called Josh Reno. Not that Josh could help him out of this situation, but he hadn't talked to the man for a few months. Since he had nothing else to do, why not talk to a former boss and close friend in New York, who could help him keep his sanity.

The woman who answered Josh's office phone sounded as though she would swoon over dead after discovering who was calling her boss. Despite his sour mood, Mason smiled. He couldn't help it. Nor could he resist the urge to flirt a little. If nothing else, he was damn good at making women feel good about themselves, not to mention habits were hard to break.

He was absolutely a man addicted to women, and he had flirtation down to an art.

"Perhaps, lovely lady," he cooed, "I will dine with you the next time I am in New York, *oui*?" He grinned, knowing American women found his accent enticing. From the heavy sigh being issued from this one, he won yet another heart without trying.

"I can't. I'm married." The woman's voice sounded as though it disappointed her.

"Does it really matter?" he asked, laying the sensuality of his voice on as thick as he could. It was like a game to him, and he played it to win.

There was a momentary pause, and for a moment, Mason hoped she was so devoted to her husband he would lose a conquest.

But when the woman purred back, "I guess not," he felt disappointed.

Well. Had he honestly believed there were any faithful women left in the world? He hadn't found one yet he couldn't sway. He never denied the fact that he had a healthy sex drive, and when he was younger, he looked for sex anywhere he could get it. However, he matured enough to understand the dangers of tumbling everything that came along. This woman sounded as though she would be willing to do that, too.

It put a sour taste in his mouth. After discovering Carol's unfaithfulness and now having a married woman hanging onto his every word, he indeed was questioning wanting anyone in his life for a long time.

A few moments later, his call was forwarded to Josh. Seconds after that, the president of Country Specialties Magazine picked up.

"Mason! Is that really you?" Josh's deep voice exclaimed across the line. "Are you in town? We'll have dinner-"

"Dinner is out," Mason interrupted. His mind pictured the man whose home shopping magazine had been his first modeling job after coming to America to make his way in the world. It was where Connie Fay, the agent for Sizzling Concepts' modeling agency, had approached him. She signed him on with her agency and rocketed him into fame when she'd landed him a contract with Citnamor Books that turned him into a household name. "I am in New Salem, North Dakota."

"Where?"

"Exactly." Josh's question summed it up rather nicely.

Silence preceded momentarily, causing Mason to wonder if, somehow, the phone had gone dead. But when Josh at last spoke, it was to restate his question.

"New Salem, North Dakota," Mason repeated, then thought he should explain its location since Josh would not understand where this was. "It is halfway between Billings, Montana and-"

"I don't believe it!" Josh cried, cutting off the explanation.

Mason chuckled. "Actually, neither do I."

"That's not what I meant." Josh's voice was serious now. "Good God, Mason. You'll never believe what I'm holding in my hand, even as we speak."

Mason's attention was diverted when he caught sight of a carload of teenage girls pulling into the gas station. He noted they arrived from the south, so perhaps there was a town around here. He just couldn't see it because of the location of this service station.

He wondered if the girls would know who he was and halfway hoped they wouldn't recognize him. He wasn't in the mood to play the part everyone expected of him.

Damn romance novels. Women believed him to be just like the man in those fantasies they were enthralled with. It would be nice to meet a woman who didn't gush all over him for a change and would allow him to be himself.

Maybe those girls didn't read romance books. At least, not the kind that sported his likeness. It wasn't as if those books would be readily available to them…

As that thought occurred, Mason's eyes caught sight of the spinner of books on sale and sighed. Among the assortment of westerns and science fiction were nestled romance books, and sure as shit, a few of them sported covers he'd posed for.

Damn it. He truly wanted to be left alone.

"Mason? Did you hear me?"

That snapped him back to the conversation. "Sorry, Josh. What were you saying?"

"I'm talking about an order my company received from there a few weeks ago!" Josh exclaimed, laughter in his voice.

Mason shook his head. If Josh could see this place, he wouldn't wonder why someone from here would shop through his home delivery publication.

Then it dawned on him. "Oh. Coincidence." It was ironic he would be here at the same time Josh was looking at an order- Why would Josh have the order? He had employees to handle those. It didn't make sense.

His curiosity pricked, he teased, "What did the guy order? Six thousand dollars worth of underwear?"

"She ordered Frank Jackson."

"Excuse me?" He disregarded the teenage girls. "It sounded as though you said someone from here ordered -Frank Jackson?" He missed the four girls' entrance into the building. He also missed them stop short, nearly colliding into one another the moment they saw him.

"That's what I said," Josh confirmed, laughing. "She filled out her order form, requesting we wrap the model on page eighty-five up, and send him to her!"

The concept of what the person had done struck Mason funny. Chuckling, he said, "If you could see this place Josh, you would not question her order. There probably are few men to choose from." Anyone who had a sense of humor to come up with a male-order-date had to be interesting.

But then, he received countless interesting letters himself through his fan club and Citnamor Books. Women sent him their panties, bras, and numerous other items. Such as the keys to their homes, along with explicit details regarding precisely what they wanted him to do once he arrived at their humble abode.

He never complied with those requests, of course. He would be dead from sheer exhaustion had he tried to satisfy their sexual pleasures. But their letters always amused him, those he bothered to read. That's what he had a secretary and fan club for. People to handle his correspondence so his admirers would continue to be happy, and he wouldn't be bothered. But occasionally, some letters were given to him for a good laugh.

A good laugh. When was the last time he'd had one of those? Other than last night when he anticipated seeing Hunter again?

"Hey. Have I got an idea!" Josh claimed. "Why don't you pop in on her and tell her you're the replacement?"

"You are joking, right?" He wasn't about to introduce himself to someone without knowing if the person was mentally stable.

"Oh, come on, Mason. You used to enjoy a good laugh. The girl would probably faint dead away if she opened her door and found Mason Lafayette on her front step. Besides, my company is known for its fast delivery and-"

It was the word dead that caused Mason to dig in his heels. It reminded him of an incident that took place last year in Huston, Texas. One crazy broad tried to shoot him. "Forget it, Josh. I will not do it."

And what did Josh mean by you used to enjoy a good laugh? He still did. He just had found nothing amusing lately.

Speaking of amusing. A girlish giggle from behind caused Mason to glance over his shoulder.

Four teenage girls waved.

Automatically, he waved back.

They looked as though they were going to faint.

So much for hoping they wouldn't recognize him. He wanted to hightail it out of there as fast as he could. The knowledge of knowing someone in this town ordered Frank Jackson, and not knowing if that person was a flake, combined with not knowing who from here had done the ordering- It could very well be one of those teenagers standing behind him- caused him to suddenly want his freedom back.

The thought of escape caused him to glance back to the area where his car was. The young mechanic shook his head and closed the Corvette's hood.

Mason cringed. That hood closing was too close to resembling someone putting a lid on a coffin.

The feeling of having just been doomed was strong.

"Josh, it has been nice talking to you, but I have to hang up and make another call. I need to be rescued. Fast!" He did not understand why he was suddenly so panicky. Maybe it was the memory of his close brush with death last year. Perhaps it was the hungry looks in those young eyes, causing him to feel as though he were about to be eaten alive. It might even be the fact the sky had become black with the storm clouds he had watched slowly moving to his location, seeming to signal his fate was no longer under his control. But whatever the reason, he didn't much care for the panic rising up in him and he wanted the hell out of there.

"Wait!" Josh exclaimed. "Her name is Anastasia Sharp. Do it as a favor to me. I'd hate to mention you owing me anything-"

"Look, Josh. I have four pairs of hungry eyes boring into my back. If I do not find a way out of this town, there will not be enough left of me for you to care whether I owe you anything, understand?"

The phone almost came off the wall when he slammed the receiver down.

He saw the mechanic standing less than three feet away from him. "Well?" Mason snapped, eager to be on his way.

The boy's eyes arched. "Well, what?"

Mason ran a hand over his face. "What did you say your name was?"

"Eric."

"Well, Eric. What is wrong with my car?"

Eric shrugged. "Damned if I know."

The sound of frustration Mason made sounded awful. "Is there anything you do know?"

Eric gave him a you're a real jerk, mister, look before saying. "Sure. We could tow your car into Bismarck." Mentally, he shook his head.

This was the guy women thought was a hunk? Brother. He was more than glad he hadn't called his cousin Anastasia the moment he recognized the guy. He sure as hell wouldn't want her to have to discover the man she thought was so great was so mean. She didn't need to meet up with another creep in her life.

Outside, the storm clouds let loose with a gentle drizzle. Inside the service station, the lights flickered as thunder cracked overhead, and a flash of lightning streaked across the sky.

Mason's feeling of doom doubled. "Let us tow it to Bismarck, then," Mason suggested, moving past the teenage boy.

Let us? Eric repeated to himself. Shaw. Right. Tow it yourself, asshole.

At the precise moment Mason brushed past Eric, the station lights went out, cloaking everyone in darkness. Outside was no brighter. Another bolt of lightning, followed by a crack of thunder, caused the four girls to split the air with high-pitched screams of fright.

Mason's heart went to his throat, and he doubted it would ever beat again.

Chapter Five

Pivoting on the balls of his boots, Mason felt disoriented. Total darkness surrounded him.

A second bolt of lightning revealed the silhouette of a figure standing inside the doorway, and it did one thing for him. He discovered his heart was still beating because it leaped to his throat. The person outlined had waist-long hair. The sudden breeze that came up caused the hair to swirl about as though it were a long flowing cape. It reminded him of a horror movie where some witch was about to destroy every living thing.

He swallowed, hard. Why he was suddenly having all these anxiety attacks, he didn't know. The conversation with Josh? Remembering there was someone in this town whose sanity was in question? He couldn't be sure. But his fear was genuine enough, and he kept telling himself to relax and get a grip. In fact, he knew damn well that if Hunter found out about this ridiculous reaction he was having, he would laugh his fool head off. Hunter didn't know the meaning of the word fear most of the time. Frankly, Mason did. At least, he was the first to admit he wasn't one of those heroes he portrayed on those romance covers. And one day, once his heart went back into place, he probably would laugh over this day when he experienced unjustifiable terror. But right now, at this moment, he was wishing to hell he had taken that goddamn plane!

Gentle laughter filled the room. Oddly enough, the sound was soothing on Mason's unwarranted fears, and he felt himself relaxing, his heartbeat slow.

"Oh, my," a woman's soft voice giggled, "It's darker than a tomb in here."

So much for the soothing effect. Mason would have preferred it if the woman had chosen some other way to describe the blackness encasing them.

"Anastasia, is that you?" Eric asked, trying to pierce the darkness with his eyes, completely forgetting the man standing next to him.

Mason wondered why that name sounded so damn familiar. Had Eric said Anastasia's last name, he might have grasped the reason. Though that probably would have panicked him all the more, so it was no doubt a good thing that he was entirely in the dark -sort of speaking. He was having trouble enough trying to see the figure standing in the doorway, assuring himself she was made up of flesh and blood.

"Of course, it's me," Anastasia laughed. "Who were you expecting? The Wicked Witch of the West?"

Mason groaned.

"Eric? Is your voice changing?"

The four teenage girls giggled.

Anastasia grinned, though no one could see the amused expression. She hadn't made it into the building before the lights went out and the garage became encased in complete darkness. She had not realized Eric wasn't alone. "Don't tell me you turned these lights off on purpose, Eric." She teased, not able to pass up this opportunity to razz her young cousin.

"Stasia!" Eric exclaimed, glad the darkness was covering the blush. "I can't believe-"

"Oh, tisk, Eric." Anastasia abolished. "Would you rather I assumed you had lured these unsuspecting girls in here, intent upon doing something sinister?"

"Enough!" Mason exploded. He'd had all he could bear of this weird conversation. "I would appreciate it, *mademoiselle*, if you would find something else to talk about."

Anastasia started. "Ah, Eric?"

"Yeah, Stasia?"

"When did you develop a French accent?"

"I haven't." Though he was seriously considering knocking the jerk over the head for snapping at his cousin like that.

"Oh." It was Anastasia's turn to glory in the darkness and be thankful it hid the color she felt rushing to her cheeks. From the sound of the guy's voice, he was no teenager. Worse, she could not see the man's face because of this darkness. It caused her to feel old anxieties of the dark beginning to rise.

His angry tone hadn't helped matters, either. But she kept telling herself it wasn't Danny waiting for her in the darkness, and there was no reason to be frightened.

Eric must have sensed her distress, for he said, "It's okay, Stasia. I'm right next to him. He's not going anywhere."

Words meant to comfort one did nothing for the other.

"What do you mean I am not going anywhere-? Ouch!" Mason exclaimed as Eric's elbow shoved into his rib cage hard enough to damn near crack one. "What in the hell was that for?" he growled, swearing in French, unable to believe the kid had the nerve to do such a stupid thing.

"Well, you're not," Eric stated, sounding as though he hadn't done a thing wrong, while inside, he was smiling up a storm because he'd wanted to punch the jerk way before this. "Your car is deader than a corpse," Mason wished these people would stop using references that complemented the weather. "And the rain out there wouldn't allow you to leave, even if your car was fixed. It's coming down so hard, the road is flooding."

It was that last statement that caused everyone to forget their personal apprehensions. Seven people turned their attention to the storm, visible through the large windows at the front of the building. Indeed, the rain was pouring down as though a dam in heaven had broken. The pavement

everywhere was becoming submerged under a thick blanket of churning water.

"My God!" Anastasia exclaimed, the first to snap out of the trance-like state everyone seemed to have gone into. She could not remember the last time this much rain had fallen all at once. And if the shower alone wasn't enough to shock her, the clouds let loose with pebble-sized hail.

Her first comprehensive thought was the fact she had left her poodle chained to its doghouse. With the way the water was flooding the pavement outside, combined with knowing the doghouse was on a slope, she was deathly afraid her dog might be in dire straits. "I've got to get home!" she exclaimed, heading out the door. She only made it as far as sticking one foot out the door before a strong hand clamped down on her shoulder, pulling her back inside.

"Do not be an idiot!" Mason told her harshly as he yanked her away from the door.

Anastasia was too filled with concern over her dog to care about who was preventing her from reaching her Mazda. "You don't understand! My dog's outside!" she jerked her shoulder away from the vice grip and headed back out the door, only to have that heavy weight clamp back down and yank her away from the door, again.

"Listen, lady," Mason gritted, "You cannot go out there! The hail is coming down too fast. You could be seriously hurt if you did something as foolish as leave this building. As soon as this passes, you can leave. But for now, relax." How could anyone be so stupid as to think about stepping out into that storm?

Anastasia whirled toward the man. She was so angry right then she wished she could see the person because at the moment, her eyes were shooting daggers toward him strong enough to have drawn blood. "If anything happens to Mason-"

"Mr. Lafayette is right, Stasia," Eric interrupted in a rush to calm his cousin. "You can't go out there. I'm sure Gale and Jeff will look after

Mas… er…" Eric's memory as to what Anastasia named her dog, coupled with the knowledge of who the dog's namesake was, and knowing who was standing behind her like some guardian angel, ready to prevent her from going out the door should she try to attempt it again, gave him the giggles. "I'm sure someone will look after… M.D." He abbreviated the name, but his laughter caused him to double over and hold his sides. He could not wait to see Anastasia's expression once the lights came back on. Above all, he wished to God he had a camera because this was going to be a priceless Kodak moment.

"Eric Miller," Anastasia snapped, "What the Sam hell is so funny?" How dare he laugh when poor Mason Divine was probably drowning at that very instant!

"I'm sorry, Stasia," Eric apologized, but his laughter did not make him sound as though he meant it. "It's just that…" he wiped tears of mirth from his face that no one could see. "It's just that… Mr. Lafayette and M.D. have soooo much in common." He couldn't help it. He laughed harder. "Mason Lafayette is French," he hinted, "and so's your poodle. Get it?" Oh, God. This was too rich.

Mason was not following this conversation, though he thought he might have just been insulted by that reference to having something in common with a dog and a poodle to boot. He hated those pampered little mutts.

He would not ask. This day was already turning into one of the oddest he'd ever had, and he really did not want to know what the joke was, though he did not doubt for a moment it was on him. Besides, the kid sounded as though he couldn't speak if his life depended upon it. His laughter was echoing throughout the building.

Anastasia, on the other hand, had a sinking feeling she knew exactly what the jest was, although she kept trying to deny it because it could not be possible that he was here.

In New Salem?

No way.

"Eric," she hissed. "You are not serious!"

"Oh God," her cousin snickered.

Anastasia paled and prayed the lights would remain off until she had the chance to escape. She doubted she would live through actually meeting the man who filled her fantasies every night. Especially when she had been ready to punch him in the nose seconds ago, had he kept interfering with her rescue attempt.

Please God, she prayed frantically, deciding that perhaps now would be a good time to talk to Gale's deity. Please, oh, please don't let those lights come back on. I'll go to church every Sunday. I'll even do a bible study! Just don't let those lights come back on until I'm out of here!

Obviously, Gale's God was in a humorous mood today and had other ideas because the lights came on at that moment, flooding the inside of the gas station in the same manner as the rain had overflowed the ground outside.

Anastasia squeezed her eyes shut. Not so much from the unexpected glare, but because she hoped that by not looking, he wouldn't see her. Kind of like the way an ostrich puts its head into the ground to avoid danger. Neither ploy worked, of course. But she hoped that this time, it would.

Thanks a lot, God, she groaned, still keeping her eyes closed. I was offering a plea bargain. The least you could have done was give me another alternative. My offer was negotiable.

Chapter Six

Anastasia slowly opened one eye, then the other. But all she could do was look at the red suede cowboy boots ten feet away from her.

One of those boots moved; its heel moving across the other to hook at the ankle of its mate.

More than anything, she wanted to be a coward, but determination got her eyes in motion. Leisurely, they traveled up the length of those form-fitting designer jeans. They outlined perfectly what she already knew from the countless photos of him she had hanging on her office wall. His legs were powerful and as thickly sculptured as the rest of him would be if she could get past that black belt surrounding the firmly tapered narrow hips. The fact he was not wearing a shirt was obvious. The sight of his navel, with a trace of hair trailing down and disappearing beneath that belt, left her mouth dry.

She had hundreds of Mason Lafayette photos blanketing her office wall, used for inspiration whenever she worked on her romantic novel. And don't forget about his calendar, with its sensual photos and romantic backgrounds. She had two of them, in fact. One in her living room, still intact, and the other ripped apart and mixed in with the other photos in her office. So, with all those pictures of him, she need not take her eyes any farther because there wasn't a spot on him she didn't already have firmly etched in her mind.

Well. That wasn't entirely true. There was one part of him she had never seen before. Only imagined when looking at a photo of him in somewhat risqué swimming trunks.

Automatically, her eyes dropped those few inches from his navel to that V between his legs. She wondered if he really was as large as those photos seemed to make him out to be and-

Her face flamed bright pink. She could not believe she was thinking about that, not when he was standing there -for real. Her head snapped up so fast, her temples throbbed because of it. She could not believe where her thoughts had taken her.

Sky-blue eyes collided with the uncanny green depths she always longed to know if they were real. And now she had her answer. They really were that cat-eyed green, and they were staring back at her as hard as she was staring at him.

She was going to die. Her heart thundered. She managed a "Hi," though it sounded too much like an "eep" and definitely like a squeak. She rolled her eyes, wishing God would comply with at least one prayer today and take her to heaven before she humiliated herself any further. Hi? Seriously? And when in the hell had that stupid mouse gotten into her throat? Surely, he thought she was an idiot, and she couldn't blame him in the least because she was feeling about as dumb as those teenage girls were looking. The only difference being, she managed not to let her mouth hang open as they were doing.

At least that was something to be thankful for. Wasn't it?

Apparently, God was still enjoying His little joke because He didn't comply with her wishes. Again. She was still standing there, and Mason Lafayette was smiling at her.

Oh, God. Don't smile! It was making him too handsome by far. It softened the lines of his rugged face and brought out a dimple she hadn't known he had. In every photo of him, he was sober faced.

Lord in heaven, Mason Lafayette was undoubtedly the handsomest man in the world, and that dimple was disarming. "Wow," she said, then about croaked because she wasn't sure if she had said it out loud or not.

Come on, Stasia. Snap out of it! He is only human, for Christ's sake! When did you begin falling all over yourself because of a man? Just think of how stupid you must look to him.

Thanks a lot, she told her conscience. How rude!

Just think about how many other women fall at his feet. He's probably nothing more than a puffed-up peacock because of those looks, so treat him like a human instead of some god.

Well, that was excellent advice. She wasn't usually flabbergasted so easily, and she took a deep breath to ease her surprise.

So, her conscience continued, tell him what you've always said you'd say to him if he ever came to New Salem.

Anastasia reminded her inner voice that she had meant it as a joke because Mason Lafayette would never set foot in New Salem, North Dakota.

But Mason Lafayette was in New Salem.

Oh, God. What next? Would there be a kangaroo in her flower garden when she arrived home? The chances were in favor of it since the most unlikely to happen, just did.

She cleared her throat and hoped that stupid mouse had gone someplace else. She could do this. No problem. "*Bonjour, monsieur Lafayette.*" Was her accent correct? "*Je accueil tu.*" She hoped she had said, "I welcome you." But with the way her luck was going, she probably said something dimwitted like, "Polly want a cracker?"

Oh, God. It wasn't the same! Her pictures didn't move. They didn't arch their brow. Oh no! Did that arched brow mean she said something other than what she intended? And for cat's sake, they did not reach out, take her hand, and press it to their lips!

She was going to die. So were the four teenage girls, if their sighs were any indication.

A dry "Oh brother" came from Eric.

"*Bonjour, mademoiselle* -Anastasia?" At her slight nod, Mason continued. "Thank you for welcoming me." He did not understand why she suddenly looked relieved. "Do you speak more than five words of French?" He did not relinquish the small hand. For some reason, he

didn't want to, and it had nothing to do with the fact beautiful women could turn him to mush.

Laughing, more at ease now that she knew she said what she intended to, she replied, "*Oui* and *Non*." But she couldn't prevent the nervous giggle that followed.

Great. She might have managed out doing the younger girls by not gaping, but she sure as hell was sounding like one. You can kill me anytime now, God. I'm ready. She wanted to crawl into a corner somewhere and disappear.

No. She didn't. She was more than liking the warmth of his hand as it continued holding hers in its gentle grasp.

To her disappointment, he released her hand.

Sweeping a few strands of his raven black hair back away from his face, one that housed high cheekbones, a long-narrow nose, and a strong chin that set off the square jaw, he asked, "Yes and no?" and looked just as confused as his voice sounded.

He looks rather cute when he's confused like that, Anastasia's inner voice noted.

She grinned, showing off a row of perfectly straight and gleaming white teeth. "You asked if I spoke over five words of French. *Oui* and *non* bring the count to seven." She shrugged, then winked. "And the extent of my French."

Mason couldn't help it. He laughed. The girl was a delight, and his earlier anxieties dimmed as though they had never been.

Girl? He shook himself mentally. This was no girl. When the lights were restored, his first look at the woman knocked the air right out of him. He would have never suspected this town would possess a knockout like that. Even Carol Gibson would have reeked with jealousy had she seen the woman, and Carol was known as one of the most captivating women in the modeling industry.

The woman's long, waist-length hair, that he had so foolishly thought of as a dark cape was dark brown with eggplant purple highlights throughout its long tress.

Eggplant purple?

Mason gave that glorious mane a second look and confirmed that yes, it definitely had eggplant purple highlights. Yet, it seemed the perfect frame for the delicate face looking back at him. The sky-blue almond-shaped eyes had thick, long black lashes outlined with black liner surrounding them. Her subtle brows were refined, arching perfectly above the twinkling eyes.

He wanted to touch that glossy hair and feel those almost too full lips against his. And had those eyes of hers continued lingering on that part of him that was always so easily aroused by the sight of a breathtaking woman, he would have done exactly that, and then some. If there hadn't been other people in the room, he just might have made love to her right there on the floor of this gas station. She affected him that strongly. The only thing that helped him prevent the bulge her eyes aroused by lingering on him from growing, and embarrassing the hell out of him, was by forcing himself to remember Carol's unfaithfulness.

Remembering Carol cooled his building lust and helped him remember his vow, of only yesterday, to steer clear of involving himself with another ravishing creature in the near future. Besides, he would not be around long enough to give in to his growing temptation to discover this woman's passion, so at least that was something to be thankful for.

So why did he feel disappointed about it?

That was easy enough to answer. He told himself it was his overly active passion for women bringing on his dismay. That, along with the deeply hidden need of his heart to find someone who would love him, not use him.

Of course, that t-shirt the woman was wearing hadn't helped matters any. With the words, Hairdressers do it with style, written over breasts

that would be more than a handful for him, and he had large hands, all sorts of images came to mind as to precisely what that style of hers might be.

He noted the hail outside had ceased and that the rain, although still coming down, was doing so more gently. He figured this would be a good way to divert the attention away from himself. And he needed a diversion if he expected to hold out on his resolve not to kiss the hell out of this woman. There was also that need to get a tow truck from Bismarck and be on his way.

That motel he spotted earlier was just too close for comfort, and so was this woman.

"The hail has stopped," he said, jerking his chin toward the window. "You may check on your dog now. I will not prevent you from trying to go outside, this time." She graced him with another of her lovely blushes. "I hope it is all right." As an afterthought, he asked, "What did you name your poodle?" He did not understand why he asked, but the question brought forth an even deeper blush from her, and now he was intrigued.

"M.D." Eric supplied, and Anastasia could have hugged him for re-minding her he had given her the out earlier when the subject first came up.

Mason nodded. He knew that. It was said just before the kid named Eric broke into that fit of laughter, which meant there was much more behind the name than simple letters. "What does M.D. mean?" Why he had this urge to know was beyond him, and yet he held his breath, wait-ing for the answer.

Anastasia wasn't about to tell him what she named her dog, and her wit worked better than ever. "My Dog," she beamed, then shot Eric a look lethal enough to kill his snort.

Mason was liking this woman more and more. He found he enjoyed her sense of humor. She seemed to have the power to make him forget

gloomy thoughts and poor relationships. Why she was avoiding the question, he doubted he would ever know. But he decided that whatever her reason for keeping the dog's name secret was her business, and he would not ask again.

Turning his attention toward the teenage mechanic, he requested, "Please find a tow truck for my car."

Anyone touching Eric with a feather right than could have knocked him over. Mason Lafayette, the guy who had been acting like nothing less than a jerk since arriving, had said please? Shocking, to be sure. "You betcha, Mr. Lafayette," he said and disappeared into the back room, still marveling over the unexpected wonder that just took place.

The teenage girls finely gathered the courage to approach Mason for an autograph, and Anastasia backed away, allowing them the charm and pleasure she just experienced. Besides, she had dinner to prepare, and she needed to assure herself that Mason Divine was all right.

Gale and Jeff would never believe this story.

Oh well. Now that the first shock had worn off, Anastasia was back to remembering that Mason Lafayette was only human. She'd done all the gaping at him she planned to. Her only regret was not being able to spend enough time with him to discover his heart. But then, it would sure be a bummer if she were to discover he really was the egotistical man many talk shows and articles made him out to be. She would prefer to hold on to her fantasy than have to face another disappointment in life.

But she was already feeling disappointed. On one hand, she was glad to have been given the chance of a lifetime by meeting him. On the other, despite not wanting to discover if he really was stuck on himself, she regretted the fact she would never know for sure.

Well, damn. Talk about your two-edged sword. With a shrug and a sigh, she walked out of the garage and headed for her car.

Chapter Seven

Mason smiled at the four teenage girls as they moved toward him. They were giggly and flirtatious, and he tried not to be annoyed. He would much rather be conversing with that delightful woman with the eggplant purple highlights.

The teenagers wanted his autograph. He had signed his name so often over the years his signature wasn't what it once had been. In his youth, it had been neat and readable; nowadays, it was a quick scribble of lines that blended together.

They asked him questions; he conversed by autopilot as they weren't asking anything out of the ordinary. Besides, his mind was thinking about Anastasia. Once he finished giving these teenagers some of his attention, he looked forward to visiting with her while he waited for a tow truck to arrive.

He was eager to be done with these teenyboppers. That funny woman intrigued him.

And okay, he wanted to take her to bed. That was a given. Perhaps he had been too hasty in making that vow yesterday. Why should he punish himself for Carol's unfaithfulness? Besides, maybe exploring the style Anastasia had in bed would be an excellent way to pass the time while he waited for the tow truck.

He glanced up in time to witness Anastasia walk out the door.

She was leaving?

To say it stunned him would be an understatement.

He could not believe it.

He doubted famous people visited this cow town that often, if ever. Wouldn't she want his autograph at least to show all her friends?

Maybe she forgot.

She will regret it later.

"Hey!" he called out as he brushed past the teens to follow Anastasia. He kept telling himself he should let her go, but his body was not accepting his mind's suggestion. It propelled him out of the door right behind her and into the rain without a shirt on or an umbrella to protect him from the elements.

It never crossed his mind that Anastasia might not care one way or the other if she had his autograph. Mainly because such a concept was beyond that of someone used to people demanding his attention wherever he went.

He caught up with her just as she reached her black Mazda. "Did you want my autograph?" He asked, using the question as a delay tactic as she opened her car door.

She yelped as her body jerked from being startled like that. "What?" she asked, staring up at him wide-eyed. It had been hard enough to fathom her fantasy man was physically in New Salem, but he'd followed her to her car, and she had no words to describe how that made her feel inside.

Warm and fuzzy, her inner voice suggested, though she did not respond to the claim. Sometimes it was best not to talk to yourself when others were around, and she certainly did not want this man to think she was crazy.

"Did you want my autograph?" he repeated, feeling the rain soaking his hair and running rivulets down his back and straight into his jeans.

"I," Anastasia opened her mouth. His autograph? She'd never been the type of woman to desire those silly things. What good was a piece of paper with someone's signature on it? Unless it was on a legal document.

He'd followed her into the rain to ask her that question, and she didn't have the heart to tell him no. But standing out here getting soaked was ridiculous. "Why don't you get into my car so we can get out of the rain," she told him, sliding in behind the steering wheel as though it didn't cross her mind he wouldn't comply.

Mason hesitated for two seconds, asking himself if it was wise to get into the vehicle of someone he just met before hurrying around the car and sliding into the passenger seat. It wasn't as though he couldn't protect himself if the woman tried to attack him.

Please attack me, his mind screamed, flashing fantasy images of Anastasia tying him up and having her way with him.

He groaned. He'd never been ashamed of his lusty nature until this day.

"Are you alright?" Anastasia asked, her eyes scanning that handsome face the gods had carved out for him.

"*Oui*," he said as his hand came up to smooth his long-wet hair away from his face.

Without hesitation, Anastasia reached into the back seat of the vehicle and grabbed one of the clean, dry towels left over from when she and Gale cleaned the salon and literally shoved it into his hands. "Really, Mason," she tisked. "Didn't your mother tell you to stay out of the rain?"

He blinked. Was she scolding him? It was the last thing he expected her to say, or do, although if you asked him what he expected her to confront him with, it would not have been about the way his parents raised him.

He felt like a two-year-old who should be ashamed of himself, rather than a fully grown man.

He cleared his throat. "*Oui*, my mother told me to stay out of the rain," he snapped, unsure why he was suddenly mad. Perhaps it was because

he came out here to convince her to go to the motel with him, and she didn't seem interested in him. At all.

Anastasia ignored his angry tone. In fact, it brought forth a chuckle from her. He reminded her of some child caught doing something wrong, and it struck her funny. "Don't worry," she patted his arm and used a voice that would be appropriate for a parent to use to soothe their child. "I shan't tell her what a naughty boy you've been." She couldn't believe she was teasing him like this, but it felt natural for her to do so regardless of having just met the man.

His eyes regarded her. For the first time in his life, a woman was not goggling over him, and even though he thought that was something he wanted, now he wasn't so sure.

A knock upon the window interrupted any comment he would have made. Both their heads turned toward the sound to discover Eric standing on Mason's side of the vehicle, protected from the subsiding drizzle by an umbrella.

Incredible. First, Anastasia had caused him to feel as though he were a small child. Now, this kid, who had brains enough to have grabbed something to prevent him from becoming drenched, made Mason feel twice the fool.

"Did you find me a tow truck?" Mason inquired as he rolled down the window and kept his self-directed disgust out of his voice.

Eric really didn't want to answer that question, so he asked one of his own instead. "How would you feel about spending the night in our humble motel?"

Mason's chin dropped to his chest. That word motel brought back all those images again of Anastasia, lying naked under him. He also had the sinking suspicion that the kid was trying to avoid something. He asked himself what more could go wrong before he reached Lake Sacajawea. "I am sure it is a nice place, Eric. But I would rather not." Okay.

So it was a lie. He just wanted Anastasia to share it with him. But he was beginning to believe that would not happen.

Damn it.

Eric fidgeted. "It's clean," he offered. "Right next door to the café. Talk about conveniences! What more could a guy want?"

"A tow truck," Mason supplied in answer to Eric's question.

"Well…." Eric tried a smile. "Do you enjoy a good joke?"

Anastasia shook her head and rolled her eyes. Leaning forward, she did not realize her breasts contacted Mason's arm until after she said, "Eric Miller. Stop beating around the bush. Mr. Lafayette doesn't have time for these games!" Then, when she realized the contact with Mason's arm, she pulled back so quickly, her head almost hit the window as a bright blush worked its way up her cheeks.

She hoped he hadn't noticed the touch.

But Mason had felt the contact and every part of his being tingled with awareness. At that moment, he could only stare out the front window of her Mazda as he fought an erection from becoming an issue.

Had she done that on purpose?

He forced himself to concentrate on the fact he still needed that tow truck. He turned his head back toward Eric, waiting for a further explanation.

However, the look on Mason's face resembled that of someone quite peeved, and Eric mistook it to mean he was angry at him, not as the frustration it was. "Oh, hell!" Eric exclaimed. "There isn't one, and that's the fricken truth! That storm that passed through here hit Bismarck about fifteen minutes ago, but ten times worse. Every tow truck available on Sundays is busy pulling cars out of the muck. It's a disaster in both Mandan and Bismarck, so…" He took a deep breath, set his jaw, and blurted, "There won't be any truck available until tomorrow

afternoon!" There. Let the rich guy figure a way out of that one. It was not his problem any longer.

Feeling lighter, now that he'd said what he had to, he squatted down beside the car, looked past Mr. Ladies' man, and told his cousin, "Gale called. M.D. is fine, and she wants to know if supper's still on." With that, he stomped away, mumbling loudly that it was not his fault that Mason Lafayette was marooned, with no salvation in sight.

Mason rubbed his hand across his face, then through his wet hair. He wished Eric hadn't put it that way. The way things were going, all that was left to happen to him was to run into that nut who had ordered Frank Jackson, and that would really be the icing on the cake.

What the devil was that name Josh had blurted out? Fantasia Carp? Some fool thing like that. And once again he questioned his decision to drive through North Dakota instead of taking a plane.

Anastasia's heart went out to him, though she was holding back a chuckle. He did not look at all as though he was having a good day. "Mason?" she tugged at her bottom lip with her teeth as an idea formed in her mind. He needed some way to get to Bismarck. "I have friends who will give you a lift to Bismarck if you'd like. I know Gale's husband, Jeff, wouldn't mind." And then, as another thought popped into her head, she wondered if she dared what she was about to ask.

The worst thing he could do was to say no.

She wondered when he had last eaten. He could be hungry. Maybe she could... Did she dare?

Why not? She'd never expected to meet him in her lifetime, so really, what was the harm in asking?

Not a darn thing. "If you're hungry, even though the café is right there," she jerked her chin toward the small diner, "I'm fixing spaghetti for my friends this evening. I always manage to make too much." She couldn't believe she was doing this! "Anyway, you're invited to join us."

She honestly doubted he would be interested in her little home-cooked meal. The man was undoubtedly used to far more flamboyant feasts. But when he asked, "You said spaghetti?" she could only nod, too stunned by the disarming smile he graced her with to speak.

"It is my favorite," he told her, and his next smile damn near had her melting through the floorboards to wash away with the slowly subsiding rainwater.

Mason Lafayette was coming to her house for dinner? Anastasia had the urge to pinch herself. She had to be dreaming again.

Chapter Eight

"I don't believe it," Gale whispered, and not for the first time. She worked alongside Anastasia, putting the finishing touches on the spaghetti dinner, complete with garlic toast and a chef's salad. "I just don't believe Mason Lafayette is sitting in your living room, talking to my husband, and letting my daughter sit on his lap!"

Anastasia rolled her eyes. If Gale said, I don't believe it, just one more time, she was going to dump the whole kettle of spaghetti sauce over the woman's damn head. "Give it a rest already," she said in a hushed tone. "He'll hear you!"

Oh, God. She didn't believe it either.

Who would have thought? Not she. And she was the dreamer.

She had not really expected him to accept her spontaneous invitation to dinner. But he had, and after making arrangements with Eric to have a tow truck pick up the disabled Corvette, he retrieved his three suitcases from its trunk and got in her vehicle. Then she'd driven them the half-mile south to her home.

Mason voiced his surprise upon discovering a town was at the bottom of the sloping hill that obstructed his view from the gas station. A town that was large enough to support a pharmacy, electronics repair shop, and an auto dealership.

"But," he told her in a bit of a scoff, "I doubt this town needs a mall."

She laughed because she had thought the same thing when the two-story building was built. Especially when the state's capital was less than an hour away via the interstate. "I know what you mean. The mall's only businesses are a grocery store, an insurance agency, two bars, and a beauty salon." She winked, adding, "The name of the salon is Shear

Delight. Like the name?" She raised a brow in warning. "It's my salon, by the way."

Mason's deep chuckle filled her small Mazda and caused Anastasia's heart to skip a beat. "In that case, *mademoiselle*, it is a *délicieux* name."

Her brows drew together. "What does *délic*…whatever you said, mean?"

"Delightful," he grinned.

She groaned. "That's an awful joke, Mason." And yet she laughed because his teasing her felt so right, so perfect. She had not suspected a teasing side of him, and she liked it. Liked it a lot.

He faked a wounded expression. "I thought it was *délicieux*… ow!" and he laughed because she punched him in the arm. "What was that for?"

She doubted her little punch did any damage. The man's arms were like solid rock. "You say that word one more time, and it will delight me to throw you out of my car!"

He'd been rude enough to remind her she stopped the car five minutes ago. They were parked in her driveway. And that he highly doubted he would suffer much damage to his person, should she make good on her threat. "Don't get technical," she told him in a laughing huff.

"You win," he told her softly. "Now, solve a mystery for me, *drôle dame*. Tell me… Why is there a big cow guarding this town?"

Had she known he had called her funny lady, she would have blushed. But she explained some history surrounding the thirty-eight feet high and fifty-foot-long statue. "We call her Salem Sue. She is the world's largest Holstein cow. The New Salem Lions Club had her built in 1974 as a tribute to the area's dairy industry."

Mason whistled and whispered silky soft, "She is a beautiful lady," just before he leaned toward her as though he were about to kiss her.

She bolted out of her car as though it suddenly caught fire. "Yes. Well… Perhaps you would like to take a quick shower and change into some dry clothes before the Martins arrive?" And she marched right into the house before he made it out of the car himself.

"You, who. Anastasia?" Gail's singsong voice snapped her back to the present. "Are you going to finish that sauce or daydream all day?"

Anastasia cleared her throat. "Finish setting the table, Gale. Ten more minutes, and this will be," she kissed her fingertips, "perfecto!"

When Gale left the room, Anastasia let out a heavy sigh. She was more than glad the Martins arrived while Mason was in the shower. When she invited the man for supper, she had not considered he might have thought she was luring him to her house to spend time in her bed.

Not that she wouldn't have wanted to explore that avenue. She would like to discover if he was as good in bed in real life as he was in her dreams, but she had never been a woman to jump into the sack with a man she just met. Besides, he had no idea how dangerous getting involved with her could be if Danny were to find out she was with anyone.

Fortunately for him, he wouldn't be here long enough to find that out.

It was for his own safety she ignored the lust she'd seen in his eyes and his invitation to join him in the shower.

Poor man. She doubted he'd ever been turned down in his life. She tried hard not to damage his ego and hoped he wouldn't take the rejection personally.

She tasted the sauce, added a touch more salt, and proclaimed it was a masterpiece. At least Mason would leave here with having sampled a good feast, and she was not being conceded about her cooking abilities. Merely stating a fact and hoped the meal would help him forget she had ignored his advances.

* * *

The shower had felt great. The dry clothes were better, but neither of those two things brought Mason comfort as he reflected on the fact, Anastasia had given him the brush off.

When was the last time his charm and sexuality had been rejected by a woman?

Never. Not once had it happened.

Bruised ego? Most definitely.

Women came easily to him. Even more so now that he'd been sky-rocketed into fame across America, where thousands of women knew his name. All of them would be more than willing to jump into the sack with him if he asked it.

And don't forget about his popularity in France. He'd been a household name there since the day he was born, and once he matured, women were giving him suggestive looks from the time he became a teenager.

To have been denied what he craved truly boggled his mind.

He might have found that refreshing if he hadn't been interested in her, but he was. Yet she actually laughed at his suggestion to join him in the shower and wash his back.

Laughed. At him!

Unbelievable.

Maybe she wasn't attracted to him, he tried to tell himself. Perhaps that was why she hadn't joined him in the shower.

Ha. He hadn't met a woman yet who hadn't wanted him unless they preferred women themselves.

His eyes glanced toward the calendar hanging on the living room wall, staring at his own image and knew that Anastasia obviously liked his looks and body.

He told himself it should relieve him to have a woman not treat him like a piece of meat for a change. Wasn't that something he had hoped

for last night? The chance to kick back with friends and not be pawed at?

Then why wasn't he relieved?

Because with everything else to have gone wrong this day, Anastasia's ignoring his cue to join him in the shower caused him to think he was now losing his touch with women.

Yes, she'd declined the offer by telling him she needed to begin the meal, but he hadn't believed her. He thought she was teasing and that she would join him, anyway. By the time he realized she really had no intention of joining him, he'd been in that shower for a good half hour.

She really had been in the kitchen preparing a meal, and guests had arrived.

It was unbelievable!

"How long are ya gonna be in North Dakota, Mason?" Jeff Martin asked, bringing the befuddled guy out from his private daze.

Mason looked across the small space that separated him from the other man. They sat facing one another in one of the smallest living rooms Mason had ever come across. Hell, Anastasia's entire house would easily fit in his own living room. "Two weeks," he answered, glancing once more at the calendar. It hadn't been turned since May, and it was now the first of July. Obviously, that picture of him standing in the shower was Anastasia's favorite. "I am visiting friends. They have a summer home on Lake Sacajawea." So, if that photo of me in the shower is her favorite, why did she not join me in participating in the real thing?

"Haven't been up there in years," Jeff told him.

"Same," Mason said and shifted a bit in the chair. "Is Anastasia seeing anyone?" and why in the hell had he just asked that question?

Maybe that would explain why she hadn't joined him in the shower if she was seeing someone. But why that would matter to her, when it didn't seem to bother any other woman he knew to cheat on the guy

they were involved with, was beyond him. "Or is she married, and her husband is out of town?" Good grief. He really was determined to make an utter ass out of himself, wasn't he?

Jeff stared. "Why?"

Why? Good question. Mason wished he knew the answer. "She is a beautiful woman," he allowed, then shrugged as though indifferent. "I would think she has a line of men knocking a path to her door."

"Not Anastasia," Jeff almost snapped. Keeping his voice low but laced with warning, he continued, "I don't know what kind of women you hang out with, Lafayette. But our Stasia is not like them, so you back off."

That sounded protective and Mason wondered why but decided to forget the whole thing. Other things needed his attention and getting out of New Salem was one of them.

If he called the Fishers now, Hunter could pick him up here, instead of Jeff Martin driving him into Bismarck. The way Hunter drove, he would be here by the time that spaghetti feast was over.

Why hadn't he thought of that before now?

"Anastasia?" his voice rose enough to be heard in the kitchen, and the moment her head appeared around the door frame, he knew the reason. She had a way of removing all thought from him. Curse the woman.

"Yes?"

He cleared his throat. "May I use your phone?" He had to get out of here before he went nuts. Her acting as though he were nothing more than a neighbor came to say howdy was really getting to him.

But that is another thing that intrigues you, his inner voice told him. She is treating you with respect. She makes you laugh-

He told his mind to shut up and allow him to wallow in his self-pity.

She had the gall to tell him to use the phone in her bedroom.

She would send me there when she has no intention of joining me, he fumed.

"She's a superb cook," Jeff sighed.

Mason gently helped the six-year-old sitting on his lap down. The child had been so quiet, playing with her two barbie dolls, he had all but completely forgotten her.

She smiled at him as he rose to his feet.

It tugged at his heart. He liked kids and hoped he would have some of his own one day. "Will you sit next to me when we eat, little one?" he asked, not realizing he was holding his breath, waiting for her answer. He was suddenly afraid his failure with Anastasia was going to extend down to even the youngest female wanting nothing to do with him.

Pattie's smile brightened, and she nodded.

He let out a sigh of relief.

When he turned to move into the bedroom, she tugged at his jeans. Squatting down and rolling onto the balls of his feet, he came to eye level with her. "I will be back, *chéri*. I promise." He patted the top of her head, then playfully pulled the single pigtail on the side of her head.

Her eyes turned serious. "Did you know Danny hurt Aunt Stasia?" she asked in a whispered voice. "She was in the hospital-"

Mason stared, and his heart twisted. The child could not possibly mean what she implied- There were so many ways for a man to hurt a woman, and he prayed Anastasia had not suffered the same fate his mother had.

Jeff Martin gasped. "Pattie! Go see if your mother needs help with setting the table!"

Pattie went. Lickety-split.

Mason's eyes trailed after the child. "Jeff?" He turned his gaze toward Pattie's father. He shouldn't ask. In fact, he didn't really want to know

the truth because if Anastasia- If she had gone through the same nightmare-

Jeff stood, snapping, "I don't believe it's any of your business!"

Maybe not, but Mason desired, deep within his soul, to know if that wonderful and delightful woman who could so quickly bring forth a laugh from him had been raped. "Pattie said-"

"I don't gossip Lafayette, and after tonight you'll be gone, so what difference does it make? Anastasia is a strong woman, and if she wanted you to know her past, she'd tell you. You've only just met her, so I doubt it's going to be part of our dinner conversation. So, go make your phone call and forget what my daughter said."

For a moment, Mason hesitated. He knew Jeff was right. That after tonight he would probably never see the woman again. But that realization caused a pain in his heart he wasn't sure he wanted to explore.

But when Mason finally turned away and left the room, walking into Anastasia's bedroom, he felt sick inside.

He moved to Anastasia's bed, picked up the phone, and dialed the Fisher's number. As he listened to it ring, his eyes found yet another photo of himself. This one framed and sitting on the dresser next to the bed. He picked it up, recognizing it as the one that went out to people when they became a member of his fan club.

"Joe's bar and grill. You kill 'em. We cook 'em," a man's cocky voice answered the Fisher's line.

He immediately forgot the photo and painful memories, replaced by overwhelming joy upon hearing the familiar voice of his best friend. "I thought you were the great and mighty hunter," he joked and felt as though the last few years roll away as though they hadn't happened.

"Mason?! Holy shit. That can't be you!" Hunter sounded as though the government had given him permission to lead a strike team to Kuwait and bomb Saddam Hussein to hell; ten times.

"*Bonjour,* Hunter!"

"I don't fucken believe it! Where in the hell are you?"

"New Salem."

"Where?"

It felt as though Mason had already had this conversation once today. "New Salem."

"North Dakota?" Hunter's voice said he didn't believe it.

"Yes, Hunter. North Dakota." And he quickly explained how he had come to be here. "Interested in playing chauffeur?"

"Are you kidding? I'd be more than happy to have an excuse to be away from your damn sister."

"Daniela?"

"Did your folks have another child I'm not aware of, Mason? Of course I mean Daniela!"

Mason shook his head and chuckled. "Hunter, you are not seriously telling me my sixteen-year-old sister is getting the best of you?"

"No," Hunter gritted. "I'm telling you that if I don't have a break from her, she's heading for an early grave."

Mason grimaced. Hunter sounded too sincere about that statement.

To distract his best friend from his upset at Daniela, Mason said off-handedly, "By the way. I heard you are now following in my footsteps, having your face grace magazine covers. Are romance books next?"

"What?!" It was a big explosion.

Mason knew he shouldn't have brought the incident up. But after feeling carefree for the first time in years, combined with knowing an American soldier magazine had snapped a picture of the one man they shouldn't have, then placed that photo on the front cover out of spite because of what Hunter did to the photographer- Well, Mason just

couldn't resist. "It is a nice picture, though you looked as though you were about to kill the photographer." That was an understatement. Hunter's expression, as Mason recalled, had been as hard as granite under the layers of camo paint covering his face.

"Mason, who in the fuck told you about that picture?"

"Your sister sent me a copy of the magazine. I liked the caption. *The Navy's SEALS. Are they worth-*"

"Which sister? I'm going to break her neck."

Mason laughed.

"I'll be there in a half-hour, Mason."

"It is over an hour's drive, Hunter."

"You say one more word about that photo, and I'll make the trip in less than fifteen minutes."

"Is it true you broke the photographer's nose, and it took fifteen men to get you under control-"

"Ten minutes, Lafayette. Then you're a dead man."

Mason wondered if the Fisher's phone survived Hunter's wrath when the line went dead.

Of course. He wondered if he would, too.

Replacing the phone to its cradle, he lifted his hand to place the framed photo of himself back onto the nightstand and froze. He hadn't seen the book before because the framed photo had been sitting on top of it.

Recovering From Domestic Violence and Abuse.

Suddenly, he wanted to puke as he contemplated why she would read a book like that if she hadn't suffered something horrible.

Chapter Nine

The conversation around Anastasia's dinner table was comprised of the recent rainstorm, how long Mason would visit his friends, and the new television show, Home Improvement. Jeff and Gale talked excitedly about the upcoming state fair in Minot, and their enthusiasm at having gotten tickets to see their favorite country-western singer, Garth Brooks, live in concert as he was scheduled to appear at the annual event.

"More spaghetti?" Anastasia asked Mason, reaching for the bowl of pasta. He'd been quiet during the meal. Taking part when asked a question, but otherwise, he was silent, and she wondered if he had received bad news during the phone call he made.

Mason pushed back from the table, patting his thin, rock hard stomach. "No. The meal was fantastic. Jeff told me you were a wonderful cook, and now I do not doubt it. I have eaten more than I am used to, and too much pasta is not good for me."

"How long have you been lifting weights?" Jeff wanted to know, eyeing Mason's biceps.

"I began weight training when I was around fifteen years old," Mason told him. "It is something my best friend was doing, and it became a habit of mine also."

"Good for you," Jeff told him. "The weights I've lifted all my life are hay bales. That's enough for me."

Mason smiled but made no comment. His own childhood memories of being on the Fisher's horse ranch and taking part in the same activity came rushing back. Even now, he could remember the smell and the dust of that job. He learned more about the importance of allowing the

alfalfa for the horses to dry out before they baled it than people would think a kid who'd grown up rich would understand.

He'd learned to be sure the baler's settings were right before starting a job of baling hay. If the settings weren't right, the bales could become far too heavy or to lose and fall apart. On average, the Fishers kept their square bales at forty pounds, but after spending all day picking them up and throwing them onto a flatbed, they felt like eighty pounds and more.

His lips twitched at the memory.

"I like to draw and paint," young Pattie Martin told him.

Looking to his right where the young girl sat next to him, he said, "Do you? My uncle Dominic enjoys that activity. They showcase his artwork around the world. Tell me, what is your favorite thing to paint? Perhaps one day, people will come from miles away to see it." He smiled at her.

"Unicorns!" she said without hesitation, laughing.

"Indeed? Do you paint them with wings and fairy dust?" he teased.

"Unicorns don't have fairy dust," Pattie informed him.

"Really?" He pretended to be shocked by the news. "I was certain the last unicorn I rode left fairy dust on me. It took me almost a week to get it all out of my hair."

Pattie's eyes widened, and she said in awe, "You rode a unicorn?!"

Anastasia chuckled at the look of magical wonder on Pattie's face. "I have a picture of him doing just that," she claimed.

Mason glanced up at her, pleased she was going along with his tall tale.

Pushing away from the table, Anastasia stood up. "Give me a moment, and I'll find it," she told Pattie, then made her way into her office and quickly rummaged through a folder in her desk drawer. Once she found what she was looking for, she gazed down at the warrior prince of the fantasy land this image had become the cover for.

It was hard to fathom he was in her house, but she would enjoy whatever little time she had left with him and would cherish the memory.

She also wished she knew what caused his mood to change from carefree to reserved.

Bringing the photo with her back into the kitchen, she handed it to Pattie. "See, honey. Mason has ridden a unicorn."

With an open mouth, Pattie stared at the picture. When her eyes moved to Mason, there was hero-worship in them. "I knew they were real," she whispered in wonderment.

"Would you like to keep the photo?" Anastasia asked the child.

"Can I, Aunt Stasia?" and Pattie held it to her chest.

"Of course, honey."

Jeff shook his head. "It amazes me how those pictures can look so real. Was that sword they had you hold heavy?"

Mason shook his head. "No. They hold a typical photoshoot from three to five hours, and the photographer wants to shoot five or six covers in one day. I have learned to be on point with the expression and poses he wants to capture. I do not have objects in my hands long enough to consider them heavy."

"When did you decide you wanted to be a model?" Gale wanted to know, and Mason was feeling as though he were on a talk show.

Anastasia laughed. "Leave the man alone. He's on vacation. And if everyone is finished eating," she began clearing plates, "I'll get started on the dishes."

"I will help," Mason informed her, also standing up from the table and began collecting the dirty silverware.

Anastasia's eyes widened at that revelation. "You will not! You're my guest and-"

"Sweetie, he wants to help," Gale scolded her as she also rose to her feet, and Jeff did likewise, raving about another marvelous feast. "The man knows he doesn't have to." She nudged her husband in the arm with her elbow. "You should take lessons, dear. See there. Mason knows how to make points with the ladies."

Jeff snorted. "I don't need to make points. I already have a wife, and dishes are for women to do."

Gale stared. "I hope you are joking-"

Jeff laughed. "Of course," he teased. "I wouldn't make a statement like that unless I was willing to become a bachelor again. Which," he kissed his wife's round cheek, "I'm not."

Anastasia reached to take the silverware from Mason's hand. "You don't need to do this." Did he really want to help with something so trivial as washing the dishes?

She was more than amazed. She would have never pictured someone as famous as him getting dishpan hands. "I don't have a dishwasher," she thought to inform him, thinking he might not realize it was manual labor he was about to find himself doing.

Mason moved his hand out of her reach and grinned as he looked down at her. She was tall enough for the top of her head to reach his chin, so he didn't have to lower his head as he did with his mother and sister to look them in the eye. They were shorter, coming only to his shoulders. "I want to help," he insisted. With that, he moved into the kitchen before she could further her protest.

Anastasia shot Gale a curious look.

Gale shrugged. "Let him help. It won't hurt him, and besides, since Mason's friend is on his way here to get him, Jeff wants to drive over to Judson and check on his parents. Now that the sun's shining again, and there are still a few hours of daylight left, he wants to see if that hail damaged their roof."

Anastasia stared. "But-" Was Gale jesting? Were they going to leave her alone with Mason? How could they? "You can't-"

"You'll be fine," Gale repeated gently. "We will lock the door on the way out, so you needn't worry about that department." Locking Anastasia's door was standard since no one knew when Danny might come to town. "And I think you deserve a little more time, however long that will be before he's gone, to talk to the man you've dreamed about for the past year."

Anastasia shook her head. "You know, I never thought for one minute I'd meet him."

"Which is exactly why Jeff and I are leaving. It's your chance of a lifetime."

"What do you mean by that?"

"Maybe he'd help you break into publishing-"

"Oh, no," Anastasia held up her hands. "I cannot believe you would suggest such a thing. I am not the type of person to use someone for my gain. If I make it into the romance writing industry and become successful, it will be because of my own hard work."

Gale shrugged. "I suppose you're right."

"Darn right, I'm right."

"Regardless, we're leaving. I look forward to tomorrow and hearing what the two of you talked about." Gale looked at her husband and daughter. "Come along, you two."

Anastasia watched the Martins as they let themselves out the front door, locking it on their way out.

With the shake of her head, she finished stacking the plates and carried them into the kitchen.

She found Mason at the counter, filling the sink with warm water. "You're really going to do this," she stated, placing her burden on the counter next to him.

He turned his head and grinned again. "Do you think I cannot do it?"

That grin, combined with that accent, was playing havoc on her senses regardless of the fact that there wasn't any sexual undertone in his voice this time. Nor a steamy gaze burning holes through her. It was as though a different person had entered his body, and she wasn't sure what to make of the new Mason Lafayette.

"I'm not used to having a man help with dishes," she told him honestly. "Danny would have never-" Her voice broke off, and she turned her head away, busying herself with finding a dish towel, hoping he hadn't noticed the catch that entered her voice. "I'm just not used to it, that's all." She shrugged and prayed he wouldn't ask who Danny was.

He didn't but wanted to. And knew he was probably better off not knowing what this Danny had done to her.

"Well, thank you for allowing me to help," Mason told her. "My mother would turn me over her knee if she found out I let a woman make me a glorious meal, then made her do all the cleanup while I sat on my ass, watching television."

A twitch began at the corner of Anastasia's mouth. "I have seen photos of you with your mother. And even though she is a beautiful woman, she isn't very tall. I doubt she would have the strength to lift you over her knee," she scoffed, and there was amusement in her voice as she made the observation.

His laugh was rich. "Oh, my mother would find a way if she was angry enough. And she is very good at scolding me when upset."

Eyes twinkling, she laughed as she eyed the six-foot-three man wearing a brown muscle shirt that was barely covering the forty-eight-inch chest as she pictured his mother scolding him. "I think I'd like to see that," she told him. "But since you seem hell-bent on getting dishpan

hands, be my guest." She moved to stand next to him in preparation of drying the dishes as he washed. "And I guess I wouldn't honestly want your mother scolding you. Especially after the bad day you've had."

Did she have to remind him of that?

They washed the dishes in silence, and strangely enough, it wasn't awkward. In truth, it felt as though they'd done this countless times together before.

After a moment, she glanced at the clock and frowned. "Mason? When did you say your friend would be here?" She did not know from which part of Lake Sacajawea his friend would arrive from, but that man-made lake was only sixty miles north of New Salem. If he was coming from the south shore, he should have been here by now.

Mason's own eyes glanced at the time.

She was right. Hunter should have arrived by now. However, knowing Hunter, he was probably having a fight with some highway patrol officer foolhardy enough to have tried pulling him over for speeding.

Mason shrugged. "I am sure he is on his way."

"Did you want to call? Find out when he left?"

Her concern touched him. "Do not worry about Hunter," he chuckled. "He can take care of himself."

Which was more than true. His best friend was responsible for Mason having received more hands-on experience in the art of self-defense than he cared to remember.

Having a friend who was a world champion in martial arts and liked to battle at the drop of a hat was the primary reason Mason had taken up bodybuilding.

Placing the dishtowel over the hanger to dry, Anastasia asked, "Would you like some coffee?" Obviously, Mason wasn't worried about his friend, and she might as well follow his lead.

Mason placed the last pan into the dish drain. "*Oui*. Coffee would be good." He glanced at her. "And Anastasia? Thank you for caring. About Hunter."

Her smile was shy. "I've been told I'm a mother hen. Guess it's showing through." She poured two cups of hot coffee and joined him at the small kitchen table.

"Who tells you that?" his voice hinted at a laugh.

"My cousin, Eric. You met him today. Remember?"

He nodded. How could he forget? "Why does he say that?"

She giggled. "Eric only says that once in a while, and only when he's grown tired of calling me weird." At his questioning look, she explained, "Whenever I do some off the wall thing, he tells me I'm weird."

"Off the wall?"

"Like the time he was talking to his girlfriend on the phone while I was at the gas station. I began singing Young Love in the background." She beamed him a smile. "Know what? Eighteen-year-old's blush so well!"

"I am sure they do," and he laughed, picturing her doing what she just claimed.

She ordered Frank Jackson.

Mason almost stopped breathing as Josh Reno's words leaped back into his thoughts, and suddenly he knew who the flake from New Salem was.

He almost laughed. Anastasia was no woman needing a one-way trip to the funny farm. But she seemed to be a lady who had maintained her sense of humor despite whatever trauma she may have suffered from the man she called Danny.

He admired her—more than he was going to admit.

"Tell me about yourself, Mason."

His gaze locked with hers, and he allowed the playful nature in him to show once again. "You have my calendar hanging on your wall, *mademoiselle*," he told her softly. "I would think you knew all about me."

Her bright red blush was incredible, and he enjoyed it. "Ask away," he encouraged with a wave of his hand, leaning back in the chair. "What do you wish to know?"

"Anything?"

He nodded.

"After what I just told you? About me being known for the strange- Anything?"

"Anything," he chuckled. "I doubt there is a question you can ask that I have not heard. Nor do I blush."

Anastasia was not about to pass this moment up. It was the chance of a lifetime, and she went for broke. "Then tell me about the real Mason Lafayette."

He stared. He could not have possibly heard her correctly. "You mean, you want to know about my career and how I got started as a model." He wasn't asking. He was clarifying.

Anastasia tugged at her bottom lip with her teeth, wondering if she should go through with it, then became determined. It wasn't as though she would see him after he left here tonight. What did she have to lose?

Not a damn thing.

Looking him straight in those cat-like green eyes that fascinated her, she told him, "I want to know about this, Mason." She placed her hand above her heart, showing him exactly what she meant.

Chapter Ten

She wanted to know his heart?

Mason was glad Anastasia's poodle chose that moment to scratch at the back door, requesting entrance.

What sort of question was that?

He watched her move to the door, open it, and let the black mutt inside. He could not meet her eyes. Not yet. He was too busy trying to come up with an answer to the one question no one had ever asked him before.

Well. She had warned him, hadn't she? But who in the hell would have thought she would ask him that unexpected question?

The poodle was dancing circles around her denim-clad legs, and he watched the scrawny thing, thinking it was cute in an ugly sort of way.

He called to it. It merely looked at him as though bored before turning its nose in the air. Somehow, it just seemed fitting that a woman as different as Anastasia Sharp would have a poodle with an attitude problem.

"What does M.D. really mean?" he asked, wanting to know, and was trying to sidestep her question at the same time.

His heart? Unbelievable!

"You don't believe it means My Dog?" Anastasia asked, eyes widening as though she really expected him to believe that crazy lie.

Mason still couldn't look at her, but a corner of his mouth twitched, and he shook his head. And she had the nerve to sound shocked at his question. God, she made him laugh.

Without warning loud banging sounded upon the front door, interrupting any reply he would have made right then.

M.D. froze, lowered his head, and began growling low in his throat.

Anastasia paled. Her heart went to her throat. The only time Mason Divine made that low, angry sound was when Danny-. "Oh, God," she whispered, her terror rising. Not now. Please, God. Not now!

M.D.'s growl became a snarl.

Without thinking about it, Anastasia hissed, "Be quiet, Mason!"

Mason Lafayette's brow arched. "I am not making that racket. Someone is knocking on your door." The word door faded as Anastasia's head snapped toward him, and his mouth damn near hit the floor. He had never witnessed actual terror before, but she was displaying, he supposed, the worst it ever got. "What is wrong?" he asked, standing. She was vibrating so profoundly he wasn't sure what he should do.

The front door rattled, forcefully.

Mason had no idea who was beating on the door, but he sure as hell was going to find out and, if it was Hunter giving Anastasia this fright, he would kill him.

Anastasia came out of her daze just as Mason headed for the living room. "No!" she screamed, grabbing his arm, nails digging into his flesh. "No!" she repeated in a frantic whisper. "Oh, God, Mason. Whatever you do, stay away from that door!"

Mason's heart squeezed. He wanted to hold her. Wanted to comfort her. "Who?"

"Damn it, Anastasia. Open this goddamn door before I break it down!"

M.D. unthawed and charged for the door, barking fiercely.

"And tell Mason to keep his ugly yap shut!" the man's angry voice added.

Inside the house, Mason Lafayette's jaw dropped. That was not Jeff Martin's voice, nor Hunter's. He had not spoken loudly enough for whoever was outside to have heard him so- Who in the hell just told him to keep his ugly -ugly? -yap shut?

Anastasia ignored Mason's bewildered look and brushed past him, entering the living room just far enough to yell, "Go home, Danny! If you don't leave this minute, I'll call the sheriff!" She reached for the phone attached to the wall in the kitchen and dialed the number, anyway. She'd gone through this scenario enough times to know Danny wouldn't leave without force.

This time, the door came close to caving in. "I told you to open this damn door, Stasia!"

Bam, bam, bam.

"Oh, God!" Anastasia's entire body quaked, and it was a struggle to hold the receiver against her ear. "Go home!" she screamed. "We have nothing to talk about!" Her heart threatened to come right out of her chest.

"Morton County Sheriff's department," a woman's voice answered the call.

"This is Anastasia Sharp. Danny's trying to break down the door!" she cried, then slammed the receiver back into place. They needed no further information. Every officer between New Salem and Bismarck had dealt with Danny at one time or another over the last two years.

Mason was at the end of his rope. This day could not possibly get worse, and after listening to the banging on the door, and Anastasia's frantic phone call, he wanted to hit something. And if the person outside was the Danny he thought it was, and he had no reason to doubt it wasn't since Anastasia was ghost white, he was going to put an end to this act of terror before the woman fainted on the spot.

His hand touched the doorknob, ready to open it and take a swing at the jerk on the other side of the door.

"No!" Anastasia screeched, grabbing his wrist. "Mason, you don't understand. If he sees you, he'll kill you!"

He met her frightened eyes. "Tell me who that man is," he all but demanded, and he did not remove his hand from the doorknob.

"My ex," she whispered, fighting the waves of emotions threatening to paralyze her. "I have a restraining order against him. But that's just a sheet of paper, and there aren't enough officers around to watch out for me night and day."

"If you don't open this door, I'll break the goddamn window!" Danny vowed.

Bam, bam, bam!

"Danny! Go home!"

"He is not leaving," Mason stated, weighing the situation. He had not been forced to use his fists in over eight years, but he knew he was in good shape. Knew his size alone could give him the added edge-

Anastasia shook her head at him as though she just read his mind, and her words confirmed it. "If you're thinking what I think you're thinking," she hissed, "forget it! Danny was in the Marines. He'll lay you out before you see his punch coming, and somehow, I doubt your agency would appreciate you showing up for a photoshoot with a broken nose!"

Mason took that as an insult. "I can take him," he told her confidently, fingers touching his broad chest. Didn't his muscles warrant even the slightest amount of faith?

She added salt to the wound by snorting. "That's what the three officers said the last time he came knocking on my door," she hissed. "Two of them wound up in the hospital!"

The shattering noise drew both of their attention to the picture window above the couch.

"Oh, God."

M.D. charged, yapping wildly.

"Mason! Come back here!" Anastasia screamed.

Mason? It finally came to him. "You named your dog, Mason?" He could not believe it!

"Hide!" Anastasia exclaimed, pushing him back toward the kitchen.

He gaped at her as though she lost her mind. "I will not!" Hide? Indeed.

"Fine!" Anastasia threw her hands in the air. "Go get yourself killed. Be my guest. See what I care." She poked a finger in his muscular chest. "Just don't come haunting me once they've buried you!"

That statement told him she didn't believe he could defend himself, which made him madder than hell.

"Thanks for the vote of confidence," he gritted, strolling past her angrily. Christ! So, the guy had been in the Marines. So, the guy had put two cops in the hospital. So, the guy was dangerous.

So, if the guy was so dangerous, why in the hell was he charging into a situation that would no doubt find his famous face rearranged at its end?

She named her poodle Mason, that's why. God! A poodle, for Christ's sake! Had it been a black lab, German shepherd, or the mighty great Dane, he would not have been so insulted, and right now, he was feeling insulted all over the place.

He wondered what the D stood for but shook the question off. After discovering what the M meant, he doubted he wanted to know if it meant dimwit. Which was precisely the way he was feeling about himself and this hair-brained idea of his to take part in the annual reunion. So far, ever since crossing that Montana/North Dakota border, he had been having nothing but a splendidly rotten day.

Well, he was going to show her he was not just something cute, by God. He was a man. One quite capable of taking care of himself; thank you very much!

Danny Sharp crawled through the broken window, bits of glass crunching together beneath his bulk.

Mason froze in mid-step. The cliché *are you a man, or a mouse*, ran through his mind as he watched the big, really big, fellow making his way into the house.

No one was ever going to know how badly he wanted to squeak at that moment.

* * *

The black jeep flew up the New Salem exit doing eighty miles an hour.

Hunter Sundance Fisher ignored the stop sign.

Having planned on arriving in this small town over an hour ago, he'd been set behind schedule because of that rainstorm. But it wasn't the reason the speedometer was above the speed limit. He simply liked traveling fast.

That storm he'd run into twenty minutes after leaving Sacajawea was the reason he was so late. Even he wasn't foolhardy enough to drive in a life-threatening sheet of rain and hail.

He was ornery. Not stupid.

The jeep squealed as it rounded the left-hand corner, and he had to fight to prevent it from jumping the bridge he needed to cross to reach New Salem. Once he had control of the vehicle, he grinned.

He liked danger.

He brushed his shoulder-length light brown hair away from his face, sweeping it off to its usual left part, only to have the wind whip it back into his eyes. He knew he should have cut the sun-kissed locks long ago, having grown it out for a recent undercover assignment. However, just knowing Uncle Cadman, who was his boss and the head of Task Force Ghost, did not like the flowing mane, Hunter had kept it, just to piss him off.

Hunter could not wait to see Mason. God. How long had it been since the last time they had seen each other? Five? Six years?

Mason was the only person whom Hunter called friend. Not that anyone else was pounding a path to his door for that honor. Which was fine with him.

Mason Lafayette. Cover boy. God, it made Hunter sick! The guy could have easily become a SEAL if he had wanted it. But no, Mason always enjoyed being in the public's eyes. Wanting attention. Wanting fame, though, Hunter supposed it was only natural for him to crave the spotlight since he'd been in it from the day he'd been born.

But why Mason would want to be on the cover of countless romance books, Hunter wasn't sure. But he speculated it had something to do with the fact there had been nothing romantic about the night he'd been conceived. But what Mason did not know, and Hunter would never tell him, was the fact Mason's face being all over the place helped the evil bastard who'd sired him lure unsuspecting young women to him.

Unfortunately, Mason was almost a mirror image of Pierre Bellefeuille, and Pierre, though showed no interest in the man who was his famous son, had no qualms about using his likeness to his advantage.

Hunter's stomach had long ago stopped throwing up when he discovered one of Bellefeuille's victims. Over the past few years, he'd learned to turn off his emotions when seeing the horror. If he hadn't, he wouldn't be effective at his job, and he'd dreamed of being one of the best of the best for longer than he could remember.

He'd been trailing Bellefeuille for the past couple of years, having gotten closer to finding him than Cadman ever did when he, too, had been looking for him. Not that Cadman had given up, but he was sixty-four now, and he'd stepped back to allow Hunter to take the lead because Hunter was like a bloodhound for tracking people over the world.

Hunter would also never tell Mason he had a half-brother a year younger than him. But Pierre had kept that son, Hadeon, at his side from the moment he'd been born, and, it seemed, Pierre was attempting to groom him to be just like him.

Just what the world needed. Another psychopath.

Hadeon was not as handsome nor tall as Mason was. Hunter knew that to be true because he'd come almost within spitting distance of him once but could not get a good enough grip on him before he lost his hold and Hadeon was whisked away by the men he was with, and Hunter's team had been fighting another group at the time.

That missed opportunity still grated on Hunter. He was not used to missing a chance to apprehend someone he'd set his eyes on to bring to justice.

Oh well. There would be another time and another place, and Hunter would be ready for it.

Hunter forced himself to snap his mind back to Mason. His best friend always liked it when women threw themselves at him, but that wasn't something Hunter enjoyed. He liked women. He just didn't need or want them throwing themselves at him.

He liked his freedom too much.

Hunter would never settle down and get married. No, sir. Not this guy. He didn't need those types of headaches. Besides, the way he conducted himself, along with what his job all entailed, he couldn't afford the luxury of opening his heart to a woman.

The thought of marriage caused Daniela Lafayette's face to form, unwanted, in his mind. Mason's kid sister was going to drive him to drink, and he hadn't been around her longer than twenty-four hours yet! It was no wonder he hadn't made a habit of attending these reunions, even if he were to have free time. The last time he saw her, she had been eight, and as far as he was concerned, she should have remained eight. She would not be following him around now, everywhere.

Hunter recognized the signs of a first crush. But why him, for Christ's sake? He was eleven years older than that little twirp. However, if she told him just once more during this reunion that when she turned eighteen, she was going to marry him; he was going to take her into the lake

and hold her ugly head underwater until the bubbles rising to the surface assured him she was quite dead.

That would take care of her little plan quite nicely, he thought with devilish certainty.

How a woman as beautiful as Mason's mother could have given birth to such an ugly duckling as Daniela, Hunter was sure he would never know. And whether or not Daniela ever turned into a swan, he doubted he would live long enough to find out. He was always one step away from death's door.

Not that he cared about either matter.

Entering New Salem, he slowed the jeep down. For Hunter, that was a miracle.

The sky was clear. The only sign that there had been rain was the water standing in the ditches. Typical North Dakota weather. It changed just like Hunter's moods. No rhyme or reason, and never predictable.

The summer's sun had not made its full descent into the west, though the sky was dimming. There was, however, plenty enough light left for him to make out the street signs. Three rights. Two lefts, and he found the proper avenue.

He had to laugh. Luck was always with him.

The jeep slowed to a crawl as he searched out the house number Mason gave him over the phone during their conversation. When he found it, the hair on his neck rose, and so did his adrenalin.

The mountain of flesh was huge, whoever he was, and he looked livid enough to kill anything, or anyone, who may cross his path.

Hunter's eyes never moved from the man as he parked the jeep. The guy was pounding on the front door of the house where Mason was sup-posed to be. Then, abruptly, Mt. Rushmore moved to the front window. Within the span of a heartbeat, he retrieved a large rock from a flower garden and hefted it through the picture window.

Hunter grinned and opened the jeep's door.

This was going to be more fun than he had hoped for!

Chapter Eleven

At six foot seven, Danny Sharp dwarfed Mason by four inches, but it was the four hundred pounds backing up the tall frame that caused Mason to reconsider Anastasia's suggestion to hide. It suddenly had merit.

Mason only admitted that to himself. He was not really going to crawl into a hole, as much as he might have wanted to. But now that he saw the size of the man who Pattie Martin alluded to having hurt Anastasia, he was determined to see this thing through. This man had done something to this woman who touched him in ways he had yet to admit. Because of that, he was not about to turn tail and run when she needed someone to protect her from more possible agony.

"Who in the hell are you?" Danny growled, hazel eyes blazing holes through Mason with scorching heat.

Mason was too busy frantically recalling every move and rule of self-defense Hunter taught him to answer the angry question.

Rule number one, Mason remembered, was, "Never, ever, let the other guy know you're scared spitless."

Okay. Fine. Mason took a deep breath and fought for that calm. "I am the guy who is going to do you a favor," he told Danny in the most unafraid voice he could muster. It impressed him that he sounded as confident as the words made him out to be.

Danny's laugh did not help his confidence any. "Yeah? What's the favor, French fry?"

That slur had Mason steaming. "I am going to give you the chance to leave nice and quiet."

And from now on, I take the fucking plane!

Obviously, Mason's forced confident tone hadn't scared Danny spitless. His saliva landed within an inch of Mason's suede cowboy boots. "And if I don't want to leave nice and quiet, pretty boy?" He took a forceful step toward Mason.

Pretty? Mason could not come up with a strong enough word in any language to describe what he thought of having that word tagged to him. Hide—ugly yap. And now, pretty. It made Mason angry enough to match the forceful step.

Anastasia gasped. What was Mason trying to do? Get himself killed?

She leaned against the door frame, needing something solid to prop her trembling body up with. She could not believe this was happening! Granted, she may have fantasized about Mason Lafayette rescuing her from Danny but, the truth was, he was going to die. Right here in her living room.

"Tell you what, asshole," Mason stated. "Stay and find out the answer to that question. I will be happy to show you the way out." And he meant it because after everything, he was ready to blow off some steam by punching this man.

Oh, God. Anastasia squeezed her eyes shut. She was going to faint. Mason was about to die, and it would serve him right. She had told him to hide. Had tried to warn him. But no. He suddenly got the idea in his head to act out a hero scene.

She could see the headlines now:

Mason Lafayette Dies From Stupidity.

She groaned pathetically. She had wanted fame, but being known as the woman whose ex-husband had killed America's biggest romance cover craze had not been part of the plan!

Danny Sharp's smile did not reach his eyes as he stood, legs apart, and beefy fists on equally large hips as he stared at Mason. "You're a dumbass, Frenchie. I'll give you that." He pointed a finger toward Anastasia,

who was still holding onto the wall as a lifeline. "First, I'm going to show you what I do to guys who sleep with my wife-"

Anastasia's nostrils flared. "Ex-wife!" she hissed. "God, Danny. When are you going to accept that?! When are you going to leave me alone?!"

"Then," Danny continued as though Anastasia had not spoken, "I'm going to kill you."

Mason knew he might only have one chance, so he didn't hesitate. He stepped back with his right foot, snapped out his left, executing a front leg kick with a powerful crack, launching his left foot high into Danny's left jaw.

Danny's head snapped to the side, and his large frame staggered back. Surprise registered on his face for a brief moment, then he shook his head as though to clear it. After that came a deadly smile as his hazel eyes locked with Mason's. "One for you, French fry," he allowed, wiping at the blood caused by Mason's boot when it contacted his cheek and left an inch long cut behind. "Now, try that again," he encouraged, then lunged.

Mason managed to get in one good uppercut before the inevitable happened. Had he continued practicing all the self-defense moves he learned years ago, he might have held his own against the bear of a man. But suddenly, those massive arms encircled his waist within their vice grip and lifted him off the floor.

Anastasia issued an ear-piercing scream.

Mason struggled, unable to breathe. The pain was unbearable, and for an instant, he thought he really would die if his back didn't break first.

A humorous chuckle coming through the broken window drew three pairs of eyes in that direction. They stared as one at the six-foot-three-inch man who's build was the same as the person dangling from Danny's grip.

"You know, Mason. You could have had him. You were doing so well." Hunter leaned himself through the window, folded his arms on the ledge, and smiled. "Did it occur to you, my friend, to try a head-butt?" Hunter waved a hand. "But then, we wouldn't want you to take the chance of injuring that handsome face, now would we?"

Danny's grip loosened just enough to allow Mason to pull air into his starving lungs. His first choked out words were, "Shut up, Hunter."

"Mind if I join in?" Hunter's grin said he was more than hoping the answer would be yes.

"Be my guest," Mason told him, still trying to break free from the tight grip holding him.

Hunter vaulted over the windowsill with the gracefulness of a cat, landing a short distance from the two men still locked together. "You wouldn't mind?" Hunter's eyes gleamed with anticipation.

Anastasia was gaping. They were crazy—all three of them.

"Do something, Hunter!" Mason's jaw clenched together tightly.

Hunter reached into one pocket of his army camo pants that had more zippers than Anastasia had ever seen on one pair of pants. From the depths of one zippered place, he withdrew a hair tie. Still holding it in his hand, he shook his head at Mason and sighed, "I see you've really been lax with all the training I gave you." He finger-combed his long locks, then formed a ponytail with the hair tie.

"Damn it, Hunter," Mason exclaimed with as much force as he could muster under the circumstances.

Hunter merely shrugged. "My. Aren't we in a testy mood," he said dryly. His almost black eyes moved to Danny. With a grin and slight wiggling of the eyebrows, he inquired, "Hey, fat boy. Wanna come out and play?" His chin jerked toward the front yard.

"Who the fuck do you think you are?" Danny snapped, holding onto Mason as though he were no more than a bothersome child.

"A teenage mutant ninja turtle?" Hunter suggested.

Mason groaned.

Anastasia stared.

Danny's eyes narrowed. "You're a real smartass, aren't you," he observed.

Hunter purposely let his jaw drop. "You don't believe me? Well, I like that." He touched his index finger to his temple as though he were considering something. "Don't suppose you would believe it if I said I was Chuck Norris?" Danny snorted and gave Mason a bounce to retain his slipping hold.

"If you two wouldn't mind?" Mason asked, feeling really stupid about being toted around as though he were a rag doll.

Hunter's arms moved out from his sides. "Well, I didn't want to use that overly used line of, I'm your worst nightmare, Mason. It's too boring."

Danny grunted. "I don't have nightmares."

"Should have used boring," Mason observed. "It got his attention."

Hunter nodded, then looked at Danny and proclaimed, "You do now," before regarding Mason once again. "That is the proper response for that corny line, isn't it?"

Mason groaned, again.

Hunter raised a brow, then asked Danny, "Did you want to put him down? Then we could step outside and have some fun. What do you say? Besides, if you win, you can come back in and finish Mason off as dessert."

"Thanks a lot," Mason gritted, just before Danny's hold released. He fell to the floor like a shelf of books, toppling over with a solid thud.

"Don't mention it." Hunter leaped back through the window with the same ease he entered with.

Danny Sharp glared down at Mason. "I'll be back."

Mason almost had the urge to laugh. The tone sounded too close to Arnold Schwarzenegger's claim in The Terminator. "Do not count on it," he warned, knowing Hunter's fighting skills.

Danny did not make it out of the window with any type of grace.

Anastasia knew she had to be dreaming all of this. That was Mason's friend, Hunter? That cocky, self-assured man whose handsome face was about to find itself on the flip side of his head?

No wonder Mason had been so sure of himself. Having friends like that often led people down the path of destruction.

Mason's groan drew her attention to him, and instantly she was at his side, helping him to his feet. "Are you all right?" she asked anxiously, checking him over for injuries. "Is anything damaged?"

Oui! My pride and self-respect! He thought to himself, but he answered verbally with, "No."

"Thank God," she sighed, wrapping her arms around his waist as he got to his feet. "And that was a stupid thing to do," she scolded firmly.

Incredible! She just had to get one more dig into his ego, didn't she? Mason doubted there was anything left of it by now.

"If your friend hadn't arrived, Danny would have-" Anastasia's eyes widened with renewed horror. "Danny's going to kill your friend!" she exclaimed, remembering why her ex-husband was no longer in the house.

"That is not likely to happen," Mason told her, glad to at least find something to be amused about, and it made him chuckle.

Anastasia's head snapped up to look at him. "How can you laugh when your friend is about to become part of my lawn?"

He had the nerve to grin. "You need not worry about Hunter," he informed her, jerking his chin toward the window.

Anastasia spun around in time to witness Mason's friend grab Danny by the collar of the t-shirt he wore, roll back onto the ground while bringing his legs up and into Danny's stomach. Danny went sailing over him with the ease of a kite. Her ex-husband landed dazed on the ground for a few seconds.

From outside, they heard Hunter say, "Oh, come on man. Put some effort into the fight, would ya?"

Anastasia gasped. No doubt about it. Hunter Fisher was just as suicidal as Mason. "He's a madman!"

"Only if he is stupid enough to get back up," Mason said.

"Not Danny!" Anastasia gritted. "I told you. Danny was in the Marines! Your friend's death is close at hand."

Mason moved closer to the window and yelled, "Hey, Hunter!" He waited until Hunter finished delivering a high kick to Danny's jaw, sending the heavier man back to the ground. "That man was in the Marines!"

"Him?" Hunter asked, face wrinkling as though he'd tasted something sour. Although Hunter respected the Marine's, he could not pass up the opportunity to egg the mountain on. He threw his hands up and exclaimed, "Well, that explains it. He fights like a little girl."

That statement brought a beet faced Danny off his knees and charging once again.

Four sheriff's cars flew down the avenue, brakes squealing as the patrol cars came to an abrupt stop in front of Anastasia's house. The officers exited their cruisers quickly, each intending to draw their weapon. But once they saw what was transpiring on the lawn, they joined the gathering crowd in staring, open-mouthed, as Danny Sharp was beaten for the very first time without a shot being fired.

The mutual thought of everyone present was, "Unfuckingbelievable!"

* * *

Anastasia watched in complete shock as the crowd gathered around the fallen giant who had once been her husband. There was a short, pregnant moment of silence as everyone, including herself, stood in awe over the fact that Danny was lying on the ground, knocked out cold.

The cheer that erupted from out of the eerie and reverent silence was deafening. Suddenly, those gathered in the street hoisted Hunter onto the shoulders of other's who witnessed the defeat of the man who held everyone in fear for almost two years.

"Show off," Mason grumbled, watching the crowd congratulating the man who would one day, without doubt, become a legend.

"I would have never believed it," Anastasia whispered, afraid speaking any louder would shatter the moment and cause it to disappear. Her eyes were glued to the hero of the day. She could not believe the man came out of the fight without hardly a scratch.

Mason wasn't smiling as his eyes watched the fanfare taking place outside. And if he were to be honest with himself, he was feeling a little pang of jealousy. Hunter had been the hero, and all he'd accomplished was to look like a damn fool. No wonder Anastasia named her dog after him. He wouldn't be surprised to discover the D stood for Disappointing.

He doubted she would renew her membership to his fan club when it came due because frankly, he wouldn't want to claim to know him, either.

"How in the world was your friend able to do something no one else has ever accomplished?" Anastasia asked, still watching the celebration going on.

Clearing his throat, trying to dislodge any signs of his damaged pride, he answered her question. "Hunter is a world top-ranking Martial Artist, and he works for the United States. Government commando." He shrugged, knowing there really wasn't any way to explain what Hunter did without telling her about Task Force Ghost.

Anastasia's eyes widened, and she laughed, "Wow. Direct from the people who brought us Desert Storm! No wonder we won that war with men like that on our side. Is he always such a cocky sucker?" She turned questioning eyes at Mason.

He blinked. A moment ago, Anastasia faced a situation that would have been more than dangerous had Hunter not arrived in time to defuse it. Now she was acting as though she hadn't been scared to death.

Perhaps her personality helped her bounce back from a stressful situation quickly, and humor was one way to release the anxiety.

Whatever the reason for her wit, her statement brought forth laughter from him. It was deep and rich in sound, and he could not remember the last time a woman managed to bring lightness to his mood when it had not been good. "I would suggest you do not say that to Hunter," he warned, chuckling. "He does not have your humor."

Anastasia felt her heart leap queerly at the sound of his laugh. The fact his smile brought out that dimple she never suspected him of having caused her breath to catch. "Thanks for the warning. I have the feeling I wouldn't want that man angry with me."

He nodded. "This is true," he allowed, then sobered. "I am glad he is my friend, and now, you will not have to worry about that man bothering you anymore." He wondered how she became involved with Danny Sharp and, least of all, marry the man.

He felt it again, the twisting of his gut. Having now seen Danny's size and knowing the man hurt this woman in some way, had Mason wanting to take her away somewhere where she would never have to face this situation again.

Anastasia's smile faded instantly. "Until he gets out of jail again," she told him dryly, then knelt down abruptly to extract broken glass from the cream-colored rug blanketing the living room. She did not want to think about what would happen once the court set bail. Someone always set him free.

Mason found a garbage can in the kitchen and brought it into the living room. Placing it close to her, he watched her trembling hands as she removed fragments of glass and wished he could take her in his arms, comfort, and soothe her fears away.

He knelt down and joined in on the cleanup detail instead. "Why do you not move?" he asked, stopping the task momentarily to watch Anastasia's bowed head as she worked.

Her back stiffened. How many times had she heard that same question? And why did people feel it necessary to give such stupid advice? "Don't you think I want to move?!" she snapped, looking up at him. Angrily, she tossed a sizeable chunk of glass into the garbage bin. "That's so easy for people to say when they have the means to do just that. But some of us in this world have to scrape by just to make it through to next week!" She stood up. "Thanks for the words of wisdom, Mason. I'll keep it in mind the next time I'm on one of my jet setting tours!" With that, she stormed away, entering the kitchen to retrieve the vacuum cleaner from its place in the broom closet.

God! If only he knew how badly she wanted to start over again!

"Anastasia?" Mason leaned against the door, watching her. "Would it help if I said I was sorry? I should not have said anything. Not when I do not know-"

"Right!" She slammed the closet door shut, then glared at him. "You don't know, Mason." She took a deep breath. The tears threatened to make themselves known, but she stubbornly refused to let them.

A few moments passed as she fought for control—that center where she could numb herself and think calmly. "You don't know, Mason," she repeated softly, not meeting his eyes. "The past two years have been hell, and one day I'm going to do that, move away from here. But right now, it's just a dream to me." Just like all my other hopes! She added to herself bitterly. She was almost angry that one of those dreams came true and was standing in front of her. In the flesh, yet still not within her reach. Her time with him was quickly coming to a close, and now she

wished she never met him because… Because she was attracted to him and knew there would be no chance to know his heart, mind, and soul.

She took several more calming breaths than caught her lower lip between her teeth as she reminded herself that he did not deserve her anger. It wasn't his fault her life had become a shamble. Nor was it his fault he had the world by the tail.

"I didn't mean to blow up at you," she told him gently, bravely meeting his cat-like eyes. "I'm the one who should apologize. Earlier, I told you you'd been stupid, standing up to Danny like that." She shook her head. "That's not true, Mason. It was the bravest thing I've ever seen." She touched the place above her heart. "And I thank you for trying. There aren't many people who would have done that."

She sighed and shrugged. "Many people have faced difficulties in their lives. My situation isn't unique. But I learned a long time ago that I can either allow those challenges to make me or break me, and I've chosen to put one foot in front of the other." She rubbed her chest. "I'm trying to be strong, Mason. And maybe you know what it's like to have something so hurtful happen in your life; you don't think you'll ever recover from it." She looked away. "Maybe you don't. Either way, I had no right blowing up at you."

Mason's heart ached so badly within his chest; he did some rubbing of his own in that place above the hurt. She was so different from anyone else, and she was touching him in ways he had never been stroked. For the first time in his life, he met the one woman who could easily steal his heart.

If a god existed, it was a cruel deity, and their humor sucked. Mason could find nothing funny about this situation. Not in the least. He opened his mouth to say something, but whatever words would have passed through his lips, neither of them would ever know. Another voice interrupted their moment, bellowing from the living room. "Hey, Mason! You going to get your ass out here, or do I have to come in there and get you?"

Chapter Twelve

Mason was not sure if he was grateful to Hunter for interrupting the emotional quiet. God, he wanted to hold her and tell her he understood what it was like to have something hurtful invade upon life, shattering the joy, the happiness that had once filled his soul.

He had never wanted to share with anyone that moment in his life when he was told Charles was not his father by blood. But something within him ached to do so now.

"Lafayette," that booming voice again, "You've got one minute before I come in there."

Mason sighed and knew his time with Anastasia was at an end. "Would you like to meet Hunter?" he asked her.

"You're sure it's safe?" And she was not trying to be funny. Hunter Fisher had danger written all over him.

Mason smiled at her. "Trust me, Anastasia. Underneath it all, Hunter is a teddy bear." And that was the biggest lie of his life. But Hunter was not the monster he made sure everyone believed him to be, either. There was a sensitive side to the man. He just didn't show it. At all. "I will guard you with my life," he claimed, reaching out his hand and took hers in his.

The picture of Danny lifting Mason off the floor formed in her mind, and she couldn't prevent the laugh that escaped from her.

"Something amuses you?" Mason asked.

She nodded but doubted he wanted to know what struck her so funny. He had not been able to overpower Danny, and here he was telling her he would protect her from the only guy to have ever beaten her ex-husband.

They walked from the kitchen into the living room and found Hunter on his knees, picking up shards of remaining glass.

Hunter stood up, stuck out his hand, and said, "Hi. It's nice to meet you, though the circumstances for our meeting weren't ideal."

"No. They weren't," Anastasia agreed, taking his hand for a brief shake. "I don't know how to thank you," she said. Her eyes glanced down at the pants he wore, wondering once again how many zippers he had sewn into them. She could guess there were at least fifteen, if not twenty.

"Actually, it was my pleasure," Hunter told her. "I thought coming here to pick up Mason was going to be a dull trip." He chuckled. "I would have stopped that bulldog from smashing your window, but it was worth seeing Mason in such a state of helplessness," He laughed and shot Mason an innocent grin.

"*Va te faire foutre*," Mason said, causing Hunter to laugh gaily.

Anastasia raised a questioning brow, feeling a little left out, not knowing what Mason had said. "What does Va-."

Chuckling, Hunter told her, "It's a vulgar suggestion and totally anatomically impossible for me to do."

"Oh," Anastasia said, having an idea now of what that expression meant.

One of the sheriff's deputies appeared at the window. "Anastasia?" He looked directly at her. "Are you all right? Danny didn't-"

Anastasia shook her head. "I'm fine, Glenn."

Glenn Anderson nodded. "We'll be taking him to Mandan. Lock him up. I can take your statement some other time. Some of your neighbors are gathering tools so they can board up your window for you."

Knowing the community was there for her touched her heart.

Glenn turned his attention to Hunter. "You'll show me some of those moves, wont'cha? I've never seen anything like that unless it was in a Chuck Norris or Bruce Lee film."

Hunter grinned, liking the complement. "Stop up at the lake sometime. I'll be there until Friday, then back Monday to finish another week with my folks. Come by anytime in between."

When Glenn disappeared from the open window, Hunter turned back to face the other two occupants of the small house, "Let's get this mess cleaned up." He looked at Mason. "Your parents damn near had frickin heart attacks when they heard you were in North Dakota and joining in on the so-called fun." He said the latter in a tone of distaste. Hunter did not have fun unless faced with danger. "Anyway, if I don't deliver you before midnight, your mom's gonna have my hide, and your mother is worse than mine when it comes to scolding. Damn near burns a person's ears off." He missed the humor-filled look that passed between Anastasia and Mason because he reached down to extract more glass from the carpet. "Unless, Mason, there is some reason I should, ah, get lost?"

"Keep it up, Hunter," Mason encouraged, knowing damn well he was giving him the chance to make love to Anastasia before they left. The offer he would have accepted any other time, but, in this case, it was an impossible dream.

"What did I say?" Hunter asked innocently.

That did it. "Hunter. I have been meaning to comment on your hair. It is as long as mine. Does this mean you are trying to follow in my footsteps and become a model?"

"Mason," Hunter's tone was deadly, and so was his expression as he reached up to undo the ponytail from the locks in question. "If you're going to bring up that magazine again, I'll warn ya now. It will piss me off."

Anastasia's brows drew together. "In your footsteps? I don't understand."

"Mason," the sound of cold steel.

Mason knew better than to continue. Hunter's warning was enough to waver him. "It is an old joke," he lied, "And I should not have mentioned it."

Anastasia's gaze roamed over Hunter's long hair. "Mason told me you work for the government. They allow hair that length?"

Hunter shrugged. "Whenever it's necessary. Besides, I'm keeping it to irritate my boss." He grinned at Mason, knowing he would understand how annoyed Cadman was by that fact.

"So, you work for the government, but you're going to become a model?" Anastasia was confused. "Is that why your pants have so many zippers in them? Are they a new fashion I haven't heard about?"

"Yes, I work for the government. No, I am not changing careers to do what Mason does." The thought made him ill. "And these pants are my own design. They work as a backpack and keep my hands free."

Anastasia raised a brow.

"In my line of work, backpacks sometimes get lost. This way, I keep basic survival gear on my person at all times."

She would not ask for clarification. The answer would probably confuse her more than she already was. "So, you are not a model?"

"Hell, no. I have no desire to prance around naked in front of a camera the way Mason does."

"I do not prance around naked!" Mason exclaimed although he was not ashamed of his body.

Anastasia cleared her throat. "I beg to differ." She could not resist pointing toward the calendar she had hanging on the living room wall and the photo of him leaning against the shower door. The picture suggested he was wearing nothing, and only the washcloth he was holding, strategically placed, covered his sex.

Hunter enjoyed the slam. "I think I like this woman!" he snickered, tears of laughter rolling down his cheeks.

"Go to hell, Hunter," and to Anastasia, he added, "And I was not naked. Not completely."

Anastasia circled the air with her finger. "So, you probably had a G-string on. What's the difference?"

Hunter grinned. "Yes, Mason. What is the difference?"

"I was not naked! That is the difference!"

Hunter rolled his eyes. "Whatever."

Mason's eyes narrowed. "Did I tell you to go to hell?"

Hunter slapped him on the back. "Yep. And rest assured, buddy ol' pal. I'll get there one day."

* * *

Anastasia watched the taillights of Hunter's jeep until they were no longer visible. Yet, she remained unmoving from her place outside the front door.

Had Mason Lafayette really been there?

She felt a lump in her throat; she did not think she could ever swallow again.

She pressed her eyelids together, fighting the tears. Life was so damn unfair! Why couldn't of he treated her like dirt? Why couldn't of he left here with her thinking he was the biggest jerk in the world? Instead, she discovered he was actually a very nice man.

She wanted to cry, and it felt as though she had lost a dear friend.

She almost laughed at the thought. A dear friend? Who was she trying to fool? Mason Lafayette had thousands of women all over the world. He would probably forget about her within a week.

Hell. He'd probably forgotten her already.

If only they could spend more time together. If only...

She sighed heavily. As always, she was dreaming of the impossible, a life that would never be.

Chapter Thirteen

The first thing that alerted Danny Sharp to the fact he was not dead was the painful throbbing in his head. The second was the feel of a hard mattress pushing into his body, which brought on the third reason he knew he was still alive. He was one enormous mass of hurt. There wasn't a place on him that did not rebel at the slightest movement.

His first thought was, he had been in a fight with Chuck Norris.

Danny groaned and rolled onto his back.

Where in the hell was he?

He opened one eye and doubted the other lid would make the trip up. The one that responded went no farther than halfway.

What in the hell happened?

The earliest thing he could remember was walking into a bar in Minot with some buddies. Now that North Dakota finally passed the Sunday opening law, it gave him seven days a week to pass the time away in the one place he could hide from all the seeing eyes.

But not the voices.

Danny did not want to know what those damn voices made him do this time.

He shifted.

He grimaced.

What had he done?

What happened at the bar?

A few drinks. A country-western band were beginning to tune their instruments when he and his friends first arrived at the establishment.

They passed some good jokes around; the liquor went down as smoothly as it ever had. Drinking helped ease the continual, mind splitting headaches which began after his accident in Kuwait.

Someone mentioned Anastasia.

Anastasia. His foggy mind grasped a faded memory, dimmed by the headaches and the voices. He remembered. He remembered he loved her. Loved her with all his heart; yet, he always hurt her. No matter how strongly he fought against the voices and the pounding in his head.

This memory was rare. Danny suffered from weeks of blackouts. Sometimes he could not remember who he was, even when given a brief reprieve from blinding insanity.

Danny remembered Anastasia now. Kind. Gentle and beautiful, physically and in heart. He had fallen in love with her the minute he met her. Her bright smile and uninhibited laughter captured his heart instantly.

A year later, after their marriage, his Marine unit was shipped to the Kuwait border to watch Iraqi troops. The accident happened there. A bomb. A flash. An explosion.

It almost cost him his life.

Danny could not remember much of anything about the accident. The details were sketchy. What he did remember did not correlate with the facts the government supplied him with while he was in the hospital. All he knew for certain was, it had taken away his career, and for Danny, that had been the same thing as death.

Military doctors declared him one hundred percent recovered from the shrapnel the bomb sent flying into his head. Regardless of their claim, he began developing slow pounding headaches. The physician said they would pass and discharged him, sending him back home to New Salem and the woman he loved.

The headaches became worse.

One year after his discharge, the voices began. After that, the last year and a half were scattered pieces of memories. Things he could recall, and images in his mind always showed him physically hurting Anastasia.

Why? Why did he always hurt her?

It's the only way to show her whose boss.

Danny's hands went to his head, praying for the relief that never came. His moment without pain was slipping away. His head began its throbbing. The voices were trying to talk to him and prevent him from piecing together what happened last night.

He wanted those voices to go away more than he did the headaches.

He hated them. Hated what they made him do.

No, you don't. We're the only true friends you've got!

"No!" Danny screamed, but it came out a choke. His throat was so dry he could barely swallow.

He wanted- No, he needed a good shot of whiskey. That always helped ease the headaches.

Why did he always hurt Anastasia?

Tears formed in his eyes as his mind flashed back to the day he'd woken up in jail, only to be told he'd beaten his wife, broken her arm, and broke her jaw.

He wanted to puke. Why had he done it? Why?!

Because she's unfaithful. We all know that. You had to show her. Show her once and for all that you're a man, and she needs to obey.

Danny groaned. "Please," he implored, tired of hearing their lies.

You know she divorced you because she was being unfaithful. One voice echoed in Danny's head.

Danny moaned and tried to tell himself that wasn't true, but he couldn't comprehend why she'd divorced him when they'd been so happy together.

She left you for someone else, the voice taunted. *She was never faithful to you.*

"That's a lie!" Danny shouted. "She loves me!"

Not anymore!

We took care of that.

You're such a fool!

You bought the lies.

"What lies?"

Ha! Ha! Ha!

Our lies!

We wanted you all to ourselves.

Now we have you.

Laughter. Mind splitting laughter.

Danny's hands pushed hard against his temples. "No!" he screamed.

"Hey! Sharp! Keep it quiet in there!"

Danny opened his half good eye once more, trying to locate the human voice. "Where am I?" he demanded of the voice that came from somewhere off to his left.

"Where do you think, ass wipe?" the voice shouted back. "Mandan's jail."

Mandan? What in the hell was he doing in Mandan when Minot was over a hundred miles north?

The voice became a man. The police officer who told him to shut up entered the narrow hall, stopping before Danny's small cell. "Hear you met your match, Sharp," he sneered. "How does it feel? How does it feel to have had the living shit kicked out of you?" The officer's laugh found its way into the outer halls.

"What happened?" Danny growled.

Since Danny was locked up safely behind bars, the officer did not give pause to the lethal tone. "I suppose you're going to say you were too drunk to remember that you stepped over the law last night and went on off to New Salem, again, even though it's a no no?"

Danny's heart felt as though it just stopped. God, no! He hadn't- Not again- "Anastasia?" he whispered in dread.

"Lucky for her, the friend of the guy she was with arrived at her place just as you broke her front window. "I'd say you probably thought you were having a frickin nightmare when Hunter Fisher showed you; you're not so damn tough after all." The officer's snickered, as he walked away, echoed in Danny's ears long after the man was gone.

Who the fuck are you?

Your worst nightmare.

I don't have nightmares.

You do now.

Danny groaned, rubbing his temples yet again as that faded memory flashed into his consciousness. Nightmare was an understatement. The cocky bastard mentioned something about being a turtle and -Chuck Norris? Shit. He had seen no one move like that in real life!

The officer said the guy's name was Hunter Fisher.

Hunter Fisher? Who in the hell was Hunter Fisher?

Your worst nightmare.

Danny tried to sit up. He grimaced at the effort but managed to pull his massive body into the vertical state.

We'll have to kill him, the voices said matter of fact.

There's no other choice, another confirmed.

He made a fool out of us, another one groaned, much like a depressed child.

Not us! Him! He's the one who failed.

Yeah. Nobody knows about us.

Danny's head throbbed.

Anastasia was with a man last night, another voice pointed out, taunting.

Danny's heartbeat faster. Anastasia? With someone else? The thought brought fresh pain—this one in his chest.

Danny recalled himself saying, "I'm gonna show you what I do to guys who sleep with my wife. Then I'm going to kill you."

Another memory, but it made little sense. The face of the man he spoke those words to was not the same face belonging to the man named Hunter Fisher.

His worst nightmare.

We told you!

She's a whore!

Danny's heart was breaking as the twisted truth worked its way into him.

She's sleeping with both of them!

Both of them.

At the same time.

She's cheating on you again!

Danny could not stop the flow of tears.

You'll have to kill them all.

Kill them!

Kill them!

Kill them all!

Danny scanned the small cell, looking for a way out, wanting liquor. Anything, anything at all, to silence those voices. But there was nothing, and all he could do was push his hands against his skull as the voices grew louder.

You hate her, hate her, hate her, they echoed.

Next time, you can't go easy on her. Next time, you need to make her suffer for cheating on you!

She deserves it.

Sleeping with two men.

Just think of what she's let them do to her, Danny boy.

Touching her.

Tasting her.

The graphic pictures forming in his mind caused him to weep.

It couldn't be true. Could it?

Oh yes, a voice whispered like a snake slithering through his mind. *It is all true, and once we are out of here, they'll see.*

They'll all see who the best man is.

Chapter Fourteen

The sky was filled with a vibrant assortment of colors as the morning sun pushed back the last of the preceding night's velvety darkness.

Daniela Lafayette watched the breathtaking sight taking place before her without noticing its splendor. She stood motionless among the thick brush and trees growing about half a mile east of the Fisher's summer home, nestled along the shores of Lake Sacajawea. In her mind, she was chastising herself for her impulsiveness, and she had to agree it hadn't been smart of her to have told Hunter she was planning to marry him when she turned eighteen.

She sighed, wondering how else she should have gone about this business of staking a claim on the one man who had caused her young heart to flutter oddly whenever he was near.

No. She shook her head. Just looking at a photo of him had the same effect. But was it her fault she was fascinated with her mother's best friend's son?

Daniela had not meant for it to happen. The fact was, until Hunter's older sister, Donna, sent a copy of the American soldier magazine with Hunter's photo gracing its front, to France, addressed to the Lafayette family, she never gave him a thought. Mainly because these reunions happened only once a year, and the last time Hunter attended one, she had been eight years old.

Then that damn magazine arrived in January of this year.

Her first glance at it, when her mother showed it to her, captured her instantly. Granted. He looked angry in the photo. Dangerous, even, and she shuttered, knowing that this man was Mason's best friend. But there was also something mesmerizing about those dark chocolate eyes staring back at her. It felt as though he looked right at her, even though it

had only been an image. After that, she knew she was in love. Not for a second had she doubted it.

She began discreetly quizzing her mother about the man she had known all of her life. She spent hours looking through family photos, at pictures of him taken throughout the years. Hunter as a baby, oh, wasn't he adorable? Hunter as a teenager. Definitely to die for.

Group family shots were her favorite because there were photos with her with him. Granted, she had been only a child then, but that did not mean she couldn't appreciate them now.

She knew Hunter liked danger. She couldn't have not known that, considering how close her parents were to his. However, something seemed to have been left out of conversations she overheard over the past few years. The undeniable fact that now that he worked for Uncle Cadman, Hunter was no longer a nice person.

Daniela tapped her foot and crossed her arms, thinking that being sixteen was definitely the pits. No one would take her love for Hunter seriously, not even him. Anything else she wanted was hers in the blink of an eye.

But not Hunter.

It hurt. It really did. The beastly man, she now knew firsthand how apt that word applied to Hunter, told her, and not in the nicest of ways either, thank you, that she was nothing more than a "bothersome twirp" and, as far as he was concerned, she could jump out of a plane without a parachute, and he would not blink an eye upon hearing about her death.

Not a pleasant thing to say to his future wife, Daniela fumed. He was hateful, spiteful, and stubborn. He did not have one single redeemable quality. She knew her life would be so much easier if she would forget him and find someone else who could cause her stomach to form butterflies whenever she saw them. And especially someone who would

not take advantage of her incredibly long hair. Using it against her by tying her to a tree branch with it because they had a short temper.

She still could not believe it.

Here she was, almost an hour since she followed him on his before dawn jog, and it did not appear as though anyone would arrive within the near future to help her out of this embarrassing predicament.

Daniela attacked the knot once more, hoping this time to set herself free, and cursed the damn man at the same time for knowing how to make knots impossible to undo.

"I will kill him!" she vowed with a vengeance, crossing her slender arms once again across her tiny waist, glaring at the worst hair snarl she'd ever had in her entire life.

The glare alone should have been enough to singe the hair free from the branch.

She felt like crying. She really did. No one had ever treated her like this before, and it was quite sobering to discover that not everyone on the planet catered to her, as she grew up believing they did.

How could she not assume the world evolved around her when all of France called her their "little Angel?"

The country showered her with love and affection. Adored her because she was Rosalinda and Charles Lafayette's daughter. Everyone worshipped Rosalinda. The woman was one of the greatest actresses the country had. Charles was an award-winning director of countless films that left people in awe of his wife's performances. Being the youngest and only child the Lafayette's conceived after Mason's birth had given her admirers of her own because of her family's fame.

Daniela never thought of herself as spoiled. It hadn't crossed her mind until he told her she was "A spoiled rich kid who needs to grow up and take a good look at the world. Not everyone has been given the life of luxury you were."

Actually, those were not Hunter's exact words. But she'd never heard so many vulgar words spoken in a single breath before, and she really did not care to repeat them, even to herself.

"Oh!" she cried, stomping her foot. The only way she would be free from this blessed tree was to have her hair cut where it twisted around the branch. That alone was enough to make her see red. Not once in her entire life had she cut her hair. And now- she would be lucky if it came to the bottom of her behind, rather than the soles of her feet, once she was out of this mess.

"I will kill him!" she repeated with a scream, pulling on her hair one more time, hoping the branch would give way.

The all too familiar amused chuckle sounded behind her and caused her back to stiffen.

"Still here, I see," he said.

"Go away."

Of course, he didn't.

"Funny. That is precisely what I told you before your hair accidentally caught on that tree."

"Accidentally!" Daniela whirled, then yelped when pain shot through her scalp because the movement caused her secured hair to pull tight, reminding her she wasn't going anywhere. "You did this to me you… you…"

Hunter grinned as though there was a joke being told. "Yes?" he encouraged.

"*Trou du cul!*" she hissed.

His right brow arched, but the smile never wavered. "Does your mother know you have such a potty mouth, twirp?"

Twirp's jaw dropped. He was accusing her of having a potty mouth? Of all the nerve! "Go away, Hunter," she repeated, turning her back to him. "I hate you."

"Well, thank whatever god showed you the light," he told her dryly, stepping closer.

She nearly jumped out of her skin when she saw the knife in his hand. "What are you going to do?!" she asked nervously, afraid he was going to make good on yesterday's threat to kill her if she did not stay away from him.

"I'm gonna cut ya free, kiddo." Hunter tisked, "You made such a mess out of your hair; it's the only way you're going to walk away from here." He moved the blade of his pocketknife as close to the knot as possible.

"I would not have a knot in my hair if you had not tied it!" she snapped, contemplating hitting him over the head somehow, but discarded the notion quickly. Until she was free, escape from her deed would be fruitless.

"If you had listened to me in the first place," he countered, "your hair would not have become tangled up."

She almost kicked him for that. How dare he continue to act as though this had not been his fault?!

Tears pooled in her green eyes as his blade sawed through her hair. "I hope you die soon!" she spat, pulling her now knee-length mass before her, mourning the loss of the two feet of hair still dangling from the limb.

Hunter grunted and pocketed the knife. "My, you truly are a member of the club, twirp. Want to be President? You could have t-shirts printed with the slogan, Pray for Hunter's death on them." He shrugged indifferently. "Rest assured, kid. Since death is unavoidable, it will happen eventually."

Daniela had to crane her neck to do it, he was so damn tall compared to her five foot four, but she stared up at him, locking her eyes with his. "Does it not bother you to be hated?" she whispered, unable to believe his apathy.

In answer, he laughed and swung his arms out to his sides. "Daniela. For it to bother me, I would have to care." His dark eyes locked again with leaf green. He could not prevent the fact he grimaced within himself. The only thing about this child he considered pretty were those eyes, a trait Rosalinda passed to both her children. Oh yes. One other thing he thought captivating. That uncommonly long, midnight black hair of hers mesmerized him. Damn shame he had to cut it to free her, but the fault lay at her feet, not his. "And Daniela. I don't give a damn what anyone thinks of me."

Daniela stared. Could his heart really have become as black as that? If so, why was she feeling those butterflies again in her stomach, instead of the fear he was trying to arouse?

She doubted she would ever know. "I bet you win many friends with that attitude," she predicted.

"Your brother is the only friend I have, little girl, and that is good enough for me."

She gaped at him. Was he joking? "Everyone needs friends, *mon coeur*."

He scowled angrily. "For Christ's sake, Daniela!" he exploded, "I am not your heart!" His hands flew through his hair in pure exasperation. "Get this through that damn head of yours!" He thumped his chest with the palm of his hand. "I don't have time to make friends. I don't need them, and I do not need a whole mess of people boohooing over my grave when the time comes. And above everything, I sure as hell don't need some lovesick idiot following me around!"

That hurt. Daniela felt the direct hit all the way to her toes. The man was impossible! "You realized that if you keep treating me like this, I

will give my heart to someone else," she sighed willfully, trying not to allow him to see how deeply he cut her by those cruel words.

"Ahhhhgggghhh!" Hunter was so frustrated, he balled his hand into a fist and threw it into a nearby tree, needing something to hit.

He spun back toward her. The fact his hand felt as though he had just broken every knuckle didn't help his mood, and the look on his face should have caused her to head for cover. But the little twirp just stood there, watching him, which only made him angrier, if that were possible. "I'm going to give you just one more warning, Daniela." The fact he was doing so was nothing less than an actual intervention from the universe. "Mason's sister or not; you keep pestering me, and I will kill you before the day is out!"

Her laughter stunned him and more than confused the hell out of him. Anyone else would have run screaming the devil himself was after them, but she just stood there laughing at him as though he had made some joke. It infuriated him, and since he was already past the point of boiling, his entire body vibrated with his anger. "What in the hell is so funny, Daniela?"

The half snort, half laugh she gave sounded awful. "Oh, Hunter. You would not hurt me, let alone kill me."

"Need I tie you back up, Daniela?" he asked tightly, ominously.

That sobered her. The miserable man would do something like that. But she noted he had not harmed her, no matter how often he threatened to do so. It fueled her belief that he would not physically abuse her.

Her mistake was voicing the belief. It sent Hunter over the edge. "No?" He said just before his hand snaked out so quickly, she hadn't seen it coming. "I've had it, twirp. I really have had it."

Dragging her with him, he sat down on a nearby log and flipped her across his lap effortlessly. Daniela was tiny. Delicately petite, and compared to Hunter's tall, powerful frame, she closely resembled a porcelain doll.

Daniela's green eyes widened in horror as she found herself unceremonially thrown across his muscular legs. "You would not dare!"

The first stinging blow said he dared.

It rendered Daniela speechless for a moment. No one had ever spanked her, and the fact that he was doing so now brought forth her earlier resolve. "I hate you!" she screamed, feeling the stinging blows through the denim of her jeans as though he were hitting bare bottom. "I really, really hate you!"

He pushed her off his lap, causing her to land with an oomph in the pile of dirt and leaves at his feet. "Good!" he growled. "That is exactly what I want from you. The only thing I want from you! Stay away from me, Daniela. Pester Wyatt. My youngest brother is a hell of a lot closer to your age, and he enjoys having people around him. I don't. Understand?"

Oh, she understood all right. She understood Hunter hoped she would forget all about him. "Perfectly!" she hissed, scrambling to her feet and rubbing her bruised backside.

"Splendid!" He yelled, walking away.

Daniela made a rude jester at his back and began planning to get revenge on the big oaf.

There was no way in hell she was going to allow him to get by with having the nerve, the utter gall to spank her!

"Brute!" she mumbled to herself. "Horrible, dreadful man!"

Chapter Fifteen

Mason, dressed in shorts and a loose-fitting t-shirt, spotted his parents through the large patio doors, eating breakfast outside on the deck along with his adopted Uncle Cadman and his wife Kasey, and Hunter's parents. Sliding open the glass doors, he stepped onto the deck of the large summer home nestled within a grove of trees along the south shore of Lake Sakakawea. The lake, named for the Shoshone-Hidatsa woman Sakakawea, who, at age 16, helped the Lewis and Clark Expedition through the Rocky Mountains to the Pacific Ocean in 1805-1806 was the largest man-made lake located entirely within the State of North Dakota.

"Good morning!" Cadman said, motioning to him to join them. "I see you decided to wake up. After you and Hunter started the bonfire when the two of you arrived last night, I figured you'd sleep until noon."

Mason grinned as it was not yet eight o'clock in the morning. "Us young people do not need as much sleep as you old folks," he said as he leaned down to kiss his mother on the cheek.

"Har, har," Cadman drolled. "Your day will come. Trust me on this. And you might recall I used to wrestle with you and the rest of the Fisher brood back when you all were little."

"Do you wish to wrestle now?" Mason asked, eyes twinkling with humor. "For old time's sake?"

"Hell, no!" Cadman told him.

Mason laughed, then looked up at the clear blue sky. "It feels as though it is going to be a beautiful day."

"Any day I'm not around horses is a beautiful day," Cadman declared. "My favorite reunions are the ones up here instead of the ranch. You'll never know how happy I was the day Colten told me they were going

to buy this place and rotate it out every other year with his siblings for our July 4th annual reunion."

His wife, Kasey, swatted his arm. "I know that deep down in your soul, you don't mean that," she told him.

"Oh, yes. I do."

"Kasey," Colten, Hunter's father, said. "You realized he hasn't been on a horse since the day he proposed to you, and the only reason he got on one that day was he wanted to make the moment memorable."

"That was fifteen years ago!" Mason chuckled. "Honestly, Uncle Cadman, why do you not like horses? They are beautiful animals."

"They sure are," Kasey agreed. "I'm looking forward to Friday when we all head to the ranch for fireworks and spend the weekend camping out under the stars."

"There is no, all. I'm not going camping." Cadman vowed.

"But, honey," his wife told him, "You love camping."

"Yep. Sure do. When I can drive to the site I've picked out. But the campsite he," Cadman pointed to Colten, "insists upon taking us to can only be reached on horseback."

The other couples around the table watched this exchange between Cadman and his wife with humor in their eyes and smiles on their faces. They all tried not to laugh at Cadman's refusal to get on a horse.

Kasey batted her eyes at him. "Please? I've gone every year without you. It leaves me the odd man out when all the other married couples are there together."

"You could stay with me at the ranch house." He suggested, trying not to feel guilty.

"Perhaps, Kasey, you could tell him he can no longer sleep with you unless he comes along this time," Mason's mother suggested.

Cadman jettisoned his finger out at his past lover. "Now, you just stay out of this, Rosalinda!"

Her smile was coy.

Turning to Rosalinda's husband, Cadman asked him, "Could you please tell your wife to mind her own business?"

Charles Lafayette chuckled. "I would never dream of doing such a thing. I enjoy sleeping with my wife, but I do not enjoy her Spanish, Italian, and French temper. This is a battle you will have to choose for yourself, my friend."

Mason watched the banter between his parents and the others gathered around the table and felt his heart stir with longing. This was what he wished he had in a relationship—the devotion, respect, and love these couples had for one another and their spouses.

His thoughts turned to Anastasia, and he wondered if she was all right after last night's upheaval.

"So," Charles said to him, "You had quite the adventure yesterday, my son." He chuckled. "Stranded on a highway in North Dakota is not an ideal situation. It could have been years before anyone ventured by to help you."

"Hey, now," Colten said, "North Dakota isn't that desolate."

"We have more people living in Paris than you have in your entire state." Charles reminded him.

True enough, Colten had to give him a point for that fact.

"Anyway," Rosalinda interrupted the two of them before another argument broke out, "Mason, we are glad you are here. It is a pleasant surprise. Carol did not come with you?" There was a singsong in her voice when she asked the question.

"I did not invite her, and I threw her out of my hotel room the other night. We are no longer together. But if we were, I would not have

brought her. This is a part of my life I do not share. You know that. It is the one place I keep private from any anyone in my life as well as the media, just as you and father have done throughout the years. And for good reason."

Yes, his mother knew what those reasons were. The fewer people who knew about the Lafayette's trips to North Dakota each year kept the knowledge from Pierre. As far as that man knew, the hitman he hired years earlier successfully killed Colten and Jacqueline. Keeping this vacation spot out of the media as much as possible kept the Fishers safe.

"Well, I am glad you kicked Carol out," Rosalinda stated. "I did not like her."

Mason raised a brow as he looked at her. "You never told me that."

She shrugged. "I have to let you find your own way," she told him as she reached out and took Charles's hand in hers. "Just like I had to discover for myself who I belonged to."

A lump formed in Mason's throat upon seeing the love they had for each other. It was there all his life, but today he felt as though he was seeing it for the first time.

"So," Rosalinda said, looking up at her son. "Are you going waterskiing this morning with the others?" She glanced around the shoreline. She saw the boat at the dock and watched the Fisher's oldest daughter and her husband playing in the sand with their four-year-old son, and their seventeen-year-old adopted son while Colten and Jacqueline's sixteen-year-old twins were enjoying a modified game of volleyball nearby.

Sadly, two of the Fisher children were not at the reunion this year. Their oldest son Clinton was in New York State visiting with his Uncle TJ.and Melissa, the Fisher's other daughter, just moved to Seattle to work for a computer software company.

Rosalinda's eyes also noted Hunter was nowhere in sight, nor was her daughter. She hoped Daniela was not tailing after him. As a mother, she

was not stupid. She knew her youngest child had a crush on Hunter and tried not to let that fact give her the willies. But, as she told Mason, she had to allow her children to find their own path, even though she knew her daughter's young crush would lead to nowhere but heartache.

However, as much as Rosalinda would have liked to tell her daughter there could be no future with Hunter, it was better she learn that truth from the man she thought she loved. A broken heart would make her a stronger person.

"Yes, we will go water skiing," Mason assured his mother as he pulled an empty chair up to the table so he could feel a part of the group of his elders. "However, Hunter has not returned from his morning jog." He studied his mother's face for a moment. She was fifty-three years old and still as beautiful as ever. The scar, almost like a C that ran from the corner of her eye, along her jaw, and ended at her chin, Pierre had carved there the night he had kidnapped, tortured, and raped her. Most of the time, the scar could not be detected because of the concealing make-up she used, but she had not applied her cosmetics yet this day.

He glanced at her arms. Those countless scars had faded. Still there, but not as prominent as they once had been. She used to wear only long sleeve shirts to cover them, but she developed a concealing cosmetic for those a few years ago. Now, if she desired, when she walked among the public, she used the concealer whenever she wanted to wear something with short sleeves.

She never wore a bathing suit or shorts in public, choosing only pants or long skirts or dresses. The scars on her legs would never fade enough to hide with concealers.

She, his mother, was the strongest woman he knew.

Once more, Anastasia's face formed in his mind, and he could not help but wonder what her ex-husband put her through and how she'd kept her humor and fighting spirit.

"I am surprised you did not join him," his mother was saying.

"Jog with a man who can run four miles in under thirty minutes, mother?" he snorted. "I think not."

Rosalinda chuckled. "There was a time when you were just as fast as Hunter," she thought to remind him.

"*Oui!*" he exclaimed, startling everyone at the table by the outburst. "When we were children, and we ran around pretending to be Navy SEALS on a rescue mission." He swept a hand through his hair. "But we are no longer children, and Hunter has me outclassed when it comes to playing the hero."

Everyone at the table looked at him as though he'd lost his mind.

Except for his mother.

She pushed away from the table, reached for his hand, and said, "Walk with me, Mason."

He felt like a child and knew a command when he heard it. He hadn't meant to erupt like that. In fact, having voiced the words surprised him as much as they had everyone else.

"Are you going to yell at me?" he asked as he stood up.

Laughing, she told him, "I would never do such a thing."

They both knew that was a lie.

Side by side they walked toward the lakeshore, then slowly began strolling along the beach as the water rolled in from the waves made by the boats speeding by farther out.

After a few moments of silence, Rosalinda asked, "What is wrong, Mason? It almost sounded as though you were jealous of Hunter, which I know is not true."

He stopped walking and scowled out at the lake. A few boats towing women in revealing bikinis behind them on skis passed by, but he did not glance their way.

Rosalinda found that interesting. Her son's head always turned to watch women in bathing suits. Especially when the suits were bikinis. But she made no comment as she allowed Mason a moment to think through what was on his mind.

"Isn't it ironic, mother?" He asked softly, turning to look down at her. "My face graces the covers of countless romance novels, portraying the larger-than-life hero's contained within, and I could not stand on my own two feet against a man hell-bent on killing me, only because I was in his ex-wife's home." He sighed. "If Hunter had not shown up, I would be dead, and Anastasia-" His voice broke off. God, he did not want to think about what could have happened if Hunter had not arrived.

"Mason, you, just like your father and I, create illusions for people to enjoy. No one should expect you to be anything other than who you are."

"And who am I, mother?"

His question was so unexpected, it rendered her speechless.

He swiped a hand over his face, then shook his head. "Lately, I have wondered. What exactly do I contribute to society? I have gained popularity only because of my looks, and the fact I've been told I resemble Pierre Bellefeuille is not cause for celebration." He looked at her, and there was anguish in his eyes. "Am I like him, too?"

Rosalinda cried out. "No! My god, Mason. Why would you even think such a thing?! You are nothing like that monster!"

"Then why am I constantly lusting over women?"

"Because you have a healthy sex drive, Mason. And you got that from me, not Pierre."

"What?"

Rosalinda sighed. "From the time I was fifteen years old, I slept with any man I wanted. I suppose you could say I had an overactive libido." She laughed. "At one time, Cadman was my lover-"

"Oh god, I did not want to know that," Mason claimed, holding up his hand to silence her.

He glanced toward the patio where Cadman sat, conversing with everyone at the table. Mason knew he would never look at his surrogate uncle again without thinking about him sharing a bed with his mother.

"My point, darling, is that when you find the one your heart recognizes as the woman you can give it to, you won't look at another. Never forget you are a Vallambrosa, and the men in my family, once they love, love forever. You may have Pierre's face, but your heart and soul are Vallambrosa. Your romantic nature comes from my family line. Please," she stepped forward, wrapped her arms around him. "Never believe you inherited anything else from Pierre. You are the opposite of that vile man."

Wrapping his arms around his mother, he rested his chin on the top of her head as he thought about what she said and felt himself relax. He had needed the reminder. Although Charles Lafayette's blood did not run through his veins, he had a family line that included nobility he could be proud of.

His great-great-grandfather, Riccardo Giovanni Maria Stefano Manca-Amat, IV Duca di Vallombrosa e dell'Asinara, founded the Yacht Club of France and the Society of Racing in Cannes, France. His great-great-grandmother, Geneviève de Pérusse des Cars, had been a duchess.

Another group of women on skis went by, but Mason did not turn his head to look at them.

Rosalinda smiled to herself. Perhaps her son's life was about to change.

"I don't mean to interrupt," they heard Jacqueline's voice and looked up to see her standing close to them. "We," she swept her hand toward the patio where the others sat watching them, "were talking about driving to Minot to do some shopping."

"Excellent idea," Rosalinda said, pulling away from her son.

Jacqueline looked at Mason. "By the way, I was wondering what the name of that man from last night was. More out of curiosity than anything else." She shrugged. "I have lived in North Dakota long enough to understand why people gossip. Perhaps I've heard of him?"

"Danny Sharp," Mason said and felt as though his tongue tasted bitter.

With a shake of her head Jacqueline said, "Unfortunately, I have heard of that devil. He's-"

"Talking about me again, Mom?" Hunter chuckled, coming up to stand with the small group.

Jacqueline gave her son a sour look. "I said, devil, dear. Not demon from hell."

Hunter grinned. "Thanks, Mom." He patted his chest and arched his back as though she had given him the ultimate compliment. "I rather like that."

"You would," Jacqueline said in disgust.

"She was about to tell us about Danny Sharp," Mason told him. "So, if you would be so kind as to shut up?"

Hunter's eyes widened with disbelief. "You were calling him a devil? Good god, mom. The guy's a wimp!"

Mason was beginning to hate his best friend. He really was. "If you do not mind, Sundance, I would like to think of the guy as being a little stronger than that wimp label you are tagging to him."

Hunter's head snapped toward Mason. The only time Mason had the nerve to call him by his middle name was when he was mad. "Having a bad day, ol' buddy pal of mine?"

Mason's jaw clenched. "You could have been kind enough to have let the man hit you, at least once!" he exclaimed.

Hunter cocked a brow. "Well, that's gratitude. Excuse me for saving your hide."

"Did I ask for help?" Mason's arms spread out to his sides.

"No," Hunter allowed. "But, I recall you telling me to do something."

"He was breaking my back!"

"So, what's the problem then?"

Mason could not argue with that logic. "Not a damn thing!"

"Glad that's all cleared up!" Hunter declared, though his face looked too humorous by far.

"You know, Fisher," Mason swept his hair from his face. "One of these days, I'm going to hire Chuck Norris to coach me, and then I will really clear this up!"

Hunter was doing some brushing back of his hair himself. But when he heard Mason's claim, his hand stopped, and his eyes widened with anticipation. "Promise?"

"Oh, go to hell."

Rosalinda cleared her throat, drawing everyone's attention to her. "If the two of you would not mind, I would like to hear what Jacqueline knows about this Danny Sharp-" She saw her daughter all but marching up the beach, and her expression told the world she was madder than hell. "Daniela! What happened to your hair?!"

Daniela strolled angrily past the group, stopping only long enough to hiss, "Someone decided it needed trimming." She shot Hunter a look potent enough to have given any man of lesser caliber pause before she continued walking toward the Fisher's two-story summer home.

"Well?" three voices asked together, turning to stare at Hunter.

Hunter merely shrugged. "It got wrapped around a tree," he explained. "I was only helping the dear girl out."

"And just how did her hair get tangled around a tree?" Mason scowled.

"I suppose someone might have reached their tolerance of the girl following them around like some lost puppy." Hunter speculated, almost laughing out loud at his use of the word puppy when he thought Daniela was a dog.

"Hunter," Mason said, and there was a lot of anger in that one word.

Hunter was not in the least bit intimidated by Mason's hard stare. "The girl is a spoiled brat, Mason," he snapped, matching the deadly look. "She didn't understand the meaning of the word no." He grinned, rubbed his wide chest in a circular motion, and explained, "I'm happy to inform everyone that she understands the word perfectly now."

Jacqueline gasped. "Hunter! What did you do?"

"Something that should have been done a long time ago." He gave Rosalinda a meaningful look. "I turned her over my knee and spanked her."

"You didn't!" Jacqueline exclaimed, face paling.

"Yes, I did,"

His mother put her hands on her hips and said with heat, "Hunter Sundance Fisher, you apologize to her this very minute!"

Hunter snorted. "Yeah. Right." Hell would freeze over before that happened.

Mason's fists clenched. "That is my sister you spanked."

"And it was long overdue, Lafayette. But," Hunter sighed, "you don't have to thank me. It was my pleasure."

"Hunter-" Mason's tone was stern.

"Mason," Rosalinda's gentle voice interrupted the tense moment. "Hunter is correct. We have all spoiled her. She needs a firm hand." She gave Hunter a half-grin. "Care to take on the job, Hunter?"

The rude sound he made told everyone he had not found the question amusing. "Care if I kill her, Rosalinda?" he inquired.

Rosalinda sighed. "That would not be acceptable."

"Mother!" Mason exclaimed, "Why would you even suggest such a thing when he is more likely to kill her if she so much as blinked wrong?!"

"I'm not that mean," Hunter protested. Regardless of having threatened to kill her, he would never follow through with it.

Okay. Disclaimer. If the child kept annoying him, he might.

Rosalinda shrugged. "Who is joking? We have catered to Daniela all her life. It needs to stop." She leveled her look at Mason. "That means no more albino tigers."

Hunter's jaw dropped, and he stared at his best friend. "You gave her an albino tiger? Are you daft?"

Mason countered with, "She wanted a wolf. Guess what she would have named it?"

"Rover," Hunter answered dryly.

Mason shook his head. "Eagle. As in Eagle's Wolf."

Hunter's eyes rounded at hearing the government's code name for him. "The brat! How did she find that out?"

Everyone present had a guilty look on their face.

Mason turned to Jacqueline, "You were telling us about Danny Sharp?"

Chapter Sixteen

Inside the Fisher's summer home, one very livid Daniela Elizabeth Geneviève Athenais Lafayette was contemplating murder. But revenge would taste so much sweeter.

"Badlands Billboard Company," a man's voice came across the telephone line after it rang five times.

Daniela's eyes made a hasty scan through the huge patio doors, assuring herself no one was on their way into the house.

She held up the American soldier magazine she retrieved from Jacqueline and Colten's bedroom, telling herself she hadn't precisely stolen it. Only borrowed it for the time being.

"I wish to order a full-sized billboard," she answered, eyes twinkling mischievously. "I need it in place by the end of next week."

"Ma'am, it takes longer than that for-"

"I need it done by the end of next week! I am sure, for the right price, you could arrange it."

There was a cough. "Do you understand those can cost up to fourteen thousand-"

"Money is of no concern, and I will pay double that if you can accomplish what I ask." Being filthy rich had its perks. She would just have to convince someone to drive her to Bismarck to arrange for her bank in Paris to transfer the funds. And to give the billboard company the picture she wanted to be displayed on the marquee.

If only she could be there to see the look on Hunter's face when he saw what she had in mind for him.

"Well," the person on the other side of this conversation said, "as soon as we receive funds, so we know this is on the up and up, we'll get to work on it."

"Excellent. I will be there sometime this afternoon." She hoped.

If she were lucky, the shock Hunter would have when he saw the billboard would send whatever vehicle he was driving at the time into the ditch.

She hung up the phone and wondered who she could convince to drive her to Bismarck.

Rolling up the magazine, she slipped it into her large handbag as she contemplated the matter.

"Daniela?"

Hearing her brother's voice behind her caused her to yelp.

Her eyes were as large as saucers when she turned to face him.

"Were you calling someone?" He leaned against the door frame, waiting for the answer.

"You frightened me half to death!" she exclaimed, holding her bag against her chest as her heart thumped rapidly.

"Who were you calling?" he asked again, wondering about the guilty look on her face.

"Well, if you must know," she told him, making it up as she went along, and tried to sound as though she had nothing to hide. "I was thinking about calling Melissa since she will not make it this year to the reunion."

Mason did not believe her for a moment but let it go. What harm could she possibly do?

"How nice of you," he said, though he did not mean it.

Hunter was right. She had become a spoiled brat.

"Did you want something, brother?"

Mason pushed away from the doorway as a grin spread across his face. "I could not help but notice that your hair needs a good trim since you allowed it to become tangled."

"I had nothing to do with it becoming entangled!" she snapped.

Shaking his head, he told her, "You obviously annoyed Hunter. The question is, what did you do?"

She pressed her lips together and was not about to tell him she followed Hunter to declare her intent to marry him. She doubted Mason would take her seriously, either.

Mason shrugged. It did not matter to him. But when he saw her hair, which very much needed a good trim so it would look halfway decent, he could not pass up the opportunity to use it as an excuse to see Anastasia again.

"I am going to drive you to a salon so they can fix your hair." He pulled the keys out of his pocket that belonged to Hunter's jeep. "While Hunter, Wyatt, Rebecca, and the others enjoy themselves water-skiing, I am borrowing Hunter's vehicle and taking you somewhere for a trim."

Her mouth formed into a pout. "I do not wish to have my hair cut shorter."

"This is not negotiable," he told her.

She raised her foot to kick him.

"Oh, no, you don't, little sister. I will carry you to the car if necessary, but you are going to get a haircut."

She realized perhaps this could be an answer to her dilemma. "Very well. I suppose I will not mind a trip into Bismarck." She patted herself on the back for not sounding eager to get there.

"New Salem," he said.

"Where?"

Mason honestly had the urge to laugh. "There is a place in New Salem I know of. I am confident they would do an excellent job of making your hair look presentable again."

"But I want to go to Bismarck!" she wailed.

"Hair cut first," he told her. "Perhaps afterward, I will drive you to Bismarck as it is only a half-hour away from New Salem."

"Fine," she told him. As long as she got there, stopped at a bank and paid the billboard company before they closed. She wondered how she would convince Mason to take her to those places without him asking questions. But getting to Bismarck was half the battle. She would just have to figure out the rest when she got there.

* * *

At noon Gale raced into Anastasia's salon with a flushed face. Her hair was windblown, and she was slightly out of breath because of the extra weight she toted. Her eyes were as wide as the prairie as they locked on Anastasia. It did not matter to her that Anastasia was in the middle of a haircut. She marched right up to her and exclaimed, "Is it true, Stasia?" She fought for breath. "Is it true Danny broke into your house last night and that Mason's friend knocked the crap out of him?!"

Anastasia groaned. "Please, Gale. I'm busy right now."

Herb Singer, whose hair Anastasia was cutting, whipped his head around, causing her to cut her finger instead of his hair. "Danny got beat up?!" Herb exclaimed. "Why didn't I hear about this?! Who is the man who decked the pig? He deserves a medal!"

Anastasia was grabbing for a towel to catch the flow of blood from her finger. "I'm sure Hunter-"

"Oh, I wish I could have been there!" Gale cried out, her disappointment clear. "And I cannot believe you didn't call me and tell me!"

"I wasn't in the mood to talk about it last night," Anastasia confessed, wrapping a bandage around the cut on the injured middle finger.

134

By now, Anastasia's two employees stopped whatever hair service they were performing to listen to the tale.

In fact, everyone in the salon was waiting with anticipation. All were wanting to hear the story of the night Danny Sharp fell.

"The way I heard it," Gale was saying, oblivious to Anastasia's shaking head, "Danny broke Stasia's front window and this friend of Mason's-"

"Whose, Mason?" someone piped up.

"Whose, Mason?" Gale exclaimed. "Whose, Mason? Why, our Stasia cooked supper last night for none other than Mason Lafayette. The one and only Mason Lafayette!"

"No!" one woman gasped. "That cover model? The one whose-" She held up the romance book she was reading while she waited for the perm she was having to finish processing and pointed to its cover. "This Mason Lafayette?" she sighed dreamily.

"Do tell," Herb grinned.

Dirty old man, Anastasia thought.

"Mason Lafayette beat up Danny?" another guy asked skeptically.

Gale shook her head. "No, idiot! His friend Hunter did. According to Harriet, you all know Harriet, nothing gets past her in this town, Hunter used some chop-chop stuff…"

"Tae Kwon do?" another guy offered.

"Karate?"

"Judo?"

"Yeah, yeah. Whatever." Gale waved a hand. "If everyone keeps interrupting, I won't be able to tell you!" she took a deep breath. "Anywho, after Jeff and I left Mason and Anastasia last night, I guess-"

"They were alone?"

"At her house?"

"Alone?"

"Do tell." Herb again.

"Oh, for Christ's sake!" Anastasia exploded. "It wasn't anything like that. All we were doing was washing the dishes when Danny showed up. Mason's friend Hunter, he's a government commando, arrived and pulverized Danny. The sheriff took Danny to Mandan. Mason and Hunter left. End of story."

"But Danny, our Danny Sharp, was on the receiving end this time?" One man waiting for a haircut whistled in disbelief. "Bet your ex is pissed as hell 'bout that."

"You had dinner with him?" the woman was gazing at her romance book, a faraway look in her eye.

"They were alone," someone restated.

Anastasia gave Herb a deadly look. "Don't."

"Well, hell," said Herb, grumbling.

"Look, everyone. I really do not need all this attention right now. And, if anyone wants their hair cut today, I'd suggest you all go about your business so I can get on with mine."

Gale was the only one who did not take the hint. "Listen, sweetie. You shouldn't even be working today. After last night, I would think your mind would be anywhere but on cutting hair."

Herb's head snapped around again. Again, Anastasia's shear found skin instead of hair.

"You're not gonna chop my hair, are ya Stasia?" he asked, looking concerned.

Anastasia clenched her jaw, reached for another bandage. "No, Herb. So far, the only chopping I'm doing is a slow amputation of my finger,

and if you move your head just one more time, I will not bother to stop the blood before it runs into your hair!"

"You wouldn't!"

"Maybe I would. A few red streaks mixed with all that gray might look good. Besides, blood is protein, and protein is good for the hair." Her eyes narrowed. "Now, turn around so I can finish your haircut." As an afterthought, she added, "And don't move!"

He didn't.

"Gale, go home. I'm busy. I'll be home around six. You can come over then."

Herb grumbled. "I don't see why she gets to hear all the good stuff."

"Keep it up, Herb. I'll be more than happy to remove one of those ears for you."

"You're a cold woman, Stasia."

Anastasia managed to keep her laugh to herself.

Gale just stood there staring at her and was more than a little hurt by the fact she'd had to hear the story from Harriet, of all people. "I just wish Jeff and I hadn't stayed so late at his parent's house," she confessed. "I could have known about this sooner."

Anastasia sighed. "Honestly, Gale. There is nothing to tell. I have to have my front window replaced," and she cursed that fact because it was yet another bill she would have to pay. "But that's really all there is to the story."

"You don't think Danny finally getting beat up isn't a big deal?"

Anastasia stopped using her shear on Herb's hair, turned toward her friend, and said, "It was the most amazing thing I've ever seen!" she confessed with a girlish squeal. "And I'm almost certain every law officer who witnessed it now have man-crushes on Hunter."

Herb almost choked. "That just doesn't sound right to my ears," he told her.

"Oh, Herb. You're so lovable." She was thinking more on the lines of a dinosaur because of his old fashion beliefs but was not about to try to change his mind. She could not afford to lose any clientele by arguing with them.

Looking back at Gale, Anastasia told her, "I can call you later. But honestly, I really need to get back to work." She motioned with her hand toward the reception area, where there were six people seated, waiting for their own turn to sit in her chair. "And I think they would like that to happen too."

Gale mumbled something under her breath but did turn to leave, and Anastasia gave a sigh of relief. However, before Gale made it to the reception desk, one woman waiting in the small lobby to have her hair colored glanced out the window and said, "Oh. My. God. It's him!"

Now everyone in the place was looking at the woman, wondering who she was talking about.

The woman pointed toward the glass. "Him!" she exclaimed.

The bell chiming above the door announced his entrance.

Mason stepped into the salon, pulling Daniela behind him. His eyes scanned the faces gaping at him, ignored them, and moved on until he found who he came to see.

The smile he directed toward Anastasia caused more than one heart to flutter.

Rooted in place, as she could not believe that once again, Mason Lafayette was in New Salem, she stared at him and could not form a coherent thought.

Herb, on the other hand, had something to say. "Apparently, my haircut will not get done anytime soon," he complained.

The women in the salon looked at him and, in unison, said, "Shut up, Herb."

Herb sat back in the chair, shook his head, and mumbled that back in his day, women had more respect for him than that.

Anastasia gained control of herself and moved toward Mason and the girl with him. "Hi," she said, having eyes only for Mason. And her own smile was as wide as Montana.

"My sister," Mason said, tugging Daniela forward, "needs a haircut."

Daniela rolled her eyes. The moment she saw the woman, she knew this was not about her brother's concern for her hair's health.

Anastasia glanced at the young teenager. She knew Mason had only one sibling because she'd read it in a magazine. However, she had not seen a photo of her, and she could easily see the resemblance to Mason. She had the same beautiful green eyes and black hair, and although she was still maturing, it was easy to see this child would one day be as beautiful, if not more so, than their mother.

However, as thrilled as she was that he had purposely sought her out and was trusting her to cut his sister's beautiful long hair, he had not made an appointment, and she was all booked until four—three hours from now.

"I would love to trim her hair, Mason. You'll just have to come back later."

He blinked. "Excuse me?"

Anastasia motioned toward the area that was hers where Herb still sat in the chair, eager to be on his way. "I need to finish his hair cut," she pointed to the woman with rollers in her hair sitting under the dryer. "Do May's comb out, finish Dawn's perm, cut and style it, and that's only the beginning. Come back at four, and I'll have an opening then."

Mason's mouth opened. "But I'm," he was not sure what he would have said. She interrupted him.

"Yes, I know. Probably in a hurry. And I know there isn't anything to do in this town for three hours. I could schedule an appointment for tomorrow. Unless you want to drive to Bismarck and hang out there for a while, then come back?"

Daniela's smile was wide enough to show her gleaming white teeth. "That is a wonderful idea!"

Mason looked at his sister and scowled.

Daniela shrugged. "Or we could stay here, and you could sign autographs all day," she suggested, noting a few of the women had already dug paper out of their handbags and were heading their way.

"*Merde*," Mason swore in a whisper only his sister could hear. He had not thought of that possibility when he'd come up with this scheme to use Daniela as an excuse to see Anastasia again. Nor had he thought for one moment she would not make time for him. But that should have dawned on him since Anastasia was not like other women he had known. They would have fallen over themselves to accommodate him. But not this woman.

His sister grinned at Anastasia. "We will be back at four," she told her, then stepped closer to the woman who so obviously had her brother's attention it was noteworthy. Rising on her tiptoes, she leaned into Anastasia and whispered in her ear. "Perhaps if you do not have other appointments after four, you would be kind enough to lock the door so my scheduled time will not be interrupted." Motioning with her head toward Mason, she continued, "And my brother can keep us company in peace?"

Realizing this teenager understood her brother's fame better than Anastasia did, she nodded. "Come back at four-thirty. I can lock the door then."

"Excellent." Turning, Daniela told her brother, "I will be in the jeep waiting for you as soon as you can break away from these admirers."

* * *

Daniela walked beside her brother along the main route of the Kirk-wood Mall in Bismarck.

Mason's first stop upon arrival at the shopping center was an outlet selling hats. Once that was done, he gathered his hair up onto the top of his head and placed the baseball cap over it to secure it all in place. Then he pulled the brim low over his face.

She'd giggled over that, and his scowl only added to her merriment. Her brother had gotten all too accustomed to women catering to him. The fact Anastasia was making him wait for an appointment truly was a breath of fresh air.

And people thought she was spoiled? Her brother was right there with her if that were true.

Daniela was thrilled to discover a bank located within the mall. Getting the transfer done, and a cashier's check for the amount she told the bill-board company she would pay them had gone smoothly -after managing to ditch her brother for a few moments by telling him she needed to use the ladies' room just to sneak away from him.

He tried to insist on waiting outside the toilet facility door so she wouldn't get lost.

Seriously? In Kirkwood Mall? When she lived in Paris and shopped the fashionable places in that city?

After she reminded him of that, they agreed to meet outside of SCHEELS, a store that sold gear for sports and outdoor recreation. By the time she finished at the bank and met up with him, he'd been sitting on a bench for almost an hour and a half.

He had not been happy about that.

Getting to the billboard company would prove a little more compli-cated, though. And as brother and sister walked the mall's main

pathway, her mind raced with how she was going to convince him to take her there without raising his suspicion.

She'd figure it out before they needed to drive back to New Salem.

She hoped.

It bored Daniela, walking this mall that offered, in her opinion, nothing she wanted to purchase. However, she was finding amusement in her brother, avoiding being recognized by anyone.

He stayed clear of the bookstore as though it had the plague. They had a life-sized cardboard cutout of his image next to a display of several new romance books hosting his likeness.

Apparently, he did not wish to be surrounded by adoring fans if, by some chance, someone in this town would recognize him as the celebrity he was.

"Perhaps we could visit Colten's parents?" Daniela suggested. Colten's parents were both in their eighties.

"Some other time," Mason said, ducking his head as two women in their thirties passed by. "I do plan to see them at some point. Just not today."

Daniela spotted a hair salon and told him, "I could get my hair trimmed there-"

"No."

"It would save time, and we could-"

"No," he said again, and she sighed.

"Perhaps," Daniela tried, "we could visit Colten's sister, Margret? Or any of his family members."

"No."

She stopped in her tracks, threw her hands in the air, and shouted, "Ooh! You make me so angry!"

People walking the mall looked their way because of the outburst.

Mason turned back to her. Three steps took him to her, and he hissed, "Are you trying to draw attention to me?"

"Well, if they recognize you, it would be more fun watching the women swarm you than what's happening now."

He looked confused. "Nothing is happening."

"Exactly! You have taken me away from the lake to use me as an excuse to see someone, and I could have been having fun water-skiing!" And spending more time with Hunter. But she would not mention that. Nor the fact he had aided in her scheme against Hunter.

"You need a haircut."

She did not hesitate to point toward yet another salon and say, "We could take care of that right now."

"I want Anastasia to do it!"

"Why? By our mother's goddess Aphrodite, you act as though you are courting the woman but are too shy to let her know!" The very idea gave her chuckles.

Incredibly, he blushed. "Do not be ridiculous," he denied his sister's observation. "I only wanted to assure myself she was all right after what happened last night at her house."

Daniela snorted. "You saw her. I saw her. She seemed fine to me."

"We made an appointment with her. I will not break it."

Daniela rolled her eyes. "I think you should send her flowers and ask her on a date. You said you were going to be here for two weeks. Which should give you plenty of time to get what you want."

"And what are you suggesting I want?" he stupidly asked.

"Sex!" she exclaimed loudly.

"Keep your voice down," he hissed, though did not understand why he was embarrassed by the word when he had never been ashamed of the act.

"Can we go now?" she asked innocently.

"Fine," he said, grabbing hold of her arm as he headed toward the exit. "Since we'll be there sooner than expected, we can take the time to view their cow statue up close."

"Oh, joy," Daniela commented dryly. "But I have something I need to do before we leave Bismarck."

He stared at her. "What could you possibly need to do?"

"Colten asked me to stop by a billboard company for him," she said, the words coming out of her mouth as fast as the lie formed in her mind. "And I told him I could do that so he wouldn't have to drive all the way down here to take care of the matter himself." Pulling the cashier's check from her purse, she said, "See? He gave me a check to give to them." She smiled innocently enough. Mason did not question how Colten could have given her a check when he, along with the older generation, had left for Minot before he and Daniela left for New Salem.

Nor did he question why Colten would have asked her to do it in the first place when the man was so organized he would have paid the bill in advance had there been one.

Mason's thought process for reasoning seemed to have dulled the moment he met Anastasia. All he knew was that he was anxious to see her for the second time that day.

* * *

"You have beautiful hair," Anastasia commented as she combed the long length out while the girl stood next to the beauty chair. It was impossible to give an accurate and even cut on hair this long unless the client stood up.

"Thank you," Daniela said, watching Anastasia's movements in the large mirror attached to the wall.

"It's too bad it got tangled in a tree. I'm sure you'll probably wrap it up to protect it the next time you walk along a path that has foliage determined to snare it." Anastasia held a small amount of hair between her fingers as she used her shear to trim the section.

"Indeed," Daniela agreed, moving her eyes toward her brother's reflection. She noted he was studying the woman cutting her hair and not paying attention to what was being said. However, since he was sitting in the lobby, he could not have heard the conversation, anyway.

She had never seen that look in her brother's eyes before, and she wondered about it.

"It was very nice of you to feed my brother yesterday," Daniela continued.

Anastasia chuckled. "We wouldn't want him to waste away, and I felt kind of sorry for him being stranded like he was."

"Are you one of his fans?"

Meeting Daniela's eyes in the mirror, Anastasia told her, "I would be a liar if I told you no. But I am not the type of woman that reads everything and anything about him. I like to form my opinion about a person by knowing them. Tabloids and the press make up things to sell papers, but," she shrugged, "I never thought for a minute I would meet the man." She laughed. "It wasn't as though I would travel to Paris anytime soon, or any other place it's been rumored he goes. And if someone told me he had friends in North Dakota, I wouldn't have believed it because, seriously, what are the odds?"

Daniela thought of Hunter's uncle TJ's wife, Tabitha, and knew what she would say about coincidences.

They happened for reasons, and, as she continued to watch her brother watching Anastasia, she wondered what the possibilities were.

Chapter Seventeen

Anastasia assumed today would be uneventful. By now, everyone in town had probably heard about what happened at her house Sunday night.

Thank goodness.

She was still in awe over the fact Mason brought his sister to her for a haircut yesterday. She knew she would never forget the look on his face when she told him they would have to come back later because she had other appointments scheduled ahead of them.

Priceless.

Anastasia doubted the man never not got what he wanted when he wanted it. But she had a business to run that would be here long after he left North Dakota, whenever that might be, and she would not risk upsetting someone by taking someone else out of turn.

And he tried to write her a check for eight hundred dollars as payment for the simple trim she did! Ridiculous! Her salon's standard fee was right in line with ninety percent of the salons in this state. Even at the ten ninety-five she charged, some people around here thought that was outrageous.

Seriously.

She refused to take more from him than what she would have charged anyone for the trim, and they'd almost gotten into an argument over it.

Perhaps someone else would have been tempted to take what he offered, but she was not someone else. And although eight hundred dollars would have paid off one bill she owed to the hospital, she held her ground and made him put his checkbook away. Especially after he tried to claim the outrageous amount was her tip.

Good grief.

Through it all, his sister watched the two of them banter back and forth about the money as though the entire thing amused her.

Last night, whenever Anastasia thought about it, she had a few laughs herself recalling his facial expressions.

He tried to explain the amount was only half the fee he would have paid if he'd gotten Daniela's hair cut at the salon he patronized in West Hollywood in California.

Did he pay sixteen thousand dollars for a haircut? For the exact same thing she could do for pennies on the dollar?

Apparently, there were a lot of rip-off artists in the world who fooled people into believing a haircut was not any good unless it was expensive.

Ha! Anastasia would put her skills with a shear up against every one of those celebrity stylists any day of the week.

All that aside, she was thrilled to see him again. And do not get her started on how her heart thumped madly, knowing he had not forgotten her!

What that second encounter did to her dreams last night was amazing. But this was today. She was back in the actual world. Getting these services done for the people waiting their turn was the only thing that would pay her bills and add to her laughable savings account. She was not foolish enough to believe Mason Lafayette was interested in her for any reason other than a distraction.

It was around noon when one man waiting for his own hair cut glanced out the window and informed everyone, "Looks as though someone is about to get some flowers." The man's hand flew to his chest as though experiencing a heart attack. "Scratch that. Someone's about to get a whole warehouse full of flowers!"

There was no preventing the twenty people occupying the salon's interior from rushing as one mass to the front window. They witnessed for themselves the florist truck parked outside, the driver, and two others, unloading a sizable amount of assorted arrangements, and then make their way into the salon. Once inside, the truck driver inquired to the gaping group of spectators, "Anastasia Sharp?"

Nineteen fingers pointed out the person belonging to that name.

Anastasia's eyes widened in disbelief as the two people with the man entered the salon, pushing a cart loaded with arrangements of different sizes. They placed them in the center of the cutting floor, and went back outside with the cart. "What?" She was having a hard time finding her voice. It seemed as though all she could do was stand opened mouth, along with everyone else, in a daze as the men returned and added still more bouquets, bringing the total number of arrangements to a mind-boggling three dozen. "I didn't order these!" she finally gasped, wishing everyone would stop staring at her as though she were some never before seen creature.

The driver of the vehicle stepped forward. He had a broad smile on his face as he introduced himself as the florist shop owner. This sale totaled more than what he usually sold in arrangements in one week that would not be going to a funeral home or a hospital. "They were ordered for you early this morning." He held out a card to the bewildered Anastasia. "The man asked me to give you this as well."

Anastasia came out of her daze. She reached for the card as she glanced once more at the colorful array of roses, baby's breath, carnations, and a variety of other flowers stretching out before her and carpeting the salon's white tiled floor.

"Who are they from?" someone asked.

Anastasia shook her head. "I still think this is a mistake."

"No mistake, ma'am," the florist was quick to assure her. "You are Anastasia Sharp?" At her half nod, he continued, "These flowers were

to be delivered to you here, and now that I have completed my mission, I leave you to enjoy." He tipped his head and headed for the door.

"Wait!" Anastasia exclaimed.

The man turned back. "No need to tip me, ma'am. It was included in the transaction."

She stared at him. That had not been what was on her mind.

"Open the card!" someone else exclaimed.

"This is absurd!" Anastasia blurted, unable to speak to the florist because everyone was crowding around her.

Quickly opening the card before someone decided to do it for her, Anastasia scanned the message.

Then reread it.

Anastasia,
You will join me tonight for dinner.
I will pick you up at seven.

Mason

Anastasia was annoyed and thrilled at the same time. Mason Lafayette sure had some nerve. Did the man honestly believe she was going to drop everything just because he was who he was? She would have appreciated it if he had asked. Not that she had anything else to do this evening, but gosh darn it! Did everyone fall over themselves whenever he snapped his fingers?

And she had vowed, after having endured Danny's personality change and abuse, that no man was going to tell her what to do ever again.

She marched up to where the florist stood and told him, "Take those with you." She pointed to the three dozen bouquets.

"I can't!" the man exclaimed, fearful of having to refund the money his business received.

"Then take them to one of the hospitals in Bismarck and distribute them to the patients," Anastasia suggested.

Yes, she wanted to be with Mason tonight. Wanted to experience an evening out. That was something she had not had for a long, long time. Always afraid Danny might find out. But it all boiled down to the fact he had not asked if she wanted to go out with him.

Well, Mason Richard Fernando Antoine Albert Lafayette was going to be in for a big surprise when he came knocking on her door tonight. Of that, she was quite certain.

* * *

Mason was stunned. He blinked several times at the door that just slammed in his face. He also wondered if it was Anastasia who possessed this bewildering power to cause him to feel like a complete ass, or if it were just New Salem in general trying to rob him of his self-esteem.

He could not believe this just happened to him.

He had looked forward to this evening and spending time with Anastasia and her delightful humor, although he refused to analyze if there was more to the tug he felt pulling him to her.

When he and Daniela left her salon yesterday, heading back to the lake, he had been a little miffed with Anastasia's refusal to take the money he wanted to pay her. He thought it was a fair amount, but she acted insulted.]

Daniela, surprisingly, pointed out that this was not where the rich and famous lived, and Anastasia probably thought he considered her a charity case.

That could not have been further from the truth.

150

He found Anastasia intriguing. A refreshing drink of water after having put up with substitutes that never seemed to quench his thirst.

Throughout the day, he could not prevent Anastasia's beautiful face from forming in his mind. Could not stop thinking about the woman's quick wit and the fact he wanted to know her better. And just because he was only going to be in North Dakota for a few weeks did not mean he could not indulge himself in a little romance.

What startled him the most was that, as much as he desired to take Anastasia to bed, that was not at the forefront of his mind. He honestly liked her. He had not respected the women he had been with in the past in ways he respected Anastasia.

Mason was not sure if he wanted to dwell on what that might mean, but for now, at least, he wanted to spend as much time with Anastasia as he could. And what better way for two people to get to know one another than by having dinner together?

Anastasia certainly was not acting like a woman who received three dozen assortments of bouquets. Nor did she appear excited about having dinner with him, which included being picked up in the luxurious limousine he rented in Bismarck that would take them to their destination.

Then again, he would be the first to admit she did not act like the women who were his fans. Many of them would have been thrilled if he looked their way. And had he invited one of them to dinner? They would have said yes in a heartbeat.

So, knowing Anastasia had yet to fall all over herself to get his attention, he should have been prepared for just about anything. But the scenarios that might have played out in his head, this response he'd gotten from her when he rang her doorbell, would not be one of them.

She slammed the door in his face.

He could not believe this happened to him.

Mason's green befuddled eyes glanced toward the waiting limousine. Then he looked down at the dozen large stemmed dark red roses, that is, what was left of them, in his hand, then back to the white door that nearly caused him a broken nose.

Why would she do such a stupid thing?

On top of it all, she opened the door, dressed in the sloppiest and oldest looking clothing he had ever seen. That fact confused him enough to inquire, "Did you not receive my flowers and invitation regarding dinner tonight?"

"Yep. Sure did," she replied matter of fact. "And the patients at St. A's in Bismarck would like to thank you for your kindness. Flowers always brighten those dull hospital rooms."

His brows narrowed. "I do not understand. I asked the florist to give you a card, telling you I would take you for dinner tonight." He explained, motioning to the waiting limo, then extended the roses. "I brought you these-"

"Oh, sure! Ask a florist, but tell me?" she replied in a huff, just before she slammed the door, leaving him to extract the roses from where they had been crushed within the door frame.

Mason glanced once more toward the limo. The driver ducked his head, pulling his hat low, and Mason knew damn well, if the man's shaking body was any indication, the guy was laughing at him.

Personally, if Anastasia thought she was being funny, he could find no way to be amused by it. None whatsoever.

Raking a hand through his hair, his male vanity attacked, he reached out a finger and depressed the doorbell once again. He was already confused and at a complete loss concerning how to deal with this situation. He felt his anger beginning to rise.

If she thought slamming the door in his face conveyed a message, she had better think again. If he had done something wrong, then she could bloody well tell him to his face.

He pounded on the door and yelled, "Anastasia! Open this goddamn door!"

Déjà vu. Hadn't this same scene taken place Sunday, but with him inside along with her?

That memory of Anastasia's ex-husband terrorizing her caused him to lower his voice. "Anastasia, please open the door. What did I do wrong?" God, this was humiliating! Never, not once, had he ever had to beg for a woman to open their door to him.

"Go away, Mason," he barely heard her say through the thickness of the door.

Issuing a heavy sigh, Mason leaned his forehead on the unmoving entrance. He noted the trembling quality of her voice. It tugged at his heart in ways it had never been pulled. "Open the door, chéri," he told her softly. "I cannot leave until you tell me why you wish me gone."

A long silence followed, and just as Mason began to think she would not acknowledge his presence, her voice came through the door. "You don't understand, Mason. I- Mason-" More silence, and then a choked out, "You're not for me."

That claim brought Mason's head snapping up, and it was the last straw. It pushed him over the edge, and his growing anger went to full bloom. Obviously, she thought him foolish for not being able to stand up against her ex-husband. Apparently, she was more intrigued with Hunter than she led him to believe.

Mason's assumption, however, could not have been more wrong.

Anastasia leaned against the closed door, moisture forming behind her eyes. Had she truly believed she could spend time with him tonight?

Yes, she planned on telling him she had not appreciated being told he was taking her for dinner. The reason she greeted him at the door, with her oldest sweatshirt and baggy pants pulled over the top of the actual clothing she planned to wear for tonight's outing, was only meant as a joke. After he laughed, she had all intentions of going with him.

She still wanted to. She just couldn't

The sight of him, decked out in a black tuxedo that matched so perfectly with his black, shining hair, while holding the dozen red roses, had nearly taken her breath away. But it was the quality of his clothing, along with the white limo, that brought reality crashing in on her. Everything about the man spoke of riches far more than she could imagine, even in her dreams. Without a doubt, Mason Lafayette was out of her league. Surely, he would be more than embarrassed to be seen with her when the dressiest clothing she owned came from Walmart, and from the clearance rack to boot.

There was something else far more devastating to her than the worldly wealth standing on the other side of the door. It was that revelation that caused her to tell him to go away. She was so attracted to him; she ached with it. But she also knew the reality. He would only be in her life for a short time, and she felt as though she were ripping apart. Her dream of meeting him had come true, but he would not remain in her life.

It was better to tell him to go away than open herself up for more loneliness and more pain. Putting an end to their evening together now, before she found herself falling in love, was the only thing she could do. The only choice she had.

"Fine, Stasia!" she heard Mason's angry tone, and the quality of hurt contained within it shook her down to her toes. "I will tell Hunter you would rather have dinner with him!"

Anastasia's eyes widened at the horrible thought. Hunter?! That dangerous man was the last person on earth she ever wanted to be alone with.

She was in motion before she realized it. Whipping around, yanking the door open, she exclaimed, "What in the hell would make you think I want to have dinner with Hunter?"

Mason was already half-way down the sidewalk when she asked that question. It caused him to stop, turn on his heel, and tell her through clenched teeth, "That is obvious, lady. He was your knight in shining armor the other night. Not I." With that observation, he turned back around and continued to the limo.

The chauffeur opened the door to the limousine as Mason reached it.

"Mason?" Anastasia watched him hesitate, as though fighting between entering the vehicle or remaining where he was. "Hunter has nothing to do with this."

Stormy green eyes locked with hers. "Really?" Mason challenged. "I have never had a door slammed in my face, and I have never had a woman turn me down for a date. The impression you just gave me, since, as you said, I am not for you, is that Hunter is more to your taste."

She blushed scarlet, knowing she had, perhaps, handled this situation completely wrong.

"I-" she began, then lowered her eyes momentarily. How could she find the right words to explain her offensive behavior?

When she looked back up, it startled her to see him standing less than two feet away. "I'm sorry, Mason, I…" she swallowed and looked away. She could not tell him she regretted the fact he would not be around very long. But he deserved an explanation.

"Tell me," he said in a voice soft as a feather. The catch in Anastasia's voice defused his anger.

She swallowed again and blinked back the tears. "You… you didn't ask," she whispered.

"Excuse me?"

She looked down at his black leather shoes. "Today. The card. You told me you were taking me to dinner. You… didn't ask, and…" she swallowed again. "It was something Danny always did in the last year of our marriage. He told me what to do. When to go grocery shopping. When to wash the clothes. When I should start dinner. When to go to work. How many appointments I could book…" She shook her head and took a deep breath. "I vowed I would never allow a man to tell me what to do ever again. Because of that, I overreacted, and I'm sorry."

Mason was not sure which touched him the most. Her apology, or her tears.

His hand reached out, gently touching her face. "Chéri," his voice was a whisper as he used his thumb to catch her tears. What was it about this woman that captivated him so?

He could not blame her for being upset. As he thought about it, the message he gave the florist could have sounded as though it were a demand. It was how he conveyed to the women he dated over the years when they should be ready. Not once had any of them complained, but he was not dealing with someone accustomed to his ways, and he was sorry he had not taken a moment to think about how she would react.

And why did his heart squeeze tight, knowing he had caused her anguish? He was not sure, but his anger was forgotten as he stood there looking at her. And knowing he did not know what she had gone through broke his heart.

"*Chéri*," he repeated. "I am the one who should apologize. And I am sorry I assumed you wanted to have dinner with me." He cupped her chin, tilted her face until her eyes met his. "Forgive me. And if you are willing, I would very much like to dine with you this evening."

Anastasia's heart squeezed. Having her dream of meeting this man come true was a double-edged sword. How could she stay angry with him when he apologized like that?

She brushed her tears away as she took a cleansing breath. "I would like that too," she confessed. "But I'm a little underdressed."

Mason eyed the sweatshirt and baggy pants. "They look comfortable," he offered, kicking himself for forgetting this was not New York or California. He was used to taking women to expensive restaurants that required formal dining. "And I am a fool for wearing this. I forgot there are no places in Bismarck where anyone would wear formal-wear."

Surprising him, she laughed. "We could find a wedding to crash." she suggested. "You'd fit right in. However, I barely would, and you'd probably agree once you see what I have on under this."

He stared at her, imagining a lacey bra and matching underwear.

Licking his lips, he questioned, "Under it?" And held his breath as he wondered if she was inviting him to her bed. If so, to hell with dinner. He wanted to feast on her.

She nodded. "I'll show you," she said as she reached down and yanked off the sweatpants.

Mason was speechless. She was taking off her pants? On the sidewalk? Where anyone could see-

Then she took off the baggy shirt and stood before him barefooted and wearing a light blue knee-length dress.

He wasn't sure if he should laugh, but it happened anyway. The chuckle started low and built until he was laughing outright.

"I know," she exclaimed, thinking he was laughing at her cheap clothing. "It's a horrible dress! And next to that tux of yours, I look like a bum. You're dressed so eloquently, and this is the best I've got."

Shaking his head, trying to speak, he said between the laughter, "*Chéri*, I am laughing because I thought you were undressing down to your underwear!"

Her eyes narrowed. "Outside?!" her face turned pink. "Never in a million years would I undress outside-" Her words trailed off as she thought about how it would have appeared to him since he had no way of knowing she'd pulled the old clothing over her dress.

She began laughing too, and to the limousine driver, they looked like two children engaged in play.

"Do you," Mason asked her once their merriment subsided, "think Jeff would lend me a shirt? Unfortunately, I can do nothing about changing these pants and shoes."

Glancing down at the demolished roses he still held, he tossed them over his shoulder, hitting the chauffeur in the face without realizing it.

Anastasia witnessed the shock on the man's face and almost started another round of laughter. "You'll look ridiculous with one of Jeff's shirts on, matched with those fancy pants of yours," she told Mason instead.

Mason shook his head. "Belle femme. If you are willing to be seen with me, I will not care what anyone thinks. I only wish to be with you."

Her heart thumped, wishing he meant those last words in a permanent way. How often had he said that to her in her dreams? But right now, at this moment, she would spend whatever time she could with him and deal with the day he walked out of her life when it came.

"Then, I would very much like to have dinner with you, Mr. Lafayette. Let's see if Jeff will loan you a shirt, and we'll be on our way."

The chauffeur watched them walk into Anastasia's house, after Mason told him to wait for them, and wondered how he had been so miserably lucky to have gotten stuck with this odd couple.

Chapter Eighteen

As luck would have it, Jeff had a shirt large enough to fit Mason. An old t-shirt with the words, Go Bison!, printed across its front. And although Jeff had pants with a waist size the same as Mason's, their length would have reached his calves. But Jeff had a pair of shorts that fit nicely, allowing Mason to change out of the tuxedo and slip into the casual wear.

Shoes proved a little more challenging to replace. However, after rummaging through some old boxes Gale and Jeff had stored in their garage, a collection of stuff they were saving for a garage sale, they unearthed a pair of flip-flops that would fit Mason's feet.

To finish the look, Jeff handed Mason a baseball cap advertising a local radio station.

Gathering his long hair up, Mason could use the hat to conceal the mass under it. Turning to Anastasia, he asked, "How do I look?"

As sexy now as the first time I saw you, Anastasia thought but did not voice it out loud. But she chuckled when she told him, "Now I'm the one overdressed!"

His smile was full of charm. "You look beautiful. Are you ready to travel to Bismarck now?"

Nodding, she took his hand, and they walked to the waiting limo.

When they arrived in Bismarck, Mason instructed the driver to take them to where the vehicle he borrowed from one of the Fishers was parked. Once there, Mason dismissed the driver, and the man was more than happy to be free of the silly couple.

Anastasia eyed the jacked-up black Ford and shook her head. "I have to admit, I never imagined you behind the wheel of a pickup."

Unlocking the passenger door and opening it to her, Mason said, "I prefer the Corvette, but when I am in North Dakota, I make do with whatever is on hand."

"Isn't your vehicle fixed yet?" she asked him, climbing into the cab.

"That was a rental." He shrugged.

She waited until he climbed behind the steering wheel and started the engine before commenting on what he said earlier. "How often do you come to North Dakota?" It still boggled her mind that he even set foot in the flat state.

Looking for traffic before easing the truck forward, he told her, "Not as often as when I was a boy." He merged onto 9th street and pointed the vehicle north on the one-way street.

They were silent for a moment as Anastasia digested that information. And the way he maneuvered the vehicle toward wherever they were heading for supper showed he knew his way around the capital of North Dakota.

Mason glanced her way and wondered what she would say if he told her about his connection to the small town of Medora in the western part of the state. "My family has always kept our trips here to themselves. Whenever the time came for our visit, my parents would let it slip they were vacationing in Italy, Spain, or anyplace other than the United States, so the paparazzi would chase the wild goose looking for us. Never do they, or I, mention this state when speaking to the media or anyone else where we vacation in the summer."

She stared at him for a moment, then chuckled, "Oh! You send them on a goose chase! I was confused for a minute when you said they chased a wild goose."

Mason cringed. He didn't slip up often on American slang as he once had. Hunter would tease him unmercifully whenever it happened in the past, and he'd worked hard to grasp the correct phrases. However, once in a while, he would say one incorrectly.

He hated when that happened.

"Some American idioms are hard to remember and are ridiculous."

He sounded like a snob, and it made her laugh. "No doubt," she agreed, earning her a quick look from him for using another slang phrase.

"Let's forget about slang for now," she told him. "I can understand wanting to keep some things private. If I were famous, I would want someplace I could go and not be hounded by the paparazzi shit heads."

Laughter erupted from him. "I have thought of them in that way all of my life."

They rode in silence for a few blocks as Mason considered that she seemed to understand privacy was a rare commodity for people in the spotlight. However, it was also a necessary evil. If the paparazzi were not hounding you, you probably weren't popular anymore.

Glancing her way again, he wondered if there was a way to spend more than an hour or two with her, and he was not thinking along the lines of sex, although he would hope it happened soon between them. Every night fantasizing about her was driving him mad, especially when he'd never deprived himself from sex before and his body was feeling it. He felt as though he was as horny now as he had been as a teenager. Ridiculous, he knew, but it was still a fact.

"Tomorrow is the fourth of July," he told her, merging into the traffic on Boulevard Avenue where ninth street ended on the south side of the capitol building. "Do you have plans?"

"Not really, though my salon is closed tomorrow and for the rest of the week. I've set money aside so I can take several days off because business is slow. People around here vacation over the weekend. Few people come to get their hair done over the fourth of July holiday. Business at my salon does not pick up until the week after."

His heart thumped. She would be free for a few days? "Taking time off from our jobs is important. Are you going somewhere?" He hoped not. He wanted her to spend the time with him.

"Not really. Tomorrow is the fourth of July parade in Mandan. I've gone with Gale and Jeff before, but I'm not interested in being in a crowd. I'm thinking about driving to Medora. It's North Dakota's number one tourist attraction, and I've never been there. I've heard so much about it I want to see what all the fuss is about." She chuckled. "I realize I grew up only an hour and a half from the place, but I just haven't made it there. This year, though, It's my goal."

"You are going alone?"

She shrugged.

"Will you go there with me?"

It was a good thing Anastasia was not the one driving. She would have wound up going into the ditch. "With you?"

Mason slowed for a stoplight, then looked at her while he waited for the light to turn green. "Hunter's family own a horse ranch south of Medora. When I was younger, it was where my family would travel every summer." The light changed to green, and he pressed down on the accelerator, then continued the conversation. "The Fishers always put on a large firework display on the fourth, and then the following day, we will head into the Badlands for a two-day camp-out."

Anastasia stared at him. Mason Lafayette camped? The concept was startling to her. "I…" She was not sure what she should say.

More than anything, she wanted to be with him. It would give her more opportunity to understand who he was under all the media's views of him. But it frightened her. Frightened her because to spend that much time with him would probably lead to heartache. She was already falling in love with him, and that was a danger zone she was not sure she wanted to travel down any farther than she had.

She cleared her throat. "May I think about it and let you know in the morning?"

Mason swung the pickup into the Red Lobster parking lot, found a parking slot, and cut the engine. Then he sat back and stared at her. Had he asked any other woman to spend a few days with him, they would have jumped through hoops to do so, but he should have known Anastasia would not follow the typical path.

"I have asked no one to accompany me into the Badlands, *belle femme*." And it shocked him he asked her to do so. "I want you to know that as you consider your decision."

Swallowing a lump in her throat, she answered, "I will."

Perhaps she was being foolish by not shouting to the rooftops a resounding yes. But even though she was a dreamer, she knew reality would crash in on her once he left North Dakota. She'd had a broken heart once. She was leery of allowing another man to shatter her world.

Trying not to be annoyed, Mason opened the driver's side door, got out, and walked around to her side of the vehicle. Opening the door for her, he reached out his hand and assisted her out of the tall truck. Once she was standing next to him, Mason closed the door, but he did not let go of her hand. "I hope you like seafood," he told her. "I am in the mood for lobster regardless of the fact this is not fresh seafood, but this is the best this town offers so," he eyed her, "unless you would prefer McDonald's-" He tried to keep the disdain out of his voice for the fast-food chain.

Liking the feel of his hand still linked with hers, she smiled up at him, then began walking toward the restaurant entrance as he followed along. "Then I guess we better get you some lobster, and yes. I do like seafood."

Their wait to be seated was not long. It was Tuesday and the day before the fourth of July celebration. Many families might have already headed

out of town for whatever traditions they partook in, or it might have been a slow day for the restaurant.

Mason and Anastasia did not care what the reason was for them being seated quickly. They were hungry, having delayed their meal by an hour while helping Gale and Jeff search for something Mason could wear.

The couple ordered quickly, and after the server left to put in their request, Anastasia asked, "So, about this camping trip your family is going on. How many RVs do you use?"

Mason chuckled and shook his head. "We use tents. The area we go to is secluded and not accessible by any other means than on horse-back."

"I have never been on a horse," she told him, trying to wrap her head around the fact this man, born to wealth, would be caught dead in the wilderness.

Mason reached across the table, took her hand in his. "*Chéri*, I would very much like to teach you how to ride." His look was sensual, and his eyes held promise.

Her face flamed. There could be no mistaking his meaning.

Whatever response Anastasia would have given was forgotten when a woman in her thirties stopped at their table. She looked at Mason and said, "Forgive me. I know I'm interrupting, and it's rude. But, has anyone ever told you that if you were to grow your hair out, you would look just like that hot romance cover model?"

Anastasia glanced at Mason, who still wore the baseball cap hiding his long hair. Smiling, she said, "Really? I don't see it."

Mason, elbow on the table, brought his fist up to his mouth to hold his laugh at bay.

The woman nodded enthusiastically at Anastasia. "He does!" she exclaimed. "I don't know if you're his wife or girlfriend, but you got one handsome guy sitting across the table from you."

"That I do," Anastasia confessed. "But I'm not sure he looks like whoever you are thinking of."

"Mason Lafayette!" the woman exclaimed, and heads turned their way.

Anastasia shook her head. "Seriously? Do you truly believe someone like that would be sitting here in the Red Lobster, in Bismarck, North Dakota?"

The woman hesitated, seeming to think that over. "Well, I suppose…" she trailed off, glancing once more at Mason. "I'm sorry to have interrupted your evening. The likeness is uncanny." And she turned to leave.

"*Passez une bonne nuit, madame*," Mason said, not able to resist speaking to the woman.

The lady spun back around. "It is you!" she gushed, grabbing her purse and rummaging through it for a paper and pen. "Please, may I have your autograph?"

Other women in the restaurant began making their way toward the booth.

Anastasia laughed and shook her head at him, "You could have said nothing, and no one would have been the wiser."

"This is true," he told her as he took the paper and pen from the woman and signed his name, "However, if giving my autograph to someone brightens their day, why not do it?"

She thought about that as she watched him interact with the dozen or so women and a couple of men who approached the table. He was charming them with that French accent of his, and oddly, she felt proud of him for caring enough to want to oblige them in their requests for an autograph.

By the time Mason was done holding court, which was how she thought of this invasion on their evening together, their dinner arrived.

"Well, that was fun," she told him as she dug her fork into the mashed potatoes on her plate.

He shrugged. "I hope it did not upset you."

Laughing, she shook her head. "Why would it upset me? You are who you are, and you are adored by a lot of people. I enjoyed watching the exchange."

Sitting back, Mason observed her. She honestly seemed not bothered by the interruption. This reminded him how different she was from the other women he dated over the past few years. They would become annoyed if he was not giving them all his attention or were irritated when no one gave them the time of day.

He was falling in love, and he knew it. As absurd as it seemed, a woman from a small town in the middle of nowhere was stealing his heart.

They fell into a comfortable silence as they consumed the meal. Each of them wondering if there could be a future together beyond the friendship that was building. Anastasia was down to earth and beautiful and not caught up in superficial things—the complete opposite of Carol Gibson and others he'd dated. They did not have a genuine bone in their body.

A server cleared their empty plates, refilled their coffee, and left them alone.

"When I was younger," Mason told her, surprised he was telling her more about his childhood, "I lived with the Fishers for a year. Their ranch offers horse riding tours into the Badlands. I helped with those and all the other daily operations of running the place while I was there. I think it took me a month to get the smell of horseshit and hay out of my nostrils once my parents brought me back to Paris."

There was something in the way he said it that told Anastasia there was more to his stay with the Fishers than he was saying. Something that

haunted him, but she would not pry. If he wanted her to know, then he would tell her.

But boy oh boy, did she have the strongest desire to wrap her arms around him and hold him tight.

She looked down at the table for a moment. Mason had shared with her. Perhaps she could share with him. "My parents died in a car accident when I was seventeen. They were driving home from visiting my aunt in Glen Ullin. They were on highway one-thirty-nine, which is just south of interstate ninety-four. They always liked to take that route, but this time someone coming up from the side road did not bother to stop at the stop sign. They just kept going. So many people think that just because they are driving in an area that isn't traveled often, they don't have to look to see if anyone is coming." She shook her head, wiped at a tear that tried to escape.

Mason reached across the table, squeezed her hand. "The sun will set soon. Perhaps if we arrive in New Salem soon enough, we can park the truck up there by that cow and watch the sun go to sleep."

She met his eyes and nodded. "I'd like that," she told him softly.

True to his word, Mason drove the pickup up the narrow dirt road that led to Salem Sue once they reached New Salem. Parking the vehicle pointing west, he and Anastasia sat quietly in the cab to watch the sun's descent.

Anastasia moved closer to him as they sat there, taking in the view. He put his arm around her, and she rested her head against his shoulder. Lazily Mason's hand stroked her arm as he wondered, and hoped, she would invite him into her house and into her bed tonight.

"Mason?"

"Hmm?"

"You said the sunsets in the Badlands were more beautiful than this?"

"Yes. They are."

She sat up, tried to see him in the cab's darkness. "Perhaps you can take me home now so I can decide what to pack. I think I would very much like to go with you to Medora tomorrow."

His heart swelled as he shifted the truck into drive and maneuvered back down the narrow dirt road, then headed for her house.

He pulled up into the driveway, cut the engine, got out of the vehicle, and helped her out.

They walked hand-in-hand up the sidewalk. When Mason noted the boarded-up window, he asked, "Will your window be replaced soon?"

"The glass company told me they could install it sometime next week." She pulled her house keys from her purse, unlocked the door. Turning to him, she said, "I had a lovely time tonight. I hope you will-"

"Yes!" he exclaimed with a smile as wide as the sky, believing she was going to invite him in.

She blinked. "I was going to say, I hope you will drive safely back to the lake tonight."

It was his turn to blink. "I.." he looked at Anastasia, then past her through the open doorway, then back to her once more. "I.."

She could easily read what was on his mind. It was on her mind too, but she was hesitant to take him to her bed. Not because she did not want to. Oh god. Everything in her wanted to know what it was like to be his lover. But she had never been someone to jump into the sack for a casual fling. And as much as she desired Mason Lafayette, he would not be around for very much longer. Sex meant something to her. Something almost spiritual, and she could not bring herself to say yes to the longing she saw in his eyes.

Rather than acknowledge the desire, she told him, "Good night, Mason."

He stared at her so long she would have sworn he x-rayed her face as he tried to comprehend, she told him no.

After a moment, he seemed to resign himself: he was not getting past that door and into her bed. He took a deep breath, reached out his hands to clasp her head between them. Gently, he kissed her on the forehead. "Good night, *belle femme*."

He turned around and seemed to walk stiffly back to the truck.

She managed not to laugh when she witnessed his hand reach down to adjust himself and hoped he did not curse her all the way back to Lake Sakakawea.

Chapter Nineteen

Twenty miles south of
Medora, North Dakota

Anastasia dropped her poodle off with Gail and Jeff, thankful they agreed to watch Mason Divine for a few days while she was away. After that, at ten in the morning, Mason, Hunter, and Hunter's siblings, Rebecca, and Wyatt drove into her driveway to pick her up for the hour and a half drive from New Salem to the F&L Ranch located south of Medora.

Sitting on the bench seat in the back of Hunter's black CJ-7 jeep, sandwiched between Mason and Rebecca, Anastasia felt like a sardine. But a happy one. And she was thankful Hunter opted to keep the vehicle's soft-top on. Otherwise, her hair would have been a bird's nest by the end of the journey.

While conversing with the Fisher's youngest daughter as the miles passed, Anastasia discovered they had a lot in common. Rebecca was an avid bookworm, and the two of them discussed their favorite authors. Realizing they read several of the same books gave them a chance to compare notes regarding which characters they liked the best and which ones they hated.

Anastasia did not mention she was writing a romance novel. Nor her desire to see the story published and on the bestsellers list. She knew the odds, but why except them? The probabilities of meeting Mason had been astronomical, and yet, here she was with him and his friends for an adventure she hadn't dreamed of.

Being this close to him, she was very much aware of their hips and thighs touching as there was not enough room in the back of the jeep to

allow space between them. Whatever the cologne he was wearing was wrapping her in a scent of something woodsy with a hint of orange. The aroma caused her to want to climb onto his lap. Those handsome features of his, combined with that fragrance, were breaking down any misgivings she might have had for accompanying him. And she knew the heat she'd seen in his eyes meant he had more on his mind than giving her a tour of Medora and the ranch.

He took her hand in his, raised it to his lips, and told her, "Thank you for accepting my invitation to join me today and for the next few days."

The feel of his mouth on her knuckles caused a shiver to go up her spine. "I'm looking forward to the fireworks." Meeting his eyes, she could clearly see he was thinking about sparks flying too, but not the kind that exploded in the air.

His smile was sensual as he told her, "I enjoy fireworks. Very much."

She swallowed. God, the man oozed testosterone. If he could harvest it and sell it, men everywhere would buy it by the gallon just so they would have no problem attracting a woman to their bed.

Rebecca reached over Anastasia, pushed Mason playfully in his chest. "You're such a flirt."

Mason grinned at the sixteen-year-old and laughed.

But Rebecca's observation had Anastasia wondering, as the miles passed, if Mason was playing a game with her affections. Why would he want to spend time with her? Someone he'd only recently met and was certainly not a member of the rich and famous.

She tried to push the questions racing through her mind aside, determined to enjoy herself on this adventure and do it one step at a time.

Upon arrival at the F&L, Anastasia learned the initials stood for the Fisher and Lafayette families. It astounded her to discover the tourist business the Fisher's ran resembled a small town. Buildings one would see on a typical ranch spread out before her as the jeep drove through

the gate. There were stables, a large barn, corrals, and other functional buildings. Those she expected. However, she had not expected the dozen cabins rented out to tourists if they wished to spend the night. Nor the mess hall with a small general store attached to it where visitors could purchase souvenirs. There was also an elaborate bunkhouse where the part-time summer help stayed, as did the four full-time employees. There was also a part-time supervisor who oversaw the running of the ranch whenever all the Fisher's were gone from the farm, although those times were rare.

Colten and Jacqueline's son-in-law Jake was the full-time Foreman. Running the spread efficiently. But every other year, when the reunion took place at Lake Sakakawea, Jake would take a few days off for relaxation. That was when the part-time supervisor was needed, which made the man's job easy enough.

But above all that grandeur, the sight to leave her speechless was the Fisher's three-story, eight-bedroom, stone-faced European-styled home at the top of a small hill. She would have never suspected to find this beautiful house nestled into the land surrounded by what people called the Badlands. She, however, thought the rugged terrain was mystical and spectacular. As far as she was concerned, there was nothing bad about this scenic area.

The jeep came to a stop in the driveway in front of the four-stall garage, and its passengers climbed out. The only luggage that needed to be taken inside were two suitcases. One belonging to Mason. The other to Anastasia. Because Wyatt and Rebecca lived here, they already had clothing hanging in their bedroom closets. Anastasia could only assume Hunter had some items here, also, as there was no bag belonging to him in the back of the jeep.

The front door of the mansion opened. From the opening stepped three women. One of them, Anastasia easily recognized as Mason's mother. She had seen a few of the woman's movies and a photo or two of her standing with her famous son. In-person, the woman was more beautiful

than those flat images of her revealed. Anastasia also recalled reading somewhere that Rosalinda was of French, Spanish and Italian heritage.

It was easy to see Mason's darker apricot skin coloring, black hair, and green eyes were inherited from her.

Rosalinda Lafayette glided forward. The woman was all grace and elegance wrapped in a small package. Dressed in a long skirt and a flowy cotton shirt, with sleeves ending at her wrists, Anastasia had only two seconds to ponder how the woman wasn't suffering in the heat of the day, before she found herself wrapped in Rosalinda's arms.

Kissing Anastasia on her cheeks, Rosalinda pulled back and said, "Welcome to the F&L." Her smile seemed to shine bright enough to compete with the sun. "My son mentioned he was bringing a guest, and now I see why." She stepped back, raked her with her eyes, then glanced at her son. "I approve, Mason. She is a beautiful woman."

Anastasia raised a brow. Approved? Should she be flattered or insulted?

Before she could contemplate the question further, the other women stepped forward. One extended her hand and said, "Hi there. I'm Jacqueline Fisher." She motioned to the other woman, who gave her a quick wave, "And this is Kasey Benson. A very good friend of our family. We are all excited you're here."

Hunter, walking past Mason, said in a low voice, but loud enough everyone heard his remark. "Hope you're ready for the noose. Your mom's going to make sure the knot gets started."

Mason scowled after Hunter's retreating back, then glanced at his mother. Rosalinda gave him such an innocent look he knew she was probably planning a wedding, and he cringed. He had been too obsessed with wanting to spend time with Anastasia to consider how his mother would view this situation.

A glance at Anastasia gave him the knowledge that she had at least a hundred questions waiting to be asked.

"Mother," Mason began, "This is not-"

Rosalinda cut him off. "Darling, son, I know what it is. Now, do not spoil the moment." She gestured toward the house, "You can show Anastasia to the guest room at the top of the stairs along with her suitcase." Smiling, she told Mason, "Since it is on the way to your old room."

He did not believe his mother thought for one minute Anastasia would spend the night there, but was willing to play whatever game she was up to. Besides, if he did not insist upon sharing a room with Anastasia, then his mother would have no fuel to stoke her wedding bell fantasies. More importantly, he had not spoken to Anastasia about sharing a room with her. Which he planned to. He was desperate to have her naked under him and begging him for release. God knew his body craved hers like an addict craved drugs.

He could not explain why, after all these years, one woman remained on his mind, not allowing another to enter. She was all he could think of, no matter how hard he tried to find interest in another.

Anastasia followed behind Mason, managing not to gape at the grandeur. The house was as beautiful on the inside as it was on the outside. The grand staircase leading upstairs left her speechless.

She was definitely out of her element here and tried not to feel like a country bumpkin.

The enormous wall near the bottom of the staircase displayed dozens of framed photos. Anastasia paused for a moment to look at them. Easy to recognize were pictures of a younger Hunter and Mason. And because she had met Rebecca and Wyatt that morning, she could spot them too. But she did not know who the other images were and continued up the stairs.

Mason stopped at a closed-door, opened it, and ushered her inside. "Where would you like me to put your suitcase?"

"On the bed is fine." She answered without looking at it, too busy gazing around her surroundings. This room alone was larger than the two

bedrooms in her house combined. "Are you sure this is a guest bedroom? It's large enough to house a family of four."

He set the suitcase down, turned to her, and shrugged. "It is the smallest bedroom."

She stared at him. The smallest? Holy shit.

"I will take my bag upstairs, then return. I would like to give you a tour if that is something you would like?"

Turning toward him, she nodded. "Yes. I would like that. I cannot believe how big this ranch is."

Mason chuckled. "There is more to it than only the buildings. The Fishers own over five thousand acres."

Her eyes widened, and she mouthed, five thousand?

"When we go camping tomorrow, you will see more of it." He wanted to wrap her in his arms but held himself back. If he touched her, there would be no tour of the ranch, and her suitcase would no longer be on that bed.

Once Mason left the room, Anastasia quickly unpacked the few items she brought with her. She hung the two sundresses in the closet, shorts and t-shirts went neatly into the dresser. Toothbrush, toothpaste, and the small amount of makeup she'd bothered with went on the counter next to the sink in the bathroom.

She could not believe she had her own bathroom. Good god, it was like being in a hotel room.

Five minutes after setting her belongings in order, there was a knock on the door. Opening it, she smiled up at Mason. He now had an unadorned baseball cap on his head, his hair pulled up under it, and dark sunglasses were hanging from the collar of the lightweight t-shirt.

"Disguising yourself again?" she questioned as she wondered why he felt the need to do so.

"Yes. Because I am going to show you around, we will be among tourists. It is better to take precautions. When I was a boy, I did not have to worry someone might recognize me but now," he shrugged, "My face is more recognizable than it had been then, in America."

"I can understand that. You've mentioned you and your family try to keep your visits here quiet. So yeah, it makes sense." She turned away from him, walked to the dresser, and picked up the beige-colored sun hat she'd brought along. Within moments, she had her own hair gathered up and tucked under it. Turning to him with a grin on her face, she told him, "I wouldn't want you to feel you were the only one who needed to be incognito. I'm a well-known hairdresser from the area. Maybe if I hide my face, no one will ask me for a haircut."

Her actions caused Mason to laugh. "Why would people do that when you are not at work?"

Chuckling, she told him, "You do not understand what hairdressers go through. No matter where I go, if a client sees me or someone finds out I do hair, I'm bombarded with questions about shampoos, conditioners, colors, hairstyles, and yes, someone almost always asks if I have my scissors with me and can I give them a trim. People do not seem to think hairdressers deserve a day off." She reached for his hand. "Come on. I can't wait to see the horses, and we can be secretive together."

Laughing, Mason took her hand in his and led her down the stairs and out the front door.

For over an hour, he weaved her through corrals and over well-worn paths while sharing stories of when he was younger and his family visited here. He entertained her with tales of some stunts he and Hunter pulled on the families, causing her to laugh at the absurdity of their antics.

She envisioned his younger version going about the daily chores expected of everyone who lived here. It gave her a better understanding of him, and now she could comprehend how someone as rich and famous as he was not afraid to get their hands dirty.

He'd learned from a young age to work hard to get a job done.

His upbringing had not been all glamor and pampering. That realization helped her see him as someone who knew what the actual world was like and gave her another view of who the man was.

While in the large barn, as Mason took her from stall to stall so she could experience the horses currently kept there, Anastasia missed a step while walking. He caught her before she would have fallen.

"Careful, funny lady. I would not wish to see you hurt." He stood in front of her, his hand coming up to touch her face as he removed his sunglasses and hooked them into the collar of his shirt.

Anastasia felt like a deer caught in headlights as she stared up at him. His eyes blazed, and she knew he was going to kiss her and her pulse quickened with anticipation.

His head slowly lowered toward hers.

"Hey, Lafayette!"

Mason cursed; his goal of feeling her lips on his sabotaged by his best friend's untimely intrusion made him mad.

"What do you want, Hunter?" he snapped over his shoulder.

Chuckling, Hunter told him, "Well, I came to tell you our mothers have the picnic ready on the back porch of the house, but the look on your face right now was worth my having to track you down."

Mason growled low in his throat.

Unintimidated, Hunter hooted out a laugh that caused a few of the surrounding horses to nicker.

Anastasia stepped from behind Mason, unsure if she felt relieved, embarrassed, or disappointed that Mason's lips had not found hers. She'd dreamed about kissing him but had not envisioned the first touch would take place in a barn where anyone would witness it.

The point in case. Hunter especially.

"Food sounds like a good idea. I'm getting a little famished," she said, heading out the barn door by herself. Needing a moment to bring her racing heart back to its normal rhythm.

Behind her she heard Mason say, "I hate you, Hunter."

Hunter's laughter followed her as she walked past corrals, and a few people doing chores as she headed towards the house, hoping she was no longer blushing. But as she walked, she remembered Rebecca's earlier comment about Mason being a flirt. She had to consider that perhaps the kiss would have meant nothing to him except to reach some goal he had.

* * *

Later in the evening, when the fireworks began, Anastasia sat next to Mason, enjoying the show. It was a spectacular hour and a half long aerial display of bursting balls of stars lighting up the night. The tourist's staying in the twelve guest cabins on the F&L Ranch gasped, clapped, and oohed as the artillery shook the ground and gunpowder exploded into brilliant colors overhead.

Next to Mason on a collapsible camping chair, Anastasia sat drinking the beer he retrieved for her from the cooler the Fishers brought for their private use. Between the gaps of the blossoming blooms, which sent out colorful showers of lights, he entertained her with stories from when he was a boy, and he and Hunter lighted the fuses to send the rockets into the air. Now the job of entertaining the small crowd belonged to Wyatt. However, Hunter joined his sibling in the merrymaking this night, for old times' sake.

Okay. Hunter did it because he liked to make things go boom, and it kept him from having Daniela smiling at him as though she were hiding something, and it bugged the shit out of him not knowing what was up the twirps sleeve if you want the truth.

When the display ended, tourists wandered back to the cabins they rented for the night, near the bottom of the slope from where the Fisher's mansion overlooked the land that made up the F&L.

Mason escorted Anastasia up the grand staircase to the room they assigned her. When he opened the bedroom door, she glanced at the bed and thought it looked more inviting now than it had the first time she saw it. As exhausted as she was, she knew she would be asleep the moment her head hit the pillow.

But he stood at the threshold, waiting, she knew, for an invitation to join her there.

Knowing she was still questioning his motives in bringing her here to this ranch, she was not ready to give in to the desire she saw in his eyes and the want her body cried out for. Her heart was afraid of the hurt it would endure once he left North Dakota. If she slept with him, it would create an emotional bond. Her heart only recently healed from Danny having shattered it. She did not want it fragmented again.

How were other women able to have sexual relationships with countless others and not have their hearts involved? That was a question she would not mind knowing the answer to.

She licked her lips and had no clue how hard it was for him not to groan as he watched her small tongue flick across it.

"Mason?"

He grinned expectantly. "Yes?"

She took a deep breath, deciding to voice the question on her mind before she lost her nerve. "At the risk of making you mad, I'm going to ask this, anyway." She looked up at him, almost in defiance. "Is the reason you seem interested in me is that I'm a conquest?"

He blinked. "Conquest?"

"Look, I'm not an idiot. I know you want to come into this room. You've been sending off testosterone since the moment we met." This

was difficult for her, but she had to say it. If he was pursuing her only because she was possibly the only woman to keep him at bay, it was better to know now. And if so, he, or someone else, could take her back to New Salem in the morning. She never had, nor ever would, jump into bed with someone she had only known less than a week. And she did not care if that person was the man who dominated her fantasies for the past year.

Mason's eyes searched her face. Placing a hand on the doorframe next to her face, he told her softly, "I will not deny I want you, Anastasia." He used his other hand to play with a few strands of her hair. "You are a beautiful woman, and sex is a wonderful thing. But it is not why I asked you to join me here."

Her chin came up a notch. "Then, why did you?"

Good question. One he was not sure he knew the answer to. But instead of telling her that, he stepped back, ran a hand through his own hair. It frustrated him, these emotions she stirred within him. Not knowing what it was about her that drew him in was driving him crazy. The fact she would question his motives caused him a little anger, and he said, "Why would you ruin a perfectly good evening by asking me that question?"

She looked away, ashamed of doing exactly what he said. It had been a wonderful night, and tomorrow they were all supposed to be going on that camping trip.

"Can I explain to you why I asked you to come here with me? Why I so willingly tell you stories of my boyhood?" He shook his head. "I cannot. I do not understand it myself. I find you interesting, but you are not a conquest. You are a puzzle. If it makes you uncomfortable that I do not hide my desire for you, I apologize. I will try to keep my nature to myself." He turned away and said over his shoulder, "Have a good night, Anastasia. I will see you in the morning at breakfast."

She watched him walk away and felt terrible for having insulted him and causing his anger.

And he was angry. It showed in the way he held his broad shoulders rigid, and his walk was soldier straight.

It was not until after he disappeared from sight, going up the second set of stairs to the third level where the room he used as a boy waited for him, she turned to walk into the room. But before she could take a step past the door, she heard Rosalinda Lafayette's voice from behind her say, "I enjoyed that."

Anastasia's face was as red as a beet, afraid the woman heard the confrontation. Slowly turning back around to face Mason's mother, she discovered the woman had a smile on her face and humor in her eyes.

"Excuse me?" Anastasia said, trying to pretend nothing just transpired between Mason and herself.

Rosalinda's smile showed off her perfectly white teeth. "I enjoyed hearing a woman tell Mason no for a change. And questioning his motives. It is refreshing."

Anastasia grimaced. "I shouldn't have said anything to him. At least, not out here where I was obviously overheard."

Rosalinda shrugged. "You said nothing wrong."

"Yeah? Well, I have the feeling I probably shouldn't have bothered unpacking. I'm sure I did not endear myself to him, and he'll take me back to New Salem tomorrow."

"Oh, I doubt that. You may have wounded him by telling him, no, but that will not change the fact he enjoys your company. And, my dear woman, if it were only sex he wanted, he would have you in that bed right now, and naked. My son knows how to seduce a woman. Reluctant or not."

Anastasia's blush deepened. She could not believe she was listening to Mason's mother talk about her son having sex so casually.

"Keep your bags unpacked, dear. You will be here until at least Sunday afternoon when our time at the ranch is over, and most of us will go back to the lake."

Rosalinda said no more and left Anastasia watching her walk down the staircase and pondering the woman's words.

Chapter Twenty

Unfortunately, the two-day camping trip was canceled the next morning. A rainstorm moved into the area during the early part of the morning and did not appear as though it would let up soon.

Anastasia was disappointed but understood why there would be no horse backing into the Badlands this day. Hopefully, there would be sunshine tomorrow, although the camping trip would no longer be an option because of scheduling issues.

Almost no one ventured outside because of the downpour. Occasionally, Colten, Hunter, Wyatt, and the Fisher's son-in-law, Jake, would take turns making trips to the bunkhouse, tourist cabins, outer buildings, and small eatery that provided meals for employees and tourists, checking on everyone to ensure they were okay and no roof sprung a leak. Other than those outings, everyone stayed inside.

Occupants of the house kept themselves entertained in various ways. A few sat down for a Monopoly game; others began a game of Clue or played Canasta. Downstairs, in the basement, was a pool table, and that too became a source of distraction from the weather.

Mason was attentive, but no longer had that hungry look in his eye when he looked at Anastasia. She was not sure if she was disappointed or relieved. However, he seemed to have formed a habit of accidentally brushing up against her now and again. During the games of pool they played, he would lean in as she held the cue stick, angling for a shot, correcting the way her fingers guided the stick before backing away without lingering. Or he would brush shoulders with her as he moved around the table as though he had not noticed the contact.

He was driving her lustfully mad with those unexpected caresses, making it harder and harder to resist the temptation he was.

She chastised herself countless times throughout the day. She either wanted him, or she didn't. If she could just decide, sleep with him or give him an absolute no would at least settle things between them.

In Anastasia's opinion, being shut in with the Fishers, Lafayettes, and Bensons turned out to be fun. It allowed her to observe each of them.

Mason's father, Charles, was a soft-spoken man who did not have his son's height and was as bald as the pool balls being played. It was easy to see how much he loved his wife in the way he would touch her now and then while doing some activity or other.

Anastasia wondered from whose side of the family Mason inherited his height and those god-like looks from. She could not find any resemblance to Charles at all. Other than hair coloring, skin coloring, and the green eyes, she did not discern any of Rosalinda's features in the man who caused hearts to flutter throughout the United States.

Daniela would be the beauty her mother was. It was easy enough to see if a person looked for it. As she aged, her features would become defined. Perhaps she would turn into a woman more beautiful than Rosalinda. However, that was hard to imagine since Rosalinda still, at fifty-three, was competition for some of the younger actresses climbing their way to fame.

Jacqueline and Colten fit well together. Jacqueline was also an attractive woman. Colten, a handsome man, although Anastasia wondered what happened to have caused him to have to permanently wear an eye patch.

Occasionally Hunter would enter the room where she, along with Mason, Cadman Benson, and his wife Kasey, played pool and made small talk with them. Enough conversation for Anastasia to comprehend Cadman was Hunter's boss, but of what she had not a clue. However, whenever Daniela entered the space, Hunter would leave almost immediately.

Which honestly amused Anastasia. It was easy to see Daniela had a crush on Hunter. The teenager was much too young to have eyes for anyone except for someone her own age. But it was enjoyable to watch Hunter avoiding her. The man was the only one to have won a fight against Danny. Yet, he seemed skittish around an adolescent's infatuation with him.

Priceless.

Colten and Jacqueline's oldest daughter and her husband also lived in this big house, along with their two children. The oldest one, Randy, was adopted and seventeen years old. He had cerebral palsy, which limited his ability to move and maintain balance without using leg braces and a hand-held mobility device. However, those facts did not damper the young man's spirits. He seemed to have a wonderful sense of humor and joined right in with the board games being played in various places in the house.

At first, Anastasia wondered why Jake and his wife Donna did not live in a separate home, away from Colten and Jacqueline, until she understood this house might become theirs one day and it was a large enough space for them to share it without crowding each other. Donna and Jake seemed the likely choice to continue one day running this horse ranch and tourist business into the coming future.

With her mind wandering, thinking of each person she met so far, Anastasia accidentally hit the Cue Ball too hard, sailing it over the edge of the table. Her face immediately flushed red, and she prayed she had broken nothing by launching the billiard ball across the room.

Mason's laughter caused her face to go another shade darker. "Interesting shot, Anastasia," he told her as he retrieved the solid mass from under a side table. "Usually, it is custom to keep it on the table."

Anastasia covered her mouth with her hand, and her eyes were wide as she gasped, "Did I break anything?!"

Kasey walked around the table, patted her shoulder. "It didn't hit anything except for the carpet. You can breathe now."

Anastasia wanted to faint.

"It has happened before," Mason tried to reassure her. "The Fisher's keep nothing of value here, in the basement. Had something broken, it would not have been expensive to replace."

Anastasia glanced across to the far side of the room, where there was a wall full of mirrors. She knew the amount she shelled out for the three wall mirrors hanging above the styling stations in her salon and could only imagine what those floor-to-ceiling sections of glass would have cost. From the setup at that end of the room, it appeared as though someone in the family might have taken ballet at one time.

Cadman racked the balls for the next game. "Your break, Mason."

The supermodel moved in for the break. Used his hand to tuck the right side of his hair behind his ear, then lined up for the shot.

And sunk the 8-Ball.

Anastasia, her earlier embarrassment forgotten, grinned. "Well, at least I didn't cause us to lose the game," she teased.

Both Cadman and Kasey laughed over that remark.

Mason accepted her observation in stride, requested a rerack, and continued with the game.

Later, as the sun set, and after they consumed the evening meal, Mason escorted Anastasia out to the wrap-around porch, where they sat down together on the swing.

"Your friends and family are wonderful," she told him, as they watched the continuing rain, although it was now a slow drizzle.

"I am sorry the weather did not cooperate. I know you were looking forward to riding a horse."

She shrugged. "Well, if this rain stops before Sunday, perhaps I will still have the chance. It's no big deal. I've had fun playing a variety of games and getting to know everyone."

"Do you have family? Brothers? Sisters?" He remembered she told him about losing her parents. Had there been someone to support her during that tragic time?

"No." She shook her head. "I'm an only child." This conversation was as gloomy as the weather, but because he seemed to want to know her better, she forged ahead with a short life story. "After my parents died, I lived with one of my aunt and uncles for a year until I turned eighteen. Thankfully, they live in Bismarck, so it was easy for me to get a job and put myself through cosmetology school." She shrugged. "One of my goals in life was to be a hairdresser. My parent's death left me a small inheritance along with the house I live in. The money helped finance the salon when I decided to open one."

Mason reached for her hand and caressed the knuckles as he said, "You are a strong woman." He wanted to ask about her marriage to Danny. He wanted to know what the man did to this beautiful woman. Perhaps whatever horror she suffered was cause for her reluctance to join him in bed, and it saddened him that something beautiful could be turned into a nightmare.

His parents never talked about their own sexual relationship. Which, honestly, he did not want to think about. What child wanted to have that image in their mind? But he could not help wondering how long it was before his mother allowed Charles into her bed after that horrible night when he was conceived.

Anastasia smiled up at him. "I don't know if I'm a strong person. I just learned to put one foot in front of the other and move forward in life."

Mason gently trailed the finger of one hand down her cheek. "It makes you someone to be admired."

Anastasia felt a shiver pass through her, and as he continued kneading and stroking her hand, she felt warmth form in the pit of her stomach.

Oh, yes. Mason was definitely an expert at seduction. She could admit that. He might not have sent her sensual looks throughout the day, but what he did with those innocent touches slowly heated her body.

Perhaps he had known all along he was breaking down her defenses, and it was on the tip of her tongue to tell him to follow her to her room.

In fact, she opened her mouth to tell him exactly that when Hunter walked onto the porch and announced, "Hey, you two want to make a run over to the mess hall with me? I think a visit with Juan would be a great idea." He glanced into the house, caught sight of Daniela walking through the living room, and said, "And I need a fucking drink."

Anastasia burst out laughing. Hunter avoiding a sixteen-year-old truly was funny to her. And his entrance threw cold water on the lust Mason kindled within her.

When she noticed the two of them looking at her, probably wondering what she found amusing, she waved a dismissive hand and told them, "Never mind. It was only something I thought was funny. But yeah, I'm up for something to drink."

Blissfully ignorant of how close he had been to his goal of getting Anastasia naked in bed, Mason stood up and told his best friend, "Sure. Why not?"

The three of them made a mad dash through the drizzle in the direction of the mess hall, staying on the walking path so they would not get their shoes muddy.

They burst through the door to the eatery, dripping wet and laughing like school children.

There were only a handful of people occupying the place. They, after glancing toward the newcomers, ignored them.

Hunter led the way to the service counter, where a man in his forties stood drying glasses while a couple of his helpers worked behind him in the kitchen, cleaning the area and getting ready to close the place down.

"You know we're about to close," the man behind the counter grumbled at the three of them in a voice that revealed he was not happy to see the late arrivals.

"Juan, why are you so grumpy?" Mason asked.

"You've had all day to come see me, Mason. Now that it's closing time, you decide to show up."

"I have been occupied."

Juan's eyes drifted toward Anastasia. "I should have known. Some things never change."

Anastasia got the impression this man assumed Mason, and she spent the entire day in bed, and it caused her to blush.

Hunter moved around the counter, heading toward one cooler. "I'm here for a beer, Juan. And we'll lock the place up for you."

One of Juan's brows lifted skyward. "You drink everything up at the main house?"

"Nope." Hunter opened the cooler, took out a six-pack of bottles, and brought them back to the counter. "Just thought I'd like to look at your ugly face for a while instead of-," he glanced at Mason; decided not to mention the person who was a thorn in his side. "Never mind."

"Would there be something else I could have?" Anastasia asked. "I'm really not a beer drinker."

Ever since Danny began drinking, she shied away from alcohol though did not mind having it occasionally. Some people could handle the beverage and have a good time. Others became addicted to it, and it ruined lives.

This time Mason walked around the counter, opened the cooler.

"Just make yourself at home, why don't 'cha?" Juan griped.

Bringing a beverage back with him, Mason uncapped it as he grinned at Juan. "I always did."

Juan shook his head. "Now that's the truth."

Handing the bottle to Anastasia, Mason told her, "You will like this."

Anastasia took a sip of the beverage labeled Pschitt. It was orange flavored and reminded her of a soda, though she never heard of the drink. "What is this?" she asked.

"It is a French soda."

Juan spoke up. "We started stocking those the year Mason lived here. The boy was not a fan of American pop."

"Soda," Mason corrected.

"Pop," Hunter said.

Sensing an argument about to unfold, Anastasia said, "Let's just call it a soda pop and move on." She thought it was silly for grown men to debate what to call a soft drink.

Taking a drink from his own beer, Mason asked, "How is your family, Juan?"

The question seemed to take away the man's upset at having late visitors. His eyes brightened, and he smiled as he answered. "My oldest girl got married last year, moved to Bismarck with her husband." Juan glanced between the couple sitting across from him and thought they looked good together. "The youngest will head to college next spring. She's going to be at the University of North Dakota in Grand Forks, studying nursing. Her main goal is to find herself a Hockey player heading for the big leagues." He laughed.

Now he glanced at Anastasia. "Where are your manners, Mason? You have not introduced me to this beautiful woman. Did you go off and get yourself-?"

"No!" Mason exclaimed, cutting off the man's statement. "She is a friend."

Hunter coughed as though he'd swallowed wrong.

Juan raised a brow. "Really?" Then slower, "A friend?" He shook his head. Apparently, the boy was in denial. He'd never brought anyone here before, and if Hunter's false cough was something to be gauged, he did not believe it either.

With a shrug, Juan extended his hand toward Anastasia for a shake. "Nice to meet you…?"

"Anastasia. Anastasia Sharp."

"Pretty name for a pretty woman." Juan smiled. "Welcome to the F&L. Are you staying long?"

"Only until Sunday."

"Well, I hope this boy treats you good. The stories I could tell you about these two could curl your hair."

"I do my own curling, thank you." Anastasia grinned.

Juan blinked.

Mason chuckled.

Hunter rolled his eyes. "That was so corny."

Juan looked confused.

"I'm a hairdresser," Anastasia explained.

It took Juan a moment to understand the joke, but his laugh rolled out when he did. "I like her!" He exclaimed with gusto. "Mason, your… friend is a delight."

Mason looked at Anastasia over the top of the bottle as he took a long pull of beer. He liked her too, but he still could not understand why he was attracted to her more than any woman he'd known in the past.

Chapter Twenty-one

The rain stopped in the middle of the night. When morning came, the sun broke through the gray clouds and forced them to pull back to allow its heat to dry the ground. It was still too wet for horseback riding; however, once the sun worked its magic, there would be a possibility for that activity later in the day. In the meantime, almost everyone decided they wanted to drive to Medora and spend the day showing Anastasia the sites.

Before leaving the ranch, Anastasia asked Mason, "So, I'm curious. Why does it appear you, your mom, and Jacqueline adore that little town we're heading to so much? It's just a town, left over from the old days."

Standing on the porch with her, Mason reached out, took a few strands of her hair between his fingers for a moment before answering. He could not seem to stop himself from always wanting to touch her. Maybe it was because he was becoming more and more sexually deprived by the minute. Being this close to a woman who joined him in his dreams, but not his bed, was driving him insane.

"Do you know any of its history?" he asked, allowing the strands of hair to fall from his fingers.

"Only what I learned in school. I know Teddy Roosevelt, the twenty-sixth President of the United States, lived there for a time. And some guy from France, who people called the Marquis de Morès, founded the town and named it after his wife. That is about all I know of the place."

The corner of Mason's lips twitched as though trying not to laugh. The way she dismissed de Morès was humorous to him. "I want to show you something," he told her and led her into the house. He maneuvered her to the bottom of the grand staircase, stopping in front of the wall of family photos the Fishers displayed.

Pointing to an old photograph, perhaps taken in the 1800s, Mason told her, "This is my third great uncle and his wife, Medora."

Staring at the photo, Anastasia said, "Wow. Medora must have been a common name way back then. I wonder if she knew there was a town that shared the name."

Mason managed not to laugh. "She knew. She is the one de Morès named it for."

Slowly, Anastasia turned toward him. Stared. "Excuse me?"

"Antoine-Amédée-Marie-Vincent Manca Amat de Vallombrosa, Marquis de Morès," he gave a slight bow. "My third great uncle." He pointed to the woman next to him. "Medora, Hunter's third great aunt."

Okay. There'd been a rabbit hole she'd stepped in somewhere between the porch and here. "You're telling me the guy who founded that historic town north of here is in your family tree?"

"A direct line, yes." He smiled. "His father, Riccardo Giovanni Maria Stefano Manca-Amat, was the second Duke of Vallombrosa and 4th Duke of Asinara. And my great, great, great grandfather."

She gasped. "You're royalty?!" Holy smokes! She almost felt like a peasant.

Mason shook his head. "From royal blood, yes, but there is no throne waiting for me to sit upon. Besides, there would be a long line of people before me before that would happen, even if it were a possibility."

"I still wish you hadn't told me that," she whispered, trying not to feel inadequate.

"Anastasia, I shared this with you because I trust you and-" He wanted to tell her she tied him up in knots. "And because I wanted you to understand why the town of Medora means so much to me. I cannot claim it to the media, and I believe you know why."

To keep it sacred and a sanctuary.

"Whether a person is rich or poor means nothing to me, nor my family, Stasia."

Anastasia thought about that for a moment, trying to read between the lines. She was not ashamed of where she'd come from. Her great grand-parents had been part of the Germans from Russia immigration in the early 1900s. They had been hard workers, determined to make a new life for themselves. They established a homestead north of New Salem, in a town called Bluegrass that no longer existed and no one would find listed on modern maps. They tilled the land and did the best they could. They might not have been rich, but they, too, were an important part of history.

Squaring her shoulders and holding her head high, she told him, "Well, I'm royalty, too. I come from a long line of farmers, and if it wasn't for us, you rich people would have starved to death."

Mason laughed, took her hand in his. "Lady Harvest," he bowed, kissed the air above her knuckles. "Would you accompany me to the town of Medora this afternoon?"

Delighted with his humor, she giggled. "Certainly, knave. I'll just grab my disguise, and we'll be off just as soon as everyone else is ready."

Mason watched her rush up the stairs, more deeply infatuated with her than before. She understood he would be incognito and seemed not to care if people knew who she was with.

It touched him in ways he could not explain.

When he saw his parents, he smiled. His mother had done nothing much to hide who she was. Usually, people did not recognize her in the United States, and especially here. But she took small precautions, such as the black western cowboy hat she now wore, with its embroidered band of dark red roses. Her middle of the back length hair was pulled to the side, held in place by a band, to hide the twenty-six-year-old scar on the left side of her face.

She wore a long slitted skirt made from the lightest cloth to cover her legs and the airy long-sleeved shirt to cover her arms.

Charles was not as recognizable as his wife, but he opted to wear a western hat today to cover his bald head and prevent sunburn. The sun was heating the air and drying out things quickly.

"Everyone is ready for the drive to Medora," Charles told Mason. "Is your young lady looking forward to the trip?"

Mason glanced up the staircase. He saw Anastasia coming down the steps in the hat she'd worn the other day, and once again, her hair was pulled up under it. He couldn't say what she was feeling about this adventure into the historic town. But watching her descending the stairs, with that broad smile on her face, he knew his heart was in more trouble than he'd thought.

* * *

"I won't do it!" Hunter exclaimed, backing away from his mother.

Currently, the small group of Fishers, along with the Lafayette's and the Benson's, stood on a sidewalk in Medora's historic town. They were stopped before a photo studio offering tourists the chance to dress up in old-time clothing and have a photo taken that would resemble an antique.

"I refuse!"

Jacqueline was fuming. "Hunter, you will join us in that photo, or I will kick you all the way back to Washington!" She wondered, and not for the first time, why the universe cursed her with a child as strong-willed and hot-tempered as this one. "Mason isn't throwing a fit about it. The least you could do, after being gone all the time, is to shut your mouth and make your mother happy without complaining about it first!"

"I could order him to do it," Cadman claimed.

"Oh, no! When you're here, you are not my boss, just my uncle, so you shut your pie hole." Hunter snapped.

196

Pointing a finger toward the place where Mason and Anastasia stood together, Hunter exclaimed. "Besides, Mason enjoys having photos of his ugly face taken. I do not, and I will not do it!" He made to move past her.

Colten grabbed his son's arm. "You will do it, son." His tone left no doubt he meant it, although exactly how he could force Hunter to do it was another matter entirely.

Mason was chuckling. "Come on, Hunter. It is not so bad. I have had millions of pictures taken, and I have come out unharmed."

"Bully for you," Hunter said dryly.

Anastasia joined in on the try to convince Hunter to have his photo taken ploy. "It will be fun!" she laughed. "I'm willing. After the family group shot, Mason and I are going to have one taken together."

"And who the hell cares?" Hunter snapped, shaking his father's hold with ease.

Anastasia's jaw dropped.

Jerk.

"Hunter," Jacqueline vowed angrily, "If you do not march your ass in there and join us," she pointed toward the photo studio, "I'll gladly tell Anastasia why your middle name is Sundance."

Hunter shook his head and rolled his eyes. "Like I care." He looked at Anastasia and said, "My parents had sex in Sundance, Wyoming, and mom got pregnant with me. There you have it."

Jacqueline punched his arm.

Wyatt snickered at his brother. "Then, maybe we should tell her about that little phobia you have, brother mine. Including why you have such a dislike for -"

Hunter's eyes widened, and he exploded, "You would not dare! Not unless you want to meet that God of yours. Today. This very minute!"

Wyatt backed up but grinned as he began singing, "The itssy bittsy-"

Hunter damn near wrapped his hands around his brother's throat before he reminded himself it was his sibling he was seriously contemplating murdering. "And you claim to have compassion, Wyatt!" he blasted, eyes becoming so dark they turned black, complimenting his mood nicely.

He turned his glare on Mason, "And you can shut the fuck up!"

Mason's attempt to cut off his laugh sounded too awful by far.

"What phobia?" Daniela asked sweetly, dearly wanting to discover Hunter's Achilles Heel.

The innocent smile she sent Hunter had him grinding his teeth.

Wyatt met his brother's lethal glare with laughter. "Well? Shall I answer her question, or will you join in on our photo?"

Hunter's jaw clenched. "All right! I'll do it!" He turned on his heel, mounted the steps, and disappeared into the building.

"I do hope there isn't anyone inside having their photo taken right now," Cadman sighed.

Jacqueline's eyes widened with horror. "Oh, no! I never thought of-" Her claim was cut short when a young couple all but flew out the door in their haste to flee the building. The look on their faces resembled that of persons having just faced the bowels of hell.

The Fisher family groaned pitifully, and Cadman winced. He was damn proud of Hunter's abilities in the field for tracking down and apprehending terrorists. But the more he put Hunter into situations that required him to go undercover, the boy seemed to forget his manners when among the general public.

Wyatt sighed. "We could either claim not to know him or tell everyone a demon entered him just now, and that he had no control over his actions."

"Are you people coming?!" Hunter's voice growled from the doorway.

No one wasted a moment's pause. They herded into the small building before Hunter came to his senses and realized they duped him into complying with their wishes.

It would not be a good time in the old town tonight once he remembered that not one of them would ever reveal that secret.

It was too unbelievable, anyway.

Later, once the photos were taken, and Hunter disappeared to only the universe knew where, a crowd began gathering outside the photo studio while Anastasia and Rebecca waited together inside for the photo's to be developed. Everyone else had gone outside to allow breathing room for others to enter the building.

"What's happening?" Anastasia asked as she glanced out one of the shop's windows.

"Well," Rebecca drawled, "I think someone recognized Mason when he took off his disguise for the photo the two of you had taken."

"No!" Anastasia gasped, appalled with the knowledge he'd lost his privacy because they'd taken part in something so innocent as a tourist photo. If she had realized the possibility, she would have refused his offer to pose with her.

Rebecca shrugged. "It isn't the first time it happened. He might take precautions, but it doesn't always work."

"But now this place will be known as somewhere he goes!"

Rebecca patted her hand. "Anastasia, no one is going to think twice about a celebrity visiting here. Medora has seen its share of famous visitors. In fact, during the summer of nineteen-sixty-five, David Soul, before he became a household name when he starred in Starsky and Hutch, sang and danced on the stage of the musical we're attending tonight."

Anastasia stared. "Get out of town. Really?" Why hadn't she known that?

Wyatt's twin nodded. "And Lawrence Welk, our famous band leader from Strasburg, often attended the musical. That's where he discovered Tom Netherton and then began having him on his show regularly."

"Oh my god," Anastasia sniggered. "Netherton was the only thing that made having to watch the Lawrence Welk show bearable when my parents turned it on every Sunday."

"So, the fact people discovered Mason Lafayette is here today isn't that big of a deal. The media might print something about it, but they will not make it front-page news."

"But he told me his family keeps it a secret."

"They do. They don't announce it to the world they come here every year. And most of the time they stay at the ranch, away from the public. But occasionally, someone recognizes them and stand in a line for an autograph. That's as far as it goes. If the paparazzi knew they frequented here, they'd set up their annoying cameras, so that's one reason the Lafayettes keep silent about this place." She lowered her voice, "And they have never disclosed their relationship to de Morès. That truth is what they hold sacred and do not talk about."

Anastasia frowned as she thought that over. She could understand why the Lafayettes would want to keep that knowledge to themselves. If word got out, the North Dakota tourism department would probably want to advertise it to draw more visitors to the area.

Rebecca glanced out the window at the sizable crowd. "It's going to be a while before Mason can get away from those admirers. The fourth of July weekend always causes this town to bust at its seams. Not that it's all that big to begin with, but you know what I mean. You'll have plenty of time to browse."

Anastasia glanced around the small space, having already seen everything this store offered.

Not sure what to do with herself while strangers occupied Mason, she stepped outside. Skirting around the gathered crowd waiting for their turn to talk with him, she found a place across the street to observe the session. She watched the way Mason interacted with these strangers. He greeted each person as though they were important to him, and not once did he appear upset by the fact they disrupted his life.

She could see some parents gathering their children around him for a photo, while others pressed paper and pen into his hand. When an older woman moved in to wrap her arms around him and kiss his cheek, he played it up for her friends, whose cameras were ready to capture the fun.

A few people gathered were handicapped in some way or another; some in wheelchairs, others mentally challenged. It was when Mason spoke with these people when Anastasia's love for him grew. The people would tell him how thrilled they were to meet him, but he would turn it around until he had them convinced, they were the ones to bring happiness to his life.

Anastasia glanced around, noticing none of the people she came here with were anywhere in sight.

Now what? She wasn't sure how long it would be before Mason was free, and she was not looking forward to standing here indefinitely.

She was about to wander over to St. Mary's Catholic Church, which she understood was paid for and built under instructions from the Marquise de Morès in eighteen eighty-four and still served the community of Medora when she felt someone tap her on the shoulder. Turning, she was more than startled to find Hunter standing there.

"We," Hunter motioned behind him toward where Wyatt, Rebecca, and Daniela stood on the sidewalk, "are going back to the ranch to go horseback riding. It's going to be a while before Mason can get away from his fans. Trust me on this. I've been through this before. So," He shoved his hands into the pockets of his jeans. "We were wondering if you would be interested in tagging along with us."

Anastasia glanced back to where Mason continued to talk to people, wondering what she should do. She wanted to stay with Mason, but it did not appear as though he would miss her. Still, she questioned, "Won't he be mad?"

"Mason?" Hunter wrinkled his nose. "I doubt he expects you to just stand here for an hour, at least, before he's free. I'll leave a message with my mom. She can tell him where you are."

Anastasia gnawed her lower lip as she thought about Hunter's offer. She almost thought about asking Mason if it would be alright for her to accompany this group. However, she'd always had to ask Danny during those last months of her marriage if she could do something, including taking a shower, and she'd vowed she'd never put up with that controlling type of personality again.

Squaring her shoulders, she told Hunter. "I'm down for that. It sounds like fun."

* * *

Five horses slowly picked their way down a narrow incline.

Wyatt Fisher was in the lead, followed closely by Mason's sister, then Rebecca. Next in line was Anastasia, with Hunter's mount bringing up the rear of the small party.

Anastasia was glad she tagged along. Roaming through the Badlands on horseback was indeed a breathtaking experience. One she would not soon forget.

Currently, no one was talking—each person lost in their own thoughts, captivated by the scenic view.

Hunter said she would have more fun riding a horse than waiting for Mason to find the right chance to leave his group of admirers, and although Anastasia admitted she was having fun, she still wished Mason was with her.

They were probably a half-hour into the ride when Wyatt's voice snapped Anastasia out of her thoughts. "Hey, Daniela! I'll race you over to that bluff!"

Daniela grinned wickedly. "Eat my dust, Wyatt!" Her mount leaped forward like a rocket.

Rebecca and Wyatt sat frozen in their saddles, watching the girl riding like a bat out of hell away from them.

Wyatt, the first one to unthaw, exclaimed, "She's gonna kill herself!" Just before he and Rebecca kicked their own mounts into action, following after Mason's sister.

"We can only hope," Hunter said wistfully.

Anastasia's head snapped around to stare at him. "You are joking, aren't you?"

Hunter shrugged in answer to her question, then eased his horse around hers until they were riding abreast. "How are you enjoying your first horse ride?"

"It has its ups and downs," she said, trying not to bounce in the saddle as the horses began a quicker pace, wanting to follow the other horses.

Hunter's deep laugh disturbed a Blue Jay, and it took to flight. "Have to admit, Mason's pet name for you hits the bull's eye." He slowed his horse back to a slow walk so the horse she was on would follow its lead, and she would no longer bounce in the saddle.

"Pet name?" she asked and felt giddy.

"Yeah. He calls you funny lady, and it suits you." He reached over and took the reins from her hand, stopping both their mounts simultaneously. "Let's take a break. Since you're not used to being on a horse, no harm in getting off and walking for a while."

Hunter dismounted and dropped her horse's reins to the ground; knowing it would go nowhere if the rider did not have control over it.

Turning to his own mount, he checked the cinch. Once satisfied he had it adjusted to a proper tension, he let the stirrup drop back down. Turning back toward Anastasia, he said, "I've got something to say. Don't care if it makes you mad."

"Well, that comes as a surprise," her sarcasm was thick. This was Hunter, after all. The man was the definition of the word dick. How he could be Mason's best friend was beyond comprehension.

Hunter laughed again. "Yep. Funny Lady." He reached for the reins of her horse, picked them up. Before handing them back to her, he said, "I haven't seen him this happy in a long time. So, I'm hoping you're for real."

Her brows furrowed. "I'm not sure what you mean."

He looked up at her for a long moment. "Are you going to dismount, or did you want me to get a kink in my neck?"

Anastasia hoped he would get a sore neck. "I'll stay where I am, thank you."

"Suit yourself."

"So, back to your question, observation, or accusation. Whatever you meant by that ridiculous statement." Anastasia laughed. "I haven't a clue what you mean. Good god, Hunter. I only met the man on Sunday. I am not a devious person. Besides, if I were, you'd probably snap my neck."

That statement brought forth another chuckle from him. "Yep. Funny lady."

"Is there a point to all of this, Hunter?" She was not sure where her bravery was coming from, but she would not have this man accuse her of whatever he was accusing her of.

"I guess, in my way, I want to tell you I hope the two of you will build on this friendship you've got going. I want to die knowing my best friend is, at last, happy again."

Anastasia gasped. "Die? What the hell, Hunter? Are you sick or something?"

He blinked, then went into another fit of laughter. "No. I'm healthy as can be. But I am making a lot of enemies in the line of work I do, and it's probably only a matter of time before one of them puts me six feet under."

She shook her head. "I do not understand what you are talking about. What type of job do you have, exactly?"

"That's hard to explain. Cadman is the head of an organization called Task Force Ghost. He works strictly for the President of the United States. They utilize his team when normal means of apprehending the bad guy can't be used, and I'm one of Cadman's top agents."

"You're a spy?" her eyes rounded like saucers.

"No." He shook his head. "I told you it was hard to explain. The bottom line is, I track down terrorists and drug lords and end them."

Anastasia shivered, knowing this man was a killer.

"It doesn't matter," he told her. "Listen, I wanted to say, when the time comes, I'll have died happy. Knowing Mason has you."

"Seriously, Hunter. We are not a couple."

Hunter shrugged. "Maybe not today." He handed her back the reins, then vaulted onto his own horse with incredible ease. "But I know you already mean a hell of a lot to him. He hasn't looked at a woman since he met you and trust me. When I witness him not glancing at an attractive woman walking by in a bikini, I know he's a goner."

His words touched her, and she wondered if it could be true that Mason Lafayette had feelings for her.

"You're a good person, Hunter." She wiped at a tear that suddenly formed as she realized this man wasn't the ogre she thought he was.

His face changed to a scowl. "You ever tell another living soul that bit of poppycock, and I'll make you eat those words!" he threatened. "Come on. Let's catch up with the others and-"

He did not have the chance to finish his suggestion. A high-pitched scream shattered the otherwise still day. "Stay here!" he ordered, more out of habit than anything else. He kicked his mount into action, heading toward the bluff where his siblings and Daniela raced toward earlier.

Anastasia watched Hunter's horse eat up the distance. She considered following, but when she glanced behind her, she dismissed the notion. A horse and rider were coming her way as though the devil himself were chasing them. The sight mesmerized her. With his past the shoulder-length black hair flying wildly out behind him, the scene almost reminded her of an Indian warrior racing across the barren plain. And even before she could make out the face, Anastasia knew who it was, and her heart leaped with joy.

Slowly, without taking her eyes off the man whose mere photo could cause her heartbeat to quicken and spark desire, she dismounted. Within seconds he was there, leaping off his own mount and pulling her into his embrace.

The kiss was more than electric.

Chapter Twenty-two

When Jacqueline informed Mason Anastasia had left with Hunter, he'd become angry, believing his best friend was trying to move in on the funny lady.

Jealousy over a woman was a new emotion to him. He'd never been possessive of one. Had never felt emotionally attached to one. It wasn't jealousy that caused him to throw Carol Gibson out of the hotel room. It was the principle that she'd broken their agreement.

The thought that perhaps Anastasia lied to him when she'd said she was not interested in Hunter had him seeing red.

But then, Hunter's mother explained the two of them were not alone. That Wyatt, Rebecca, and Daniela would be with them. It helped calm him down enough that his blood no longer boiled as he walked to the vehicle he had driven here. Although it simmered as he drove back to the ranch. By the time he arrived, Mason calmed down enough to console himself with the fact they had not ridden off to be by themselves.

Then, knowing Hunter's explosive temper, Mason was afraid he would do something to cause Anastasia stress.

Mason was definitely in a whirlwind of conflicting emotions.

Upon arriving at the F&L, it surprised Mason to find a horse already saddled and waiting for him. Because his mind kept wanting to taunt him into believing the worst, he'd expected he would have to waste time securing his own mount.

He was leery about traveling into the Badlands by himself. It had been years since he'd done so. But once mounted and heading out of the corral, memories flashed before his eyes. Countless times he'd helped escort tourists over trails through the gullies and buttes, and as he rode the

path the note Hunter left with one of the trail guides telling him the route they would take, he recognized landmarks and terrain and relaxed.

The fact Hunter made sure he knew which direction to go eased Mason's brooding about there having been a ploy on his friends' part to be alone with Anastasia. However, the moment he topped still another butte and saw the two people, who were at the forefront of his mind, stopped in the distance, his earlier thought of Hunter wanting to be alone with Anastasia came rushing down on him in huge waves.

When he witnessed Anastasia wipe at her face, he assumed she was crying. His anger that Hunter would dare cause her heartache spurred him into action. It tested the riding skills he had not used in years, and he pushed the brown Quarter horse to its limit as he raced down the butte at a breakneck speed, intent upon socking Hunter in the nose.

Witnessing Hunter's horse abruptly takeoff, leaving Anastasia alone, confused him. By the time he reached her, she was already dismounted. The desire to soothe away whatever hurt Hunter caused out-weighed his need to confront his best friend.

Dismounting, it only took four steps to reach her. He had no words when he saw the moisture in her eyes, and his heart twisted. All he wanted to do was comfort. He opened his arms to wrap her in his embrace, but the moment he touched her, she raised her face and crushed her lips to his.

He had not expected it. Was jolted by it. Something in his heart rejoiced.

He could not identify the emotion as he held her, consumed her, and was not sure he wanted to investigate the feeling or acknowledge it.

But he recognized lust. That familiar passion had him pulling her body firmly against his as he invaded and explored the depths of her mouth.

He heard her groan, and it stoked his fire. His hand moved down between them to the front of her shirt, needing to feel the firmness of those tantalizing breasts.

His lust filled brain took a moment to register the fact she was fighting against his onslaught, pushing against his chest as though trying to pull away from him.

Good god. He still did not know what her ex-husband had done to her. Did not know if Danny had raped her. And here he was, close to pulling her to the ground, spreading her legs and entering her in one thrust.

Appalled at his behavior, he pulled back so abruptly she almost fell when the wall she'd been pushing against gave way. His hand clasped her arm as she stumbled forward, preventing her from landing on her face.

She stared up at him with eyes gone wild. "Holy. Shit." She said, panting for breath as she took a step back away from him.

"*Pardonne moi, chérie*," he told her. "I have wanted to kiss you from the moment I saw you. But it is no excuse for my behavior. Please, forgive me."

"That was a kiss?!" she exclaimed. Never in her life had she imagined something like what he claimed was a kiss.

Apparently, she had a lot to learn about writing a passionate scene. The chapter in the romance novel she was crafting, where the couple first kissed had been sweet in its description, but holy cow. Mason's real-life kiss put that fantasy kiss into the dullsville zone.

He'd almost eaten her alive.

He raked a hand through his hair, not liking the sexual frustration he'd been experiencing ever since meeting this woman. Never in his life had he abstained from sex when he felt the urge, but since meeting her, none of the women he met this week at the Fisher's lake cabin caught his attention enough to want to be with them. That included having no desire to be naked in bed with them, and it was all because of this funny lady with the eggplant purple highlights in her hair.

"I apologize for my loss of control. It will not happen again."

"Hey," she told him, "You don't have to threaten me like that."

He blinked. "Threaten...?"

Her smile was a grin. "I didn't say I didn't like it. But for cat's sake, I sure as hell wasn't prepared for it. Next time I'll at least know what's coming."

He stared at her for two seconds before a chuckle built low in his chest, then gave way to full laughter. She was a true treasure to him.

When his laughter subsided, he asked gently, "What did Hunter say to you that caused your tears?"

She looked confused by his question. "What do you mean? He didn't do anything-"

"Chérie, do not lie for him."

Shaking her head, she told him, "I'm not lying, Mason. If you saw tears, they were caused only because I discovered how much Hunter loves you."

"I..." He began, almost embarrassed by her statement. He loved Hunter like a brother and knew Hunter felt the same way about him.

He cleared his throat. "We have always been close," he told her. "We-"

Whatever Mason would have said was cut off when the sound of a horse approaching at a gallop got their attention.

Together Anastasia and Mason watched as the animal and its rider closed the distance between them.

Wyatt reined in on his horse hard enough to cause it to rear momentarily. His face looked ashen, and suddenly Anastasia remembered the scream she heard moments before Mason's arrival. She felt dread wash over her, and Wyatt's words did nothing to rid her of the impression that something was terribly wrong.

"Daniela fell down a butte!" he exclaimed breathlessly. "She's not moving. She won't answer when we call down to her. Hunter's trying

to climb down to her now. I'm going back to the stables to call for the air ambulance!" He did not wait for them to question him but spurred his horseback into a run as he continued his quest for help.

"Oh, god," Mason moaned in anguish as he quickly mounted his horse at the exact moment Anastasia was going for her own mount.

By the time the couple reached the butte, Hunter had finished his descent into the deep crevice where Daniela lay motionless on the hard, rocky floor.

Mason leaped off his horse before it came to a complete stop, rushing forward to look over the side of the steep incline. For a moment, he too almost slid off the side when he lost his footing in his haste to assure himself his sister was alright.

The rock fragments his boot dislodged showered down onto the two people below. Instinct caused Hunter to throw himself over Daniela's small body, protecting her from the falling mass. It was too bad Daniela was unconscious at that particular moment. She would have basked in the close contact of the man who filled her girlish dreams. As it was, she missed the feel of his body pressed against her, shielding her from the debris raining down on them.

Once the dust settled, Hunter snapped his head up to discover who the culprit was to have just given him a dust bath. "Lafayette!" he yelled angrily, "Get your ass away from that ledge before you come tumbling down and join your sister!"

Mason did not budge. "How is she?" His voice trembled with concern.

"I'll let you know as soon as you use that brain you supposedly have. Lay yourself out flat if you're going to insist on staying where you are!" Hunter did not wait for Mason to comply before he began his slow examination of the young girl. She'd been a thorn in his side for a week, and, for an instant, he was suspicious. Could this be yet another trick of the blasted girl's attempts to gain his attention? But once he felt the

lump on her head and saw the odd angle in which her left leg lay, he did not question the girl's motives any farther.

Quickly, he felt for a pulse. Finding one, he breathed a sigh of relief, though he was not about to ever tell anyone he was thankful the twirp was still alive. "Daniela," he called gently, slapping her face lightly, hoping to arouse the unconscious girl. "Hey, twirp. Wake up."

Daniela's eyelids flickered, opened on a moan, then closed almost as quickly. She groaned as a sharp assault of pain ripped through her. "Why could you have not left me alone?" Her voice was only a whispered sound of anguish. "I did not feel pain then."

"Want me to knock you back out?"

Her eyes flew open. "That is not funny!"

"Wasn't meant to be."

She groaned as another stab of pain worked its way through her small body. "Am I going to die?"

"Unfortunately, no." He knew he was being unjustifiably nasty to her, but he sure as hell was not about to let her know how glad he was she had not fallen to her death. But he would not give fuel to add to her infatuation with him by telling her otherwise either.

Daniela glared up at him. "Have I told you yet today that you are an âne trou?"

Hunter merrily laughed at that question. He could not seem to help himself. Here she was, lying in the bottom of a crevice, obviously in a great deal of pain, and she was calling him names instead of screaming her fool head off. At that moment, he admired her for her bravery and thought maybe, just maybe, she was not quite as ugly as he first believed.

Nah. What was he thinking?

"Hunter?" Mason's anguished voice snapped him from his thoughts. "How is she?"

Hunter stood, then moved back enough so he would see Mason's face. "Lump on her head 'bout the size of a goose egg," he answered. "Lots of cuts, bruises, and one very broken leg. Other than that, I'd say your sister's fine dandy."

Closing his eyes, Mason expelled a sigh of relief through his lips and silently gave thanks to the gods. He did not want to think about how close he had just come to losing the sister he loved.

Pushing himself backward away from the edge, he slowly stood up. He'd done as Hunter commanded. Laying down on his stomach to see over the edge so he would not be at risk of slipping over the ledge. When he turned, he found Anastasia at his side. She looked as worried as he had felt, and when she wrapped her arms around his waist and leaned into him, he reeled her in and held her tight.

"She'll be all right," Anastasia said, trying to reassure him.

"Yes," he agreed, then glanced at Rebecca, who was standing a short distance away, chewing on her thumb with worry in her own eyes.

"How did this happen?!" Mason asked her. "Daniela knows better than to stand that close to the edge of a ravine!"

Rebecca looked at him and cried out, "I don't know! Once we finished the race, we dismounted and were just walking along and looking at the view. Daniela was hanging onto her horse's reins, leading it behind her, and we were laughing over some dumb joke Wyatt told…" she shook her head. "The next thing we knew, she fell over the ledge!"

They would have to ask Daniela what happened once they brought her up from the bottom of the butte.

Mason untangled himself from Anastasia, took a couple of steps toward the drop-off. But this time stopped far enough away from the edge,

so he was at no risk of sliding down there himself. "Hunter!" he called out, "What can we do?"

"Not much until Wyatt gets back here with some ropes, although you could look around for some two-foot-long branches about two inches thick and pass them down here."

Mason's brow knit in his confusion. "What do you need those for?"

"I'm going to stabilize her leg. It's a closed break. No bone sticking out, and no swelling, numbness, or discoloration, so that's a good sign. And send a canteen down here. There is one attached to my saddle if Wyatt and Rebecca didn't bother to bring water with them."

Indignant, Rebecca stomped almost to the edge and shouted, "We aren't stupid! We've lived here all our lives if you recall. We always bring water with us whenever we ride."

"Great! Did you pack a rope?" Hunter shouted back up.

Sarcastically, because they had not, she asked, "Did you?"

"Not one long enough to do any good pulling her out, but if you look on the saddle, there's one long enough to tie the canteen to and lower it down."

Rebecca made a face. Of course he would have brought a rope. Her older brother had always taken the boy scout motto of being prepared to heart long before she and Wyatt were born.

Later, once the air ambulance arrived, the paramedics lowered a stretcher down and allowed Hunter to secure Daniela to it. The ledge at the bottom was narrow, and because Hunter could do the job, they did not see any point in climbing down there themselves.

Everyone grabbed the ropes and pulled the stretcher up. The moment Mason saw his sister, he went to her, leaned down to hug her the best he could, and began speaking to her in French. Anastasia could not understand the words, but the emotion in Mason's speech pattern let her know he was assuring Daniela she would be alright.

They loaded Daniela into the helicopter, and Mason moved toward it to climb onboard. The air ambulance would transport her to the Dickinson hospital, and he did not want his sister to make the trip alone. It would be a while before their parents were located and told what happened.

Before he left, he kissed Anastasia and told her, "I am sorry I have to leave you."

"Considering your sister needs you more," Anastasia said, "please don't worry about me. I'm sure I can find someone to take me back to New Salem." She glanced at Hunter, and when he nodded that yes, he would take her home, she grinned. "See. I won't have to hitchhike. But please, call me to let me know how she is doing. Okay?"

Mason held her for a moment, looking at her face as though trying to memorize it. "I will do that, chérie." His kiss was soft as he told her goodbye.

Anastasia stood back with the others as the helicopter's blades began rotating. Soon, a storm of dust formed, and shortly after that, the copter lifted off the ground.

Once the copter was a speck in the sky, Hunter told Anastasia, "Come on. Let's ride back to the ranch, and I'll take you home."

With a nod, Anastasia climbed into the saddle of the horse she'd been riding and hoped Daniela's recovery would not be too painful.
And damn it, she missed Mason already.

Chapter Twenty-three

Early that following Monday morning, Danny Sharp sat quietly in the back seat of the patrol car; biding his time until the officer transporting him to the courthouse for his preliminary hearing stopped and opened the door to let him out.

Don't be frightened, Danny boy.

We're with ya, buddy boy.

You'll be free in no time.

It's going to be so much fun, fun, fun!

Danny's head throbbed. The past week had been hell on earth. These damn voices had not given him a moment's peace. He could not dull the headaches with liqueur, and the voices tormented him unmercifully as he ranted and raged inside that shit hole of a cell.

If the voices lied to him, he no longer cared. His head felt as though it would explode at any given moment.

Not much longer, buddy boy.

Stay alert.

We're almost there.

Anastasia won't forget, once we're through with her, who's the man of the house.

Oh, what fun we'll have! -in a one-horse open sleigh!

Danny groaned and cursed the handcuffs preventing him from pressing his hands against his temples to counteract the pressure from within.

"Shut up, Sharp," the young officer told him, observing his charge in the rearview mirror.

"My fucking head hurts!"

"Whimper," the officer tisked, not in the least sympathetic to the man's pain.

Asshole.

We should kill him too, too, too.

"No!" Danny screamed, trying to hold on to whatever amount of sanity he could. He could not, would not, allow the voices to have their way. If he lost the battle he was fighting, there would be no way to prevent himself from carrying out the evil plan the voices were plotting.

"Shut up, Sharp," the officer snapped.

Oh, he's a dead man.

No pity in him.

No life either, once we're through. Snicker, snicker.

Can't wait, wait, wait.

Not much longer. We're almost there.

It's going to be an adventure!

It's going to be fun.

I wish we had a gun, one voice whined.

A gun?

What a pun!

Fun?

No. Gun.

Danny shook his head, hard. Hard enough to make himself dizzy. He was losing the little amount of control he'd hung onto these past days.

Soon, Danny. Soon.

It's all right. First the nightmare, then your wife.

Snicker. Snicker. *No more Chuck Norris!*

Shhh. *That's a secret!*

Who will know? No one knows we're here.

Not even the nightmare!

Oh, I can't wait to see the look on his face.

Beat us up, will he?

We'll show him he's not so great.

Yeah, see. We're gonna stuff him back into that shell, see.

It was nice of those officers, telling us where we could find the Fisher man.

Oh! Ha! Ha! Fisher. Man. I get it! And on a lake, too!

Of course, silly. Where else would a fisherman be?

Danny could no longer stand the pain. It swallowed him completely, forcing the man he had once been to retreat and escape the never-ending torture.

The voices were going to have their way after all.

Hahahahahahaha!

Chapter Twenty-four

On that same Monday morning, Charles Lafayette found his son sitting on one of the medium-sized boulders lining the shoreline close to the Fisher's summer home, gazing out onto lake Sakakawea. Obviously, Mason was deep in thought, and Charles felt he knew what was on the boy's mind.

Approaching the area, Charles stopped beside the formation. Without a word, he turned his eyes to view the deep waters stretching out before them as he waited patiently for Mason to speak, if he had anything to say at all.

Charles was a patient man when he was not behind a camera lens, directing a movie. He demanded perfection on a set, but when he was around family and friends, he could be patient enough to drive them insane.

"When did you know you were in love with my mother?" Mason asked quietly.

Chuckling, Charles told him, "I knew I was in love with her the first time I watched her perform on the stage. Elegance and grace radiated from her, and suddenly, my heart was lost to her." He turned to look at Mason. "She was young the first time I met her. Perhaps you will recall I attended college with your Uncle Dominic?" At Mason's nod, Charles continued. "Rosalinda would visit him on campus, and he introduced us, but I thought nothing remarkable about the encounter."

Charles sighed. "And then one day by chance I saw her in that play, and suddenly, my heart would not allow me to look at another from that day forward."

Mason thought about that for a moment and could admit that his own heart seemed to be doing the same thing to him.

"I do not recall hearing stories of when the two of you dated," Mason told him.

Laughing, Charles said, "There was no dating, Mason. I was in love with your mother for nine years before she finally came around to admitting she loved me too."

Mason raised a brow. "I do not understand."

"Have you noticed how stubborn your mother is, Mason?"

With a grin, Mason answered, "The very definition."

"Amen."

They shared a laugh over that, both knowing the statement was gospel truth.

Once the amusement subsided, Mason asked, "Did you have many lovers in those nine years?"

The subject did not shock Charles. He and Rosalinda always encouraged their children to say what was on their minds. Besides, this was the one child who took after Rosalinda in so many ways. The subject of sex was always on the boy's mind.

Before answering, Charles climbed onto the rock next to him and sat down. It was amazing the man, who was now sixty-four years old, was spry enough to accomplish the task, but he did. "Mason, I had no lovers once your mother came into my life."

Mason could only gape at him. "I thought the two of you did not have sex until your wedding night." No lovers? Mason could not fathom it.

Charles' amusement was rich as he looked back onto the lake. "We did not have sex that night, either."

"What?" No sex on their wedding night?

"And I do not wish to talk about that time as I do not want to upset you."

"Why would it upset me…?" Mason trailed off as it occurred to him the timing of his mother's abduction would have been around the same time as their wedding.

Rosalinda and Charles had not talked about when Pierre kidnapped her, and Mason was glad for it. Growing up, he saw daily what the man had done to her. The scars on her arms. Her legs. And when she did not wear makeup, the one on her face. However, he never asked how long they were married before his mother's nightmare began.

Charles saw the understanding in Mason's eyes.

He had wanted the child from the moment they discovered Pierre had impregnated Rosalinda.

Softly Charles said, "I honestly did not know if I would ever have sex with your mother because of that night. But I loved her enough to allow her to heal and come to me on her own terms. And yes, I knew she might never want to have a man touch her again. Cold, cold showers became my normal daily routine for a long, long time."

Mason frowned. "You are telling me you did not turn to another woman, and you had not had sex with anyone for over nine years?" Mason, having been sexually active most of his life, found that hard to believe.

"I loved your mother, Mason. No one else interested me enough to want to take them to bed."

For a moment, Mason said nothing as he pondered that and compared it with what he felt was happening to him. After a few minutes, he whispered, "Perhaps even though your blood does not run through me, I am your son after all."

Charles swallowed a lump in his throat, and moisture formed in his eyes upon hearing Mason's declaration. "You have always been my son in my heart," he choked, wrapping Mason in his embrace.

They sat there a moment, father and son, holding each other, not ashamed of their open display of affection for each other.

"So," Charles said, pulling back and wiping at his eyes to remove the tears that had fallen, "Are you saying you are in love?"

Mason shrugged. "I do not know what to think. I cannot get Anastasia out of my head." Seven days. He'd gone seven days without sex, and it was an all-time record for him.

Once again, Charles' laugh was heartfelt. "Cold showers, my boy. I think they are in your future."

"Do not say that!" Mason exclaimed as his hand went to his heart.

Charles chuckled at the pained look on Mason's face.

Hunter walked up to the grouping of boulders and asked, "Did I miss a good joke?"

Charles shook his head. "Not one Mason finds amusing."

Hunter wanted to ask, but shrugged instead. And then, for politeness' sake, because he honestly did not care, which is what he told himself, he asked, "How is Daniela doing?"

"She is getting used to the crutches." Charles eyed him. "Thank you for what you did for her."

Uncomfortable with that small amount of gratitude, Hunter waved it away. "Anyway, Mason. I was wondering if you wanted to-"

His sentence was cut off when they heard his mother yelling at them. Looking toward the house, they saw Jacqueline running down the beach, waving her arms as she continued to call their names.

She was breathless by the time she reached them.

"Mom?" Hunter asked, concerned.

"Report… On the news," she gasped, motioning with her hand toward the house. "Channel nine is broadcasting a special report. There was an

escape this morning." She looked at Mason. "Danny Sharp is on the loose!"

"What?!" Mason and Hunter exclaimed in unison, disbelief in their voices.

They did not wait for her to repeat herself. Mason slid off the rock and raced for the house. If he had not been in shock, he would have taken pleasure in the fact he matched Hunter's powerful strides as he too ran toward the patio doors to hear the broadcast for himself.

They entered the house at the same time. Already there was a group gathered around the small television Jacqueline had on the counter in the kitchen. Among them were Cadman and his wife, Kasey.

Meeting Hunter's eyes, Cadman shook his head, conveying the news was not good.

The news bulletin continued. "… earlier this morning. Killed was officer Ted Rossman. Rossman had been with law enforcement three years when he fell victim to the prisoner he was transporting to the Mandan courthouse. Officials have confirmed that officer Rossman's patrol car and gun were taken by the fugitive, twenty-five-year-old Daniel Sharp."

Mason's dark-apricot tan left his face. "What?" he sat down on the nearby barstool before his legs buckled.

"Sssh!" Hunter hissed, eyes glued to the television.

Charles entered the house to join his wife and the others as they listened intently to the reporter's information to the community.

"The public," the reporter continued, "is warned Sharp is dangerous." They displayed a mug shot of Danny on the screen. "If anyone sees this man, please contact the Mandan Police department. Sharp was last seen driving the stolen police car north on highway eighty-three."

The broadcast ended, and Mason stood up. Looking at Hunter, he told him, "Give me the keys to your jeep. I need to drive to New Salem."

When Hunter met his eyes, he could easily see the worry and fear on his friend's face. Was Sharp already there, in New Salem, with Anastasia?

Glancing to Cadman, Hunter asked, "Will you call the Mandan police department and see if you can find out any more information?"

"I'll do one better than that," Cadman reached for the telephone attached to the wall, picked up the receiver. "I'll get someone to New Salem to stay with Anastasia until the two of you get there. It's a two-hour drive, and we want her protected. Now."

Hunter cocked a brow at him. "I can't believe you said that to me."

Cadman's eyebrow rose in question.

"Two hours? Me?"

Colten shook his head at his son's inquiry. "Cadman forgets you got your need for speed from your Uncle TJ."

"Alright, an hour," Cadman amended. "Once I make this call, I'll head down to Mandan and see what I can find out from the locals that the media didn't tell us. But if you stand here any longer talking about it, you're not going to have your jeep to drive." He pointed toward the patio doors where Mason could be seen slipping out. "He took your keys to the jeep from the wall."

"Son of a bitch," Hunter hissed, sprinting into action. He exited the house and ran for his jeep. He was just in time to stop Mason from climbing behind the wheel. "I'll drive, thank you very much."

"Fine," Mason told him, rushing around to the passenger seat. "I do not care who drives. I only want to make sure Anastasia is all right." He glanced at Hunter. "I think I might love her."

Breaking into a fit of laughter, Hunter had a hard time putting the key into the ignition. "You think you love her? My god, don't you suppose you would know the answer to that?"

Mason glared at him. "I have never loved a woman before. How should I know if what I feel is love or lust?"

Hunter backed the jeep up, stopped. "You're talking to the wrong guy, Lafayette. You know I'm not going to let that happen to me."

He caught sight of Daniela slowly hobbling along the dirt road with her crutches as Wyatt and Rebecca accompanied her. He could not have prevented the evil gleam coming to his eyes, even if he had wanted to.

The jeep bolted forward.

"For Christ's sake, Hunter! That was my sister you almost ran over!"

"I missed her, didn't I? And besides, how do you know I wasn't toying with my youngest siblings? They had the same look of horror as she did." Hunter stated dryly. But it had been worth the wide-eyed expression of total and complete horror on the twirps face. Ever since he had more or less rescued her, the girl's infatuation with him had doubled, and for the life of him, he could not understand why when he did everything in his power to pick on the kid.

Mason's eyes looked upward, and he shook his head. Hunter's logic was incredibly unlogical.

"Well, hell, Mason! I'm only trying to do the girl a favor. Hopefully, by the time she's headed back to Paris, she'll hate my guts."

Exactly one hour later, they arrived in New Salem. They first drove to the salon Anastasia owned but were told a Sheriff's deputy had escorted her home.

At least they knew she was, for the moment, safe.

* * *

"Anastasia," Mason snapped as he ran his hands through his hair, "Why are you being so difficult about this?"

Stubborn woman.

He and Hunter had been at her house for almost an hour and a half. Both were trying to convince her to go to California with Mason. It was Hunter's idea. One Mason liked immensely. He had been thinking about asking her to go with him when he brought her back from Medora, but Daniela's accident put a kibosh to that plan. Now, knowing Danny was somewhere out there, possibly watching her house at this very minute, this became the perfect excuse to bring the subject up.

And what had her answer been?

A resounding no.

Yep. Mason should have considered the fact she was not like any other woman on this planet. Hundreds of them would have jumped at the chance to spend time with him at his California residence. But not her. And he was beginning to curse the very day he met the non-conforming woman.

"And why can't you just leave me alone, Mason?" Anastasia snapped back.

He scanned her face. Thick, long black lashes framed her blue eyes. Her dark brows were perfectly shaped and arched gently above the al-mond-shaped eyes. Her nose was narrow but not overly long. The way it turned slightly up at the tip set off the naturally dark pink lips he'd had the pleasure of tasting and wanted to taste again. But he doubted that desire would become a reality any time soon.

"Because I want you to be safe!" he shouted back.

His words touched her and deflated her anger. Issuing a heavy sigh, she sat back in the straight-back chair she was sitting on at her kitchen table. "Mason," she told him gently, as though he were a child. "I can't afford to take off for an indefinite amount of time. I have bills to pay and a business to run and-"

Until then, Hunter had been sitting at the table, watching their argu-ment with amusement. They were bickering like an old married couple. But when Anastasia mentioned her concern regarding finances, he

figured he had the best solution in the world to take that argument out of her list of excuses. Glancing to Mason, he asked, "She is a barber, right?"

"Beautician!" Anastasia gritted. The one thing she really hated was when people called her a barber. She was a licensed cosmetologist, damn it. Her license gave her a broader spectrum than that of a barber who strictly focused on hair and facial hair. The State of North Dakota licensed her to do all of that, including working on nails, skin, and more, not just hair.

Hunter stared at her as though she were crazy before turning his attention back on Mason. "You need a haircut, Mason. Why don't you hire her?"

"I need a haircut?" Mason asked in astonishment as he stared at Hunter's own long mane.

Hunter rolled his eyes. "Did you suddenly get stupid?"

It was Mason's turn to stare, not appreciating the slur. "I may not have your photographic memory or speak the ten languages you do, but that does not make me stupid."

Sitting back in his chair, Hunter sighed. "Figure of speech. I know you're not dumb. But you're missing my point."

"Which is?"

"Hire Stasia as your personal stylist!"

The smile on Mason's face started off slowly as the idea took root. Looking now at Anastasia, he told her, "Anastasia, I would like to hire you as my personal stylist and will pay you sixty thousand dollars."

Anastasia felt as though someone just slapped her. In fact, her body jerked back from hearing the staggering amount, rendering her momentarily speechless.

Hunter gaped at his best friend. "Are you nuts?"

Slowly, Anastasia said, "No. Thank. You."

No, thank you? Mason was glad he was sitting down. He doubted he would have been able to endure his shock at her refusal. "That is a lot of money-"

"Exactly! So glad you noticed!" She told him. "Do you believe I am a charity case?"

Mason's eyes blazed. "Why would you think such a thing?!"

"Because ever since I met you, you keep trying to throw money at me as though I'm some prostitute that can be bought!"

Mason jerked. He stared at her so long; she thought he would burn a hole into her brain from the anger she saw coming from those beautiful green eyes of his that were so dark now they were the color of a dark green sea.

Without a word, Mason got up and walked out of the room.

Hunter broke the static-filled silence by placing his hands together and applauding loudly. "Bravo!" He sneered. "That has got to be the best display of prideful stupidity I have ever seen."

"Shut up, Hunter!" Anastasia cried as she turned her head to glare at him.

Leaning forward in the chair, he told her, "Listen to me very closely, Anastasia. That man you just insulted only wanted to remove your financial excuse for not going with him. He's frightened for you. Especially because he saw what your ex is capable of, and he wants to protect you in the one way he knows how. He's got a shit ton of money. A thousand dollars to him is a dollar bill to you, and he sure as hell does not think of you as a prostitute or a charity case. Why can't you trust him enough to go with him?"

Anastasia burst into tears. She had dreamed of meeting Mason Lafayette, and now all she had done was offend him because of her own pride and fears.

"You can trust, Mason," Hunter told her, and his voice was incredibly soft.

"I trusted Danny, too!" She cried, tears leaping to her eyes. "He was kind; gentle. I never thought he would hurt me!" And then, it poured out of her; what she had gone through with her now ex-husband. "After Danny was involved in an explosion during Desert Storm, he became abusive. The doctors said he was recovered one hundred percent, but he kept having headaches, but they discharged him anyway. He was never the same after that. His personality began slowly changing, and sometimes I thought he was someone else. I tried to get help for him, but every one of my letters to his Marine superiors was answered with a standard form letter or returned to me unopened." She wrapped her arms around herself tightly, trying to still her quivering body. "When Danny found out about the letters, he blew sky high, and that's when the beatings began. After that, he began accusing me of having affairs with practically every man in New Salem! Including the seventy-five-year-old grandfather down the street!"

Hunter moved from the chair. In a rare display of sensitivity, he wrapped his arms around the woman, stroking her head gently while she continued to cry.

"I don't even know what set him off the last time," Anastasia whispered, resting her head on Hunter's shoulder as she continued to weep. "I honestly thought he was going to kill me. Perhaps he would have, but Gale's husband Jeff had seen him pull into my driveway, and he ran for his house and came back with a baseball bat. He knocked Danny out with it just after he broke my jaw, which was after he broke my arm."

Anastasia took a deep breath. "I was in the hospital for a week. The doctors had to wire my jaw shut, and my diet for six weeks was nothing more than liquids and very soft foods." She wrapped her arms around him, lay her forehead onto his chest. "I hate soup and gelatin so badly now the thought of them makes me want to puke."

Hunter almost had the urge to laugh at that last statement of hers. It amazed him she still had a sense of humor after going through something like that.

"Oh, this is a touching scene," came a cynical sneer from the doorway, and Hunter's head snapped up to find Mason standing rigid in the doorway with his fists clenching at his sides. "Do you wish for me to leave so the two of you can be alone?"

Hunter slowly untangled himself from Anastasia's arms and stood to his feet. Turning to look at his best friend, he said, "Lafayette, don't be an ass." Then he looked at Anastasia. "I think it would be a good idea for you to tell him what you just told me. And when you're done, pack your bags. You're going to California."

Chapter Twenty-five

Hunter had not slept in almost twelve hours. He was too consumed with shifting through a puzzle where none of the pieces fit than to waste time by giving his body rest. Not that going without sleep was new to him. He had done it before. Countless times, beginning when he was young, he began conditioning himself to function on less sleep than most people need.

Growing up, listening to his Uncle Cadman's tales of adventures around the world, capturing criminals only added more determination to accomplishing a mission he seemed to have been born with. To become one of the best of the best. While studying up on what it took to become a Navy SEAL, Hunter discovered functioning on a small amount of sleep was a part of hell week. An aptly named time frame that SEAL want-a-be's went through. It was a grueling week of physical exertion consisting of runs, swims, boat drills, and calisthenics on four to six hours of sleep during the entire week and were still required to perform academically.

Thank god for his eidetic memory. But for those who did not have his gift for the ability to recall things from memory after seeing it only once, Hunter gave them the respect they were due.

Mason and Anastasia would have arrived in California almost sixteen hours ago. Within that time frame, there still had been no trace of Danny. It was as though the man disappeared off the face of the earth, and that bothered Hunter.

A lot.

Authorities found the stolen squad car in an abandoned barn thirty miles north of Bismarck. Other than that, there was no way of knowing which direction the guy was heading, and for some reason Hunter did not believe Danny was on his way to New Salem; yet. Not that he had

anything other than gut instincts to base the impression on, but he learned a long time ago that more often than not, his gut was usually right.

Danny was obsessed with his ex-wife. That much Hunter knew from the countless people he interviewed over the last thirteen hours. Everything showed a pattern, which meant Danny should have headed directly for New Salem when he escaped.

He hadn't.

Where was he going?

Hunter sighed and leaned back in the chair as his eyes roamed the wall blanketed with photos of Mason. It felt sort of weird having countless pairs of his best friends' eyes staring at him from those images. Anastasia said this room was off-limits to him, just before law enforcement escorted her and Mason to Bismarck where they boarded the private plane Mason secured to fly them to California.

Naturally, Hunter wouldn't have listened to her, anyway. But the bright red blush flooding her face when she made that decree had him going in there the moment she and Mason were in the escort car.

The second he opened the door and saw the walls littered with photos of Mason, he burst into laughter.

Now, sitting at her desk, going through the drawers, he discovered dozens of unopened letters marked, return to sender.

All addressed to some of the top brass in the military.

Not afraid to snoop, he tore one open and read the contents. All handwritten in a flowing cursive style that was easy to decipher. It backed up what Anastasia told him about her quest to get help for Danny.

Something was definitely amiss and sent up red flags that said a coverup was at work.

Putting the envelopes back in the drawer, determined to do a little research into Danny's time with the Marines, Hunter reached forward with his right hand and turned on Anastasia's dinosaur of a computer.

The system was so old it required Floppy disks to boot it up.

Digging through the desk drawers, he found disks used to save whatever information she wanted to keep. Out of a pack of twenty, two were missing.

He shrugged. For the moment, that detail was not important. He was more interested in the disk labeled diary than with the absent disks. Somewhere was the key to Danny's erratic behavior, and perhaps it was here in Anastasia's reminisces.

"Those are personal to Anastasia," a woman's displeased voice informed him from behind.

Recognizing the voice, he knew who it was. He did not turn to look at her, nor did he stop loading the disk and recalling the first document up on the computer's monochrome screen. "Hello, Mrs. Martin." He greeted Gale casually.

Gale moved forward until she stood beside him. "Did Stasia give you permission to go through her things?"

"Nope." He began scanning the information displayed on the screen.

Gale's hand reached out and covered the display. "Then I guess that means you should not be in here."

Hunter leaned back in the chair, stretching his long powerful legs out and hooking them at the ankles, regarding her. He gave her credit for her boldness. "How long have you known Anastasia, Gale?" He had not found the time to question the Martins yet, busy with other interviews. Now that one of them presented themselves, this was as good of time as any to conclude the eyewitness sessions.

"For about five years," Gale answered but did not remove her hand from the monitor. "Ever since Jeff and I moved out here to escape the hustle of Bismarck. We like peace and quiet."

"And how long have you known Danny?"

"Practically since the day Anastasia met the monster."

Hunter's brows raised. "So why did Anastasia marry him if he was such a monster?"

With a sigh, accepting the idea this man was only trying to help, Gale removed her hand from blocking his view of whatever words Anastasia may have written and moved to the twin-sized bed that was pushed up against the wall, and sat down. "She was in love, and to be honest, I adored him back then. He was a very gentle man. All trim and handsome. No one guessed he had an evil side to him."

Hunter was quiet for a moment. She was not telling him anything new. Countless others, including Danny's distressed parents, aunts, uncles, and numerous family members, said the same thing. Danny had been a nice guy.

What made him change? Hunter asked himself for the hundredth time.

Reaching into the drawer for the box of disks, he asked Gale, "Have any idea why there would be two disks missing from here?"

She shrugged. "I don't know. Could be Stasia took them with her. Since she had no way of knowing how long she would be gone, she probably thought she'd use this as a vacation and work on her book if the opportunity came along."

"Book?" That was additional information.

"Didn't you know?" Gale shook her head. "No, I guess you wouldn't. She keeps it to herself. I'm probably the only one she confides in regarding it. Anastasia has this big dream of becoming a romance writer. She started writing as part of her therapy. It helps her express herself, let out emotions she's bottled up." She looked at him. "And she's a

talented writer, though you would probably think I was being biased because she's my friend. But she won a competition in a national magazine recently. They are going to publish the short story next year in their January issue."

Hunter glanced once more at the photos of Mason hanging on the wall and almost laughed again. Mr. Romance meets Miss Romance writer by chance. Now there was a fictional tale if there ever was one.

"If you are wondering if Anastasia is the type of person who would use your friend to reach her goal, I can set you straight on that. She isn't that kind of woman."

Actually, that thought hadn't entered his mind. Being around Anastasia in Medora was enough time to have sized her up. She wore her feelings for Mason on her sleeve. No. She was not the sort of woman who would use someone for her own gain.

"I understand it was your husband who took a baseball bat after Danny the night he beat Anastasia severe enough to put her in the hospital. My hat off to him as I physically fought the guy-"

Gale chuckled. "Jeff was scared to death, and who could blame him? But when he came into the house with that bat, Danny's back was turned away from him, and Jeff did not stop to make conversation with him. He knew how dangerous Danny was," she shook her head, "Is," she amended. "Jeff swung that bat as though his life depended upon it and knocked Danny out with the first blow."

Hunter laughed. "Wish I would have had a bat last Sunday."

Gale stared at him. "Listen. Why are you sitting here investigating Anastasia when you should be talking to whatever government people you work for? People accuse me of liking conspiracy theories, but I'm telling you. I think something happened over there in Iraq the military doesn't want anyone to know about. Why else would everyone ignore Anastasia's pleas for help?!"

Hunter agreed with her. The more he dug into this, the more it felt like someone had something to hide. He did not want to believe the government would do such a thing, but he was also well aware that they did. Wasn't his own existence proof of that? Whenever they needed help, they called him friend. If he got caught, they would deny any knowledge of him.

Not much of a friendship, but he loved every minute of it.

"Excuse me, Gale. I need to make a phone call." He hoped he could reach Cadman at the police station in Mandan, as that was where his uncle/boss was hanging out at while doing his own investigation into Danny's escape. He needed Cadman to unearth the records regarding Daniel Sharp's time while overseas.

* * *

North Dakota was not known for more than grasslands and low rolling hills, but there was plenty of foliage where Danny lay hidden from anyone looking for him.

His breathing was heavy. His forehead, lined with sweat, caused him to continually wipe at his eyes to remove the salty liquid as it flowed down his face. Every muscle in his body ached from having closed the remaining distance to his intended goal on foot. But the pain was nothing compared to the agony raging within his head.

He groaned as he rolled onto his side.

Ssssh, you big dope! An inner voice hissed.

They'll hear us!

Not us! No one knows about us!

Danny licked his dry lips. Christ, it must be at least eighty-five above zero, and the sun blazing down on him, as he lay hidden in this shallow ditch, was merciless.

A child's laughter sounded, and Danny's eyes moved toward the five-year-old playing near the patio doors.

Should we take him?

He's not the one we want, you ninny. He's too young.

What if he isn't here?

Danny spotted the teenage girl on crutches slowly make her way to a beach chair; sit down, then place the leg with the cast on it up on the second chair to elevate it.

How 'bout her?

Well, if he isn't here, then she'll do. It could be lots of fun, snicker snicker.

Oh, I can hardly wait! One cried gleefully.

Danny closed his eyes. He did not know where he was or how he'd gotten here, but he knew he was powerless to stop the voices from having their way.

Couldn't someone put a bullet through his head and end his suffering? He hoped so. He really did.

He felt the solid mass of the stolen police 9mm in his hand and wished he had the guts to turn it on himself before it was too late. The problem with that was he was afraid of dying as much as he was of living.

If there was a hell, he was in it.

* * *

"I have a national guard helicopter on the way to New Salem to pick you up now," Cadman's voice informed Hunter while they conversed on the phone. "I have a few details to finish up here, then I'll order a bird for myself and be right behind you."

"Son of a bitch," Hunter hissed, "Are you certain that's where he's heading?"

"From what I've gathered from here, I do not doubt it. It is unfortunate some officers talked about you, and where you're staying at the lake, within Sharp's hearing, but in their defense, no one thought he would escape."

"If anything happens to my family-"

"Hunter, I know. That's why I sent the copter for you. I have tried calling up there to warn them, but no one answers the phone. I'll keep trying. I have authorities headed there now. A sheriff's cruiser will be waiting for you at the drop off point. If anyone can stop him, you can."

"A fucking bullet through his eyes would stop him."

"Any other time, I would agree with you, but in this case, I believe the man doesn't deserve the one-way ticket. He was a victim, Hunter. I read the files the brass sealed up. That explosion he was involved in was not caused by Iraqi forces. It was our military's fuck up."

"Yeah, and now my family could become victims because of the Marines' reluctance to take responsibility."

"Get to Sakakawea. Apprehend him. If my gut is right, Danny has scar tissue from his head injury, putting pressure on his brain. With surgery, it's treatable."

"I hear the copter approaching. Got to go." Hunter slammed the phone down and headed out the door. Yeah. Maybe Sharp's personality change was not the man's fault. But if he hurt anyone at the lake house, Hunter would do what it took to bring the man down, and if that meant killing him, so be it.

Chapter Twenty-six

Anastasia stood motionless in the doorway. The room was slowly becoming bathed in light as the morning sun's rays pushed their way through the tall glass doors located across the room.

She shouldn't be here. How many times she told herself to leave, she did not know. But still, she lingered, watching the sleeping man, mesmerized by the pure maleness of him.

He slept on his back with his left arm bent, covering his eyes. His deep, even breathing, told her he was not aware of her presence. If she left now, he would never know she had stood in his doorway, held captive by his thickly sculptured chest, powerful arms, and rock-hard stomach. The rest of him was hidden from her view, covered by a dark blue satin sheet. The same color of the pillowcase encasing the pillow cushioning his head. His past shoulder length midnight black hair fanned over it, and her fingers itched to run through the strands.

She knew he was naked beneath those sheets. Knew he would welcome her there; hold her, make love to her. All she had to do was take those few steps, and she would be there, in the warm embrace of his arms.

Her heart raced. Her body trembled. She felt an unquestionable desire for him. She had dared to fantasize and dream about being with him, kissing him and him kissing her. Dreamt of feeling his hands stroking her body until she called out and begged for release.

He would be a gentle lover and take her to ecstasy. In her dreams, at least, this was true.

Did she dare make her fantasies a reality, knowing that once Danny was back behind bars, their time together would end?

Some women in this world would think she was crazy for hesitating. But she had never been a woman to have casual sex. Her heart wanted love involved with the act, and although Mason did not love her, he had shown her in many ways he cared for her.

That was something. Wasn't it? A reason to give into her desires even though she knew that they would go their separate ways when this nightmare with Danny was over and all she would have left were the memories.

Oh, but sweet memories they would be, and certainly unforgettable.

They arrived last night, early in the evening. A limousine had been waiting for them when their plane landed at LAX. The arrangements having been made before leaving the Bismarck airport.

The limousine driver drove them to a clothing store. A surprise Mason bestowed on her. A gift of an entirely new wardrobe.

At first, Anastasia protested such an outlandish shopping spree. He was already going to pay her wages while she was with him, so she would have no income loss. Allowing him to spend more on her had not felt right. But then, he had given her such a pitifully wounded puppy dog expression because of her refusal, she'd felt guilty for not allowing him his desire.

But she recalled Hunter's words. That to Mason, a thousand dollars to him was a dollar to her, and that giving gifts was something the man enjoyed doing.

She would never forget the look of pleasure that crossed his face when she finally said yes to the clothing. Never in her life had she seen someone so joyous to squander money that he'd reminded her of a little boy who'd been given the moon.

She left the expensive boutique wearing a black tank dress cut low enough to show more than a little cleavage and it was set off by several gold bangles and matching gold earrings he'd added to the bill. She felt as though she were a princess, if not a bit risqué one. She'd never been

daring with her clothing before, but Mason's eyes seemed to devour her, and because she knew it pleased him, she was happy to allow him the pleasure of seeing her dressed in one of the items he picked out for her.

After the shopping binge, the limo took them to Mason's home, though the word home did not accurately describe his residence. Far from it. It was a thirty-eight-room mansion on two thousand acres of well cared for lawn and exotic floral gardens.

Then he'd told her the house he grew up in was larger than this masterpiece.

Without setting foot inside the structure, she felt totally out of her league.

Once the beautiful mahogany arched door, surrounded with decorative glass, opened, the wealth displayed on the interior attested to the fortune that was obviously his. And she damn near fainted when she discovered the living room in his home was larger than the combined square footage of her little house on the prairie back in New Salem.

She was almost overwhelmed, and yet she had a strange sense of belonging as well.

Her favorite room in this massive house, with its seven bedrooms, ten bathrooms, eleven fireplaces, and multiple entertaining rooms, was not the marble-floored entry or the ivory lined living room. Nor was it the enormous kitchen, although she could envision herself cooking there as it appealed to her love of baking and cooking.

Her preferred room was used to display a few of the book covers his image graced over the years; half of them she'd not been aware of, and oddly, she felt a sense of pride for him and his accomplishment.

There were photos of him with movie and television stars, which she expected considering who his parents were. There were images of him with other famous models and even one of him with the last President of the United States.

Mason's beautiful and luxurious home's tour ended with Mason showing her to the bedroom she could use while she was there. He did not mention her sharing his room, but she'd seen the message in his eyes. A message that told her she was welcome in his bed whenever she wanted.

She wanted it then. She wanted it now.

Anastasia's blue eyes roamed lazily over Mason's naked torso once again. He had not changed positions since she first entered his room this early morning, and that had been almost twenty minutes ago.

She could hear her heartbeat pounding in her ears. Was she willing to risk her heart farther to this man by sharing his bed?

Knowing the answer, she took a step forward and froze.

A sigh escaped through Mason's lips, and he rolled onto his side, away from her.

She almost had the stupid urge to laugh, although she did not know why.

Another step. But a sudden rocket of fur flying past her leg almost had her screaming. But when her eyes focused in on the culprit responsible for giving her this fright, she contemplated wringing her poodle's little neck. Her stupid dog beat her to her goal. She seriously considered switching its initials around to D.M. and rename the thing Dumb Mutt.

The unexpected intrusion of M.D. leaping upon his person startled Mason out from the peaceful slumber, and he was not pleased to have been jolted awake like that. Especially when he spent most of the night tossing and turning. Having Anastasia in his home and just across the hall played havoc on his mind and sexually deprived body. It had taken every ounce of sheer willpower not to slip into her room during the night. He craved making love to her like a drug addict craving narcotics. But he wanted her to come to him on her own accord, which was a decision only she could make.

The dream he'd been having before the sudden interruption was a fantasy involving Anastasia, and he sure as hell would have liked to have finished that dream. Now he faced more sexual frustration because the source of his arousal wasn't close at hand for him to reach for and get lost in her warm depths.

He reached out his hand and grabbed M.D. by his collar. "Listen, mutt," he growled in a tone to match his spirit, "You may very well share my name, but you do not share my bed!"

"Then- can- I?"

Mason froze. Every part of his being wanted to roll over to see for himself if the person belonging to that quiet voice was actually in the room.

His bedroom, to be precise.

He hesitated only because he knew he'd roll over and discover the room empty. But he forced himself to do it anyway because he hoped this wasn't a fantasy and he would see her standing there.

He did. He just didn't believe it. Not at first, and he blinked several times, thinking he was still sleeping.

When it did finally dawn on him that this was no dream, he almost did the unthinkable and laughed at the reality. Not that he found it funny that Anastasia was standing in his room watching him. But she simply did not appear the way he had envisioned her coming to him.

In his dream, she wore a sheer negligee of seductive red and plenty of lace. But somehow, the reality seemed far more interesting. In fact, he doubted he had ever witnessed a woman looking quite this sexy before, regardless of the fact there was nothing sensual or seductive about that oversized pink t-shirt hanging loosely on her body, hiding every delicate curve. The sloppy looking shirt ended above her knees, giving him a marvelous view of the shapely legs he so admired. But the best part of all, and the reason the urge to laugh was on the brink of coming forth, were the tiger faced slippers gracing her feet.

He snapped his eyes back up to her face before the laughter had its way.

He concentrated for a moment on her dark brown hair with its eggplant purple highlights cascading around her in soft waves, falling freely to her hips.

His eyes stopped their roaming once they found her breasts pushing out on the material, and his palms almost broke into a sweat from wanting to touch them. Caress them until the nipples were hard and erect. Better still was the thought of taking one into his mouth, and that idea caused his mouth to go dry.

Then he noticed there was something written on the shirt. It took him a moment to focus on the design, as interested as he was with what was being hidden from his view. Once he saw what the shirt bore, a cartoon drawing of three blue teddy bears sitting on top of a curling iron and the words, curl up with me, written across it, he gave into a smile. After all, he should have known Anastasia would be a woman who would not wear frilly things to bed.

Slowly, his eyes met hers. A very sensual and seductive smile spread across his face, and his husky voice was seductively smooth when he said, "*Chéri*, you may curl up with me anytime."

He had the sexiest smile and come hither look she'd ever seen. Combined with those cat-like green eyes that had become a dark shade of jade, her desire for him increased tenfold. His huskily spoken words, whisper-soft, yet oh so seductively male, carried upon the heavily accented and deep vibration of his speech caused her to tremble from desire.

Mason rolled onto his right side, placed an elbow on the pillow, and rested his head lazily on his hand. His left leg raised slightly, bending at the knee. The movement caused the remainder of the silken sheets to slide away, just covering his already aroused member.

Slowly he extended his left hand toward her, coaxing without words.

Before she knew it, she was in his arms, enclosed within his powerful embrace. He rolled onto his back, placing her full weight on top of him, and rained kisses upon her face. He whispered gentle words in his native French, and although Anastasia did not understand the words, the meaning was clear. His hands interpreted the message in slow, easy caresses, cherishing her with his hands, his mouth.

When his mouth once again claimed hers, she opened for him, returning the probing of his tongue as her senses marveled and reeled at the taste of him.

The kiss lingered, deepened, as though they were afraid there would be nothing as joyous and beautiful as this moment ever again.

When they broke apart, they took deep gulps of air as though they had been drowning; consumed under the turbulent waves of passion crashing in on them.

Green eyes locked with Anastasia's blue depths that were so dark from her desire they were almost black.

He reached up, lightly trailing a finger along her cheekbone. "You are so beautiful, *mon chéri*," he whispered, his hand continuing down her throat, over her shoulder, and across the length of her arm.

Saying not a word, Anastasia bent her head and kissed the flesh of his neck, then began tasting and licking a trail slowly down to the wide expanse of his hairless chest. Inch by inch, she traveled until she reached one of his nipples. There she stopped, circling it with her tongue then covered it with her mouth.

Air hissed through Mason's lips, and he almost grabbed her than to turn her onto her back. Some men were not sensitive in that area, but he was, and he basked in the feel of her licking him there.

God in heaven, he was going to explode if she did not do something real soon to ease his growing need. He had not had sex for over a week. For a man accustomed to sex every day, his body felt as though it had gone to hell and now wanted to explode with pent up desire.

Whether Anastasia read his mind, he couldn't be sure. But she suddenly sat up and removed the pink t-shirt, revealing every delicious curve of her body. His mouth went dry. He couldn't swallow. He was captivated by the beauty displayed before him. The ample breasts he had only imagined with his mind's eye danced in front of him, and when she placed her hands on them, leaned forward and whispered, "Mason," the husky way she said his name was his undoing. His hand came up, accepting the gift she gave, and as soon as their weight rested entirely in his care, she arched forward, still farther. He needed no more encouragement than that. He raised his head, capturing one of the brown nipples between his teeth, licking, tasting, and suckling on the soft flesh until the tips were hard and swollen, and still he continued to feast on the large mounds.

Anastasia gasped and moaned out her pleasure. She placed her hands into the thickness of his hair, holding him close as his mouth continued with its magic. It felt so good, so right, and she trembled in her pleasure, keening his name over and over.

Another moan and Mason went out of his mind. With one swift move, he had her on her back, spread her legs, and thrust into her in one powerful motion, burying his large and swollen member to her limit and still wanted to go beyond.

Her gasp froze him. Had he hurt her? It was the last thing he wanted to do, and when he felt her body begin to shake, his heart felt as though it would shred in half. "I'm sorry," he whispered, cursing his impatience, and felt as though he were a young boy making love to a woman for the first time. Perhaps she had not been ready for their joining. Usually, he took his time to ensure the women he bedded in the past were withering from desire.

"Did I hurt you?" He could not fathom how he could have. Her passageway had been slick, accommodating him without resistance.

When she didn't respond, except to continue to shake. He forced himself to his elbows so he could look down at her regardless of the fact he very much wanted to play the coward and not face a woman's tears.

The last thing he expected to see was a Cheshire cat grin on her face. When he realized she was laughing, not a good thing to do to a guy at this particular moment, his jaw clenched tight, and his brows narrowed. Somehow, he found the strength to growl, "What is so funny?!"

That question brought on a harder bout of laughter from her. In fact, she snorted, and Mason had to once again remind himself she was like no other woman he had known. But that did not prevent him from simply not believing this was happening to him!

"Oh Mason," she snickered. "I'm sorry. I can't seem to help it. You were taking so long to get around to this part of it, I thought I was going to die. And to be quite honest, if you hadn't done this soon, I would have. But once you did, and you froze like that, thinking you hurt me, though I admit it was really sweet of you to think of my feelings, I just hadn't realized you were this big and well, it took me by surprise. That's all. I'm sorry, I laughed."

He stared at the lunatic he was falling in love with. "Stasia?" Mason's tone and smile were tight.

She managed to bring her laughter under control. "Yes, Mason?" she asked softly, searching his handsome face.

He lowered his mouth to hers until there was only a breath separating them. "Shut up," he whispered, lowering his mouth the rest of the way to hers.

She did, for a time. But once his artful hands and mouth stoked the burning flame within her, bringing out passions and feeling she never knew she possessed, she called out as their bodies reached a fevered pitch; reaching heights neither had soared before. She could not abide by his softly spoken command. His name tore from her lips as her body arched into his and a kaleidoscope of colors exploded behind her eyes

as she found the release she had never experienced before. And as she reached her bliss, that moment when bodies go tight and then liquid, Mason drove himself deeper into her as he found his own rapture.

There would never be another woman in his life except for this one, and he vowed to never let her go.

* * *

Later, as they lay entwined, cocooned in the mattress's softness, Mason gently stroked her hair and asked, "Stasia. What does the D stand for?"

She rested her cheek against his chest. "The D?" she asked and pretended not to know what he referred to.

"Do not play stupid, *chéri*. I have waited long enough to learn what M.D. really means."

"Could I claim amnesia?" she asked but said it in a suggestive tone.

"No."

"If I tell you, will you tell me what Hunter's phobia is?"

"No."

"I didn't think so," she grumbled.

He chuckled. "If I told you that secret, funny lady, and Hunter found out, I would not live to see another day." He gently pulled the hair at the nape of her neck, forcing her to look up at him. "Now, tell me."

"Divine," she answered with a grin as she raised up to kiss his chest. "Mason Divine."

For a moment, he stared at her. Then as the silliness of it struck him and knowing only she would have the gall to name such an ugly-looking mutt something like that, he felt laughter bubble up and released it.

"Hey," she scolded, swatting his chest. "I thought it was rather original myself, not to mention complementary considering his namesake is also French."

"But a poodle?" he cried, tears rolling down his face.

"Well," she huffed, sitting up and folding her arms across her breasts. "If you don't like the fact I chose a name very suiting to you, then pooh on you!"

"Pooh?" And he laughed all the harder.

"Divine as in, supremely good. Superb." Her tone turned seductive. "Heavenly, even." She leaned forward and kissed him. "Definitely heavenly."

His hand snaked out, and he pulled her down to him. "You are going to kill me, woman."

Her brow arched.

"I have already made love to you twice, and now I want to make love to you again."

"Is that so bad?" She asked, batting her eyes.

He flipped her onto her back, kissing her soundly, and then looked at her as though he were in serious thought. Finally, he spoke, and when he did, it was to say one word. "Spiders."

She looked at him as though he lost his mind. "Spiders?" she asked, wondering what on earth he was talking about.

"Spiders," he repeated. "Hunter has arachnophobia." He grinned at her still puzzled look. "He is frightened to death of spiders."

"Spiders?!" Her eyes widened with disbelief. "Hunter? Hunter, I'll kill anything that sneezes wrong, Hunter?" She chuckled. "You're joking."

He shook his head. "During his basic training, he used an outdoor toilet. However, there was a poisonous spider in there with him. It bit him on his penis. He was in the hospital for a week. He had an erection that

lasted for hours, but there was no pleasure from it. Ever since that day, when he sees a spider, he breaks into a sweat."

It was too unbelievable to believe. "Mason, you better make love to me before I break out in a long bout of laughter."

He did not need to be told twice.

Chapter twenty-seven

Daniela Lafayette was not in a good mood. But then, she hadn't had an incredibly wonderful vacation, either. To date, nothing but disaster had befallen her since setting foot on North Dakota's soil this year. As far as she was concerned, she would not care if she ever saw this blessed state again.

"Want to go for a walk?"

The, have you lost your mind? Look, she gave Wyatt Fisher was enough to cause the seventeen-year-old to flinch. "You are almost as funny as Hunter, Wyatt." She told him and pointed to her neon hot pink cast.

Wyatt sighed heavily before running a hand through his collar-length light brown hair. It was the same habit Hunter had, and noting the fact did nothing to appease Daniela's foul mood. Perhaps the only thing she had to be grateful for was the habit was where the similarities between the two brothers ended. Wyatt, although youthfully handsome in his own right, simply did not have the build or rugged male features that so captivated her all those months ago. Thank God. Otherwise, she would have probably given into her urge to hit him over the head with one of her crutches. At this point in her misguided vacation, she was ready to commit some form of mayhem. The question was, what. The, to whom was already answered since she was placing all the blame for her rotten luck at Hunter's feet. She was convinced it was his rudeness toward her that began the domino effect of misfortune tumbling down on her. The fact she was the one to knock that first domino over by telling him she planned to marry him in three years was irrelevant.

Wyatt squatted down beside the beach chair. "Okay. I chose the wrong words. You needn't snap my head off." He looked at her cast, propped up on another beach chair, then back to her face. "What I meant was,

why don't we blow this pop stand and go exploring? Since everyone else is fishing or water skiing, I thought you and I could do something together. I'm sure you've seen that old, weather-worn building down the road. It's actually a hundred-year-old farm-stead, and I thought you'd get a kick out of seeing the place close up." At her cocked brow, he hurried on. "I've already figured out a way to get you from here to there without your having to use your crutches to go the distance, so you can't use your broken leg as an excuse."

"Why would I want to look at some old house when I have already seen it?"

He smiled. "Why not? I realize you're having a real blast just sitting here doing nothing, but that place is kind of interesting. It's still in fairly good shape, considering how ancient it is. "Besides," his face took on a mysterious quality as he said, "I have something I want to show you."

The idea of having something to do rather than sit on the beach all day watching everyone else having fun in the sun was a pleasant thought. She very much liked the idea, so it didn't take long before she agreed to accompany him on his little adventure. In fact, he managed to bring forth a laugh from her once he showed her the solution to her inability to walk without the aid of crutches. He made a makeshift wheelchair, converting a wheelbarrow into something that could be used as a one passenger buggy.

He placed pillows within the metal contraption so they would cushion her ride. His thoughtfulness and willingness to help her achieve some form of fun eased her foul mood. She vowed to be more attentive to him during the rest of this vacation than she had been. It would be the least she could do considering he was the one to always seek out her company since this reunion began last week. If she had not been spending all her time mooning over Hunter, she would have noticed sooner that Wyatt had a very gentle spirit about him.

So, if Wyatt was so attentive and gentle with her, why couldn't she see him in any other light than that of a dear friend? She even admitted to

herself that it was sort of nice to have this Fisher being civil to her. Hunter certainly had not been kind. But the problem was her young heart still hung onto its fantasy that one day Hunter would lose his heart to her.

Not long after she and Wyatt arrived at the old homestead, located less than a fourth of a mile from the cabin, her fellow teen revealed his surprise. Spreading out the blanket he brought along and helping Daniela move to it, he reached into an old wooden crate and pulled out a baby gray-haired rabbit.

Squealing with delight, she took the soft animal into her hands and nuzzled it. "When did you find it?" she asked, stroking the fluff ball.

"The other day." He shrugged. "I'm keeping it in the box for now, but I'm thinking about bringing it back to the ranch with me when we go home on Friday."

"It is adorable," Daniela said and cooed to the thing.

"Daniela," Wyatt said, "I love you."

She froze. That had been an unexpected revelation, and it almost made her cry because it was the wrong Fisher proclaiming his love, damn it.

Unsure how to respond, she handed the rabbit back to him. "Wyatt," she licked her lips. "We have been friends since we were born, and although I am flattered, my heart belongs to someone else."

Wyatt put the rabbit back into the box, then glared at her. "You haven't talked about having a boyfriend back in France."

"He does not live in France."

"Yeah? Then where does he live?" Wyatt's voice snapped out, believing she was making this fantasy boyfriend up so she wouldn't have to tell him directly to his face she wasn't interested in him.

She shrugged because, honestly; she did not know where Hunter called home.

"Damn it, Daniela! You don't have to lie to me!"

"I am telling the truth!" Once those words left her mouth, she realized it was a half-truth. Her heart still belonged to another; he just was not her boyfriend.

"Yeah? Then what's the guy's name?"

"All right!" she snapped. "If you must know, I am in love with Hunter!"

"My brother?!" he boomed in a voice that hissed out disbelief.

She nodded.

The look on Wyatt's face resembled someone having just caught the scent of something offensive smelling. "For the love of Mike, Daniela! Have you lost your mind? He is eleven years older than you!"

"My parents have eleven years between them," she waved a hand to say that point was so trivial he shouldn't waste his breath arguing that point.

He extended his arms out to his sides. "Okay. Forget the age differ-ence."

"It never bothered me in the first place."

He ignored that statement. "How about the fact Hunter doesn't like you?"

The worst part about hearing the truth spoken out loud was having it cut through her heart like a hot knife, and there was not a way to prevent the tear that slipped past her eyes. "I did not expect you to understand," she whispered.

Her distress worked its way on Wyatt's gentle heart. There was far less bite when he continued. "My brother isn't exactly the marriageable kind of guy, Daniela. And I didn't mean he doesn't like you specifically. He's just not a very friendly person towards anyone, even on his best day. But have you forgotten what he does for America? Good god, it rips my

family apart, knowing he may never come back. Knowing this reunion might be the last time we see him at all for that matter, because if he dies out there," he waved his arm to indicate the world, "during an assignment, the government won't retrieve his body. And it will be Uncle Cadman who has to tell us the news." He shook his head. "Daniela, forget Hunter. It wouldn't be anything less than painful because of his job. Also, he vowed never to marry for that very reason. He doesn't want to leave a wife and kids behind to struggle through without him. Besides, the chances of any woman penetrating that thick iron wall he has around his heart is as unlikely to happen as Christ returning this very second!" He paused for a moment, proving his point. No bugle sounded, and Jesus Christ did not appear.

She wanted to say, where is your faith? But since she was lacking in that department herself, she skipped the question.

That last bit of information about Hunter's vow confirmed her suspicion about why he seemed to purposefully push people away. The statement he made last week to her, I don't need anyone boohooing over my grave, just before he'd spanked her, yet another crime against the beast, clearly made sense to her now.

She wondered if she dared quiz Wyatt for more information regarding his ill-tempered brother but thought better of it since she already hurt his feelings by rejecting his attraction to her. "I suppose you are right," she allowed, deciding there was no point carrying on this conversation any longer. The best thing to do was to change the subject. But she could not think of anything because she noticed movement outside of the building through the gaps in the exterior walls.

"Who is that?" She asked, then shifted uncomfortably on the blanket. The unknown person's large silhouette filled the opening that at one time had been the front door. She had no idea why she felt afraid, but she began looking around for some type of weapon.

Wyatt spun around the moment Daniela implied someone was outside and came face to face with one of the meanest looking, not to mention

largest men he had ever seen. "You lost, mister?" He asked and did not like the uneasy feeling that came over him.

"That depends." The man's deep voice stated.

"On what?" Wyatt asked, purposefully placing himself between Daniela and the stranger.

"You people know Hunter Fisher?"

"What do you want him for?" The moment he said it, Wyatt wanted to kick himself for having been so stupid. Everything about this man spoke of danger, and had he used his head, he should have realized he should not have disclosed knowing Hunter until after he discovered what the man wanted.

"My name is Danny Sharp," he informed them, then brought his left arm from behind his back; the police 9mm clenched in his fist, and he pointed it at Wyatt. An evil smile twisted his lips. "I want you to go get him for me. If you don't," he jerked his chin toward Daniela, "you can say goodbye to your girlfriend."

"Hunter isn't here!" Wyatt exclaimed, paling. He recognized the name and did not doubt for a moment the guy meant what he said.

Wyatt's distress was nothing compared to the ashen look on Daniela's face behind him.

"You've got one hour," Danny said. "After that, bye-bye, girlfriend." He motioned Wyatt out of the building with the gun. "Now, go!"

For the first time in his life, Wyatt regretted not being the fighter his brother was. There was absolutely nothing he could do but comply with the man's instructions, and he did. Faster than he thought himself capable of, he exited the structure with lightning speed.

Danny turned his attention to the young and very helpless girl trembling on the blanket before him. "You better hope your boyfriend finds the fisherman quick. I meant what I said." He pointed the gun at her head. "I'll pull the trigger if he's not here in an hour."

Shaking like a leaf, but not without a voice, she asked, "What, what do you want with Hunter?"

Danny's smile was grotesque. "I'm going to kill the son-of-a-bitch."

Despite her fear, Daniela could not help thinking about doing that same thing herself if she came out of this alive. Wretched man! He was responsible for every mishap to have befallen her, and now here was solid proof. She would not be in this situation if it was not for him, and in her anger, she hissed. "Good luck. I hope you do kill the ass!" Her eyes focused on the man standing before her, swallowed hard, and reversed her wish. Besides, she would rather have that pleasure herself.

Danny's eyes took on a puzzled look, not because of her words, but Daniela's accent pricked another memory. One involving a similar accent belonging to the other man who had been with Anastasia that night. And that reminder caused him more anger. "You any relation to that other man screwing my wife?"

Daniela stared and played dumb. "I do not know what you are talking about."

Danny grunted. "You must be related to that French fry. You're as stupid as he is."

Daniela doubted her brother had appreciated that slam. She also did not like the way this man was continuing to look at her. "Sir," she put forth the bravest voice she could muster, "if you know Hunter, then do you think it wise waiting for him to rearrange your face?"

"He already tried that, sweet thing. That's why I'm here." He moved closer. "Time to start counting. Times running out for you, little girl."

Daniela damned bravery and let loose with a terror-filled scream that felt as though it would rip her vocal cords from her throat.

* * *

A half an hour ago, a national guard helicopter landed one mile from Colten and Jacqueline's' lakeside home, dropping Hunter off where a

257

county sheriff's deputy waited for him. One minute later, the un-marked car was picking its way over a less traveled dirt road toward Hunter's parents' home. Twenty minutes after that and nearing the long-ago abandoned homestead, Hunter's eyes witnessed Wyatt exit the building as though Satan himself were in hot pursuit of his religious brother.

"Stop the car!" Hunter exclaimed, opening the passenger door before the vehicle had slowed.

Wyatt felt hope rise in his chest, seeing Hunter's form materializing from the car. Instantly he changed directions and reached the now stopped vehicle before Hunter had taken five steps. He did not have the endurance his brother had, and it took him a while before he caught his breath. "Danny- Shar-," he gasped, pointing through the trees concealing them from the old shack.

Hunter grabbed the front of his brother's t-shirt, jerking him forward. "What about him?" He growled, fearing the worst.

Wyatt's eyes rounded like saucers at seeing his brother's fury, knowing what he was capable of and fearing Hunter would pulverize him before he realized whom he was holding onto. "He's in there!" He cried, motioning with his hand. "He's got Daniela and…"

"What?!" Hunter's explosion set birds nestled in the trees to flight. He was thankful, ecstatic even, that it wasn't any member of his family, but triple damned pissed that once again, it was Mason's sister who needed rescuing. It was as though the girl was a walking magnet, attracting every possible means of danger to her.

Unbelievable!

"He, Sharp, Danny," Wyatt sputtered. "He told me I had one hour to get you there." He shook down to his toes, having never seen his brother this livid, and he wished, no, he prayed, Hunter would let go of his shirt, just in case, he needed to duck. "If I don't bring you by then, he's going to kill her."

"Goddamn it!" Hunter let go of his brother's shirt and almost considered letting the man do just that. It would certainly solve his headaches regarding the girl. But then, once this week was up, she would be on her way back to France, he'd be on his way to South America, and life would be fine dandy once more.

Praise the damn lord!

Wyatt stumbled back from that sudden though welcome release, and he also silently asked God to forgive his pigheaded brother for that direct line of blasphemy. "Well?" He asked, throwing in a forgive him father; he knows not what he does prayer because of Hunter's demonic facial expression. "Aren't you going to do something?"

Hunter's hands stilled in their labor of securing the ponytail at the nape of his neck. "I'm thinking about it!" He snapped.

Wyatt stared.

Brushing past his brother, Hunter began walking toward the run-down shack. As much as Daniela bugged the hell out of him, he was not that big of heel to actually want harm to come to her. "Get to the house, Wyatt." He threw over his shoulder. "Find everyone and let them know what's going on." He directed his next order to the deputy. "Radio the others. Tell them to get their asses here yesterday. After that, you keep my family inside the house until I say it's okay to come out!"

The terror-laced scream expelling from the rickety building sent Hunter into a full run. He reached the opening in less than a minute. "Sharp!" His voice boomed. Any sympathy he might have harbored for the man because of the injustice served him was forgotten as his eyes took in the scene before him.

Danny had a gun pressed against Daniela's temple, and she was sobbing uncontrollably.

At the sound of Hunter's voice, Danny turned, grabbed Daniela around the neck, and pressed her face firmly against his stomach as he

continued to push the 9 mm against her temple. "Back off, or I will kill her," Danny warned.

Hunter held his ground. "Thought you wanted to see me."

Danny forced Daniela to her feet by pulling her up with one beefy arm. "That was before I found a relation to the other man who's been screwing my wife." He cocked the gun. "Now, back off. Perhaps I will kill her instead."

There was no outward sign to reveal the panic raging war inside Hunter. This situation was almost beyond him. Not because he had never come up against someone as dangerous as Danny before; there had been plenty enough over the years. But this was the first time he knew, personally, the person counting on him to defuse the situation. It made his palms sweat, and he tried desperately to detach himself from all emotion. He knew that if he reacted on feelings rather than gut instincts, Daniela would have no hope of living past this day. This moment and so he forced himself to shrug indifferently and say, "Suit yourself."

The anguish filled gasp that tore from Daniela ripped at his heart. He wanted to reassure her he had not meant he did not care, but he forced himself not to look at her. He needed to watch Danny's eyes. Needed to concentrate. But the hell of it was, throughout this reunion, he had been doing everything in his power to get the girl to hate him, and now that she did, he could hear it in her voice as she sobbed and cursed him in French; he felt a twinge of guilt flood through his heart. He should have handled her infatuation totally different from what he had, and having finally achieved his intended goal, it left him feeling strangely empty inside.

A long silence, broken only by Daniela's heart-wrenching sobs, stretched between the two equally dangerous men. Hunter held his breath, amazed by what he witnessed in Danny's eyes, his face, and his actions. The man appeared to be listening to something, or someone

and, whoever that someone was, it controlled the deranged man's actions.

"You want me to kill her?" Danny asked suspiciously.

Again, Hunter shrugged. "Didn't say that Sharp. But since you came here to find me in the first place, why don't you and I have at it first? Remember the last time? Remember how I beat the crap out of you without breaking into a sweat?" He continued the baiting, drawing on Danny's fury toward him and hoping the man would become furious enough to forget about Daniela and come after him.

The ploy seemed to work when Danny exclaimed, "I was drunk!" The gun moved away from Daniela and leveled at Hunter's chest.

"But you're not now. Let's go outside. Think you can beat me now that you're sober?"

Silence. Hunter watched Danny listening to the unseen voice, wondering how a person dealt with someone who was not thinking for themselves.

"We think you should die now," Danny claimed matter-of-factly, his eyes looking at but not focusing on Hunter.

Daniela's horror-filled eyes watched as Danny's finger slowly began pulling back on the trigger. In the blink of an eye and despite her heart having been ripped into thousands of fragments by Hunter's final and most devastating rejection, she resolved to aid him in whatever way she could and only because unfortunately Hunter was her only way out of this building alive. If not for that, she would dearly love to see him die. He had already killed her.

With as much force as her slight frame could manage against someone as tall and heavily built as the man holding her, she pushed against Danny just as he pulled the trigger. The discharge was deafening. Her ears rang from being so close to the boom.

Her action saved Hunter's life, though. The bullet harmlessly embedded in the wood behind his left shoulder, and before Danny could comprehend the fact he missed, and why, Hunter was on the move.

Everything happened in a blur of movement—Hunter threw himself at Danny, knocking the bigger man to the ground. Miraculously, Daniela managed to avoid the collision, though pain shot through her broken leg as she put pressure on it to prevent herself from falling, which caused her to fall to the ground anyway. Sobbing and crying, she began crawling away from the two men locked in a struggle that, quite possibly, was to the death. She was not about to stay around to congratulate the victor. The only thing on her mind was to get the hell out of there.

Outside of the building, it took her a while to struggle to her feet. Placing her weight on her good leg, she began hopping away from the building as quickly as possible. The tears streaming down her face almost made it impossible to see where she was going. When arms wrapped around her, lifting her off her feet, she screamed anew.

"Sssh, I've got you, pumpkin," Cadman's voice soothed in her ear. "We'll get you back to the house. Your folks are there, waiting for you."

"Uncle Cadman!" she wailed, collapsing against him in her relief.

"Yes, pumpkin," he said, kissing her on the temple, then carried her to the sheriff's car that brought him to the scene.

At the house, Cadman carried her inside and placed her on the couch. Her parents rushed to her, wrapping her in their loving embrace. And as they soothed, assuring her and themselves, she was al-right, she cried out, "*Prendre moi maison*!" Burying her face in her mother's breast, she begged her parents to take her home. "Today! This minute!" She suffered enough ill-fortune to last her a lifetime and enough heartache to vow, at that moment, never again to love a man as she had, in her young girl's heart, loved Hunter.

Rosalinda stroked her daughter's hair as her own tears flowed down her cheeks and matched Daniela's unstoppable river. "We will leave as soon as possible," Rosalinda assured her, then turned to her husband.

"I will make the arrangements," Charles vowed, turning away to use the Fisher's phone. He would make sure that by this same time tomorrow, his precious little daughter would be sleeping safely in her own bed in Paris.

While Rosalinda and Charles comforted their daughter, the entire Fisher clan rushed outside, despite Cadman's and the deputy's protests. They wanted to see for themselves what was going on.

Eight people came to an abrupt halt once they reached the end of the driveway, and they saw the figure staggering toward them. If not for the fact they each knew him, knew that long golden-brown hair and muscular build, they would never have recognized him because of the amount of blood and bruises covering his face and body.

"Hunter!" Jacqueline screamed, running toward him.

He shook off his mother's hold, though it almost brought him to his knees; he was that weak. Christ, Danny certainly was not the wimp he had been the first time, and it had taken almost every ounce of his strength to finally knock the man out.

Colten stepped forward. "Sharp?" he asked, eyeing his son, and wondered if Hunter were about to drop.

Hunter's cut and swelling lip did not allow the smile to come easy. "He looks worse than I do. I knocked him out, finally. The officers on scene had to carry him to a cruiser. He's on his way back to Mandan."

"Honey," Jacqueline whispered, "You need to see a doctor-"

He cut her off. "Where's Daniela?" Hunter asked, swaying somewhat.

Colten backed up his wife. "Son, your mother's right. We need to take you to the hospital."

"Daniela!" Hunter snapped.

God! She saved his life, and he owed her for that. Owed her for having treated her so poorly all this time when she really had not deserved it. Saved him despite the fact she should have wanted nothing more than to have the pleasure of watching him die.

It loathed him to death, having witnessed her courage for a second time. The first having been when he pulled her from the bottom of that butte so the air ambulance could transport her to the Dickinson hospital. She gritted her teeth against her pain, and now he found himself respecting the little twirp.

Damn it to everlasting hell! How had that happened?

"She's in the house," Colten told him and stepped aside, knowing that when Hunter was determined, there was no reasoning with him.

It took him longer to get there than he would have liked. Longer still before he could gather the strength to walk the remaining distance to where she lay, curled in her mother's lap. So small. So fragile-looking, and yet she caused Danny's shot to go wild when she'd pushed against him.

There was no doubt in his mind she saved his life today.

Well, goddamn it; he was about to do the one thing he was not known to do often. He was going to apologize and hopefully explain to her he had not really meant to sound so indifferent regarding Danny's threat to kill her. He wanted her to know that, had he pleaded for her life, Danny would have killed her in that moment.

It took all his remaining strength to squat down on the balls of his feet before her. "Daniela," he croaked out.

Daniela's tears stopped instantly. Her body stiffened. "Go away!" she screamed.

Of course, he didn't. He never did what she asked.

"You… saved… my… life... and…"

She almost came off her mother's lap. "I had to!" She hissed, every ounce of her hatred for him coming through. "If he had killed you, you, you, son-of-a bitch," her parents both gasped at her choice of words, "I would not have been able to do this!" And before anyone, including Hunter, knew her intent, she balled her hand into a tight fist and socked him with all her might, right between the eyes.

If they had not seen it, no one would have believed it. Hunter's head snapped back. His already weak and spent body rolled, and he landed sprawled out on the floor; passed out to the world.

Daniela doubted she had ever felt better in her entire life.

"I'll be damned," Cadman said, staring at the unconscious man sprawled out before them. His twenty-six-year-old top fighter had just been knocked out by a sixteen-year-old girl that did not weigh over one hundred pounds.

Then he looked at Rosalinda and told her, "It would probably be a good thing for her not to be here when he wakes up."

"I will help you pack your things," Jacqueline said, knowing Cadman was probably right. Hunter would not be happy about having been knocked out by Daniela.

Chapter Twenty-eight

Two weeks passed before Hunter felt strong enough to do what he must. After the close brush with danger Danny placed his family in because of him, there was no doubt in his mind concerning what would be the best for them.

He had not expected them to understand, and they hadn't

His mother's tears, brought on by his announcement, almost ripped him apart. But it was for their safety, after all. There were too many people in the world who might try to seek revenge against him in the same manner Danny Sharp had if they began searching for him through his background. If his enemies found out where he was from, they could go after his family. And if those people could unearth information about him, then Pierre Bellefeuille could too. Jacqueline and Colten had stayed off that man's radar for almost thirty years, and Hunter would not lead the man to them.

He was never coming back.

Cadman, once back in Washington D.C., began erasing as much information about him as humanly possible. If anyone tried to find out who Hunter Sundance Fisher was, they would discover the man did not exist. The only copy of a birth certificate would be the one his mother had in his baby book. If something happened to it, a duplicate would not be an option. Cadman made sure of that. Erasing even that detail.

Hunter's resolve to cut all ties with his family left him feeling empty inside, but it could not be helped. He always had it in his mind to bring down Pierre Bellefeuille. Cadman had never gotten close enough in his days of searching for the man, but Hunter knew it was only a matter of time before he himself would bring Pierre to justice or die trying.

The fact Hunter had gotten close to Pierre's son during that mission allowed him to believe he would succeed where Cadman failed.

Hunter made one stop in Bismarck before heading his jeep east. That was to get a haircut. It was time to get serious in his quest.

Once his hair was no longer hanging past his shoulders, and he was on the highway heading east out of Bismarck, he drove with the radio tuned to a country-western station without really listening to it. His mind kept going back to Daniela. No matter how much of a pain in the ass she'd been, she hadn't deserved his treatment of her.

Too late to make amends. Not that it would matter. He wouldn't be seeing her again, either.

Fourteen miles outside of Bismarck, he saw the billboard. At any other time, he would have probably demolished the thing by hand. But now, all he did was ease the jeep to the shoulder of the road and stare at the enormous display, showcasing his face. The photo was the same one that stupid publication had taken, and now it was probably going to haunt him for the rest of his life.

The words, *Hunter Fisher-North Dakota's own pride and joy* were plastered above it, and a very bold and very black, *NOT*! Was stamped across the image sideways.

There was no doubt in his mind as to whom was responsible for that sign. There was only one person he knew foolhardy enough to have done it, without fearing whatever consequences there would have been.

Daniela.

Damn the little twirp to hell. Despite the odds, she sneaked into his heart without his realizing it until he saw the hatred he thought he wanted from her, radiate from those emerald green eyes of hers.

He sat parked along the shoulder of the road for at least ten minutes, not knowing if he should laugh or cry.

"Touché," he said with a sorrowful sigh, shifting his jeep into drive and said goodbye to North Dakota.

Chapter Twenty-nine

Leaning with his shoulder against the door frame, Mason watched silently as Anastasia sat in his study at his desk, typing away on the keyboard of the computer he purchased for her the day after the one spent in his bed. A glorious day of loving, sleeping, and sharing dreams.

That had been almost four weeks ago, and she still had no idea that it was safe for her to return to North Dakota. He had not told her. He couldn't. He was too afraid he would lose her. Too afraid to find out if she would return to Danny once she discovered the truth. That the accident the man suffered was the cause for the ninety-degree personality change.

He knew he had to tell her.

He had not thought it would be this hard. But then, he hadn't bargained on Danny's having been a victim himself, and now that a surgeon had removed the scar tissue, easing the pressure on his brain, it was likely he would once again be the man Anastasia had fallen in love with before the explosion. He would be at the VA hospital in North Dakota for months while he recovered. Not only because of surgery, but he was receiving counseling for the trauma he suffered upon discovering everything he'd done over the past two years, especially what he'd done to Anastasia.

Would she go back to him?

Mason continued to watch her type. His heart ached. No. It did not ache. It hurt like hell because if she left him…

He could not lose her! She made his life complete. His home felt as though it truly was a home for the first time since he purchased it two years ago. God, it felt wonderful to come home after taping a talk show or after filming a guest appearance on a television series. Or after

spending hours posing for book covers. Coming home to Anastasia's bright smile and warm embrace was the highlight of his day. And whenever she smiled that Cheshire Cat grin of hers, he knew he would find himself laughing over some insane thing she'd done.

Like the day he invited friends over, and she appointed herself guardian over the children. The adults walked into the kitchen to raid the refrigerator and discovered Anastasia having a colored macaroni and cheese party with the kids. They were on a blanket laid out on the kitchen floor enjoying a colorful feast unlike any the adults had seen before.

With the aid of food coloring, she tinted the pasta blue, the butter for the bread red, and the beverage, which was milk, black. When she saw the adults, she looked up at them and said in a natural helium sounding voice, "Oh no! The grownups have discovered our hiding place!" And she grinned that grin at him. The children laughed hysterically. His friends gaped, and he joined her on the blanket because she coaxed him there.

She just had a way of making him do things he never envisioned himself taking part in before.

Anastasia loved children. He wanted her to have his.

How would he survive if she went back to Danny?

She had no idea he was standing behind her. He hadn't announced his arrival, and because that stupid mutt of hers was not in the house for a change, it hadn't yapped and alerted her to his presence. It was outside, with his dogs running wild over the estate grounds. It still amazed him that M.D. -he refused to call it Mason Divine- had been accepted by his six Great Dane's as though it were their long-lost brother.

Mason almost hated having to break the spell he was in. He enjoyed watching her when she was unaware of him being there. The way she would sometimes talk to herself while working at the computer, putting together the romance story she was writing often caused him to chuckle.

She would pull at her hair, glare at the screen, and exclaim, "Oh, that is just too stupid for words!" Before deleting the entire paragraph, to begin anew.

She wanted to be a romance author. Why it surprised him, when by now nothing the woman did should catch him off guard anymore, he did not know. But when she confessed the one dream that kept her going, kept her from buckling in when her world was falling apart, he encouraged her; offering to help her secure a contract with Citnamor Books.

She'd flat out refused that offer, saying she would welcome his help with being put in touch with the right people who could review her work, but that was the only help she wanted from him. "I want to make it because I have talent, Mason," she'd told him. "Not because of what you can do for me. That wouldn't be right, and I would never use you for selfish gain."

If he had not known he loved her before that statement, he would have known it then. She had a quality about her that set her apart from the other women he had been with, and the thought of having to give that up if she went back to Danny caused him agonizing grief.

He would die a thousand deaths before he let her go. "Stasia."

His single spoken word, though voiced gently, caused her to jerk. She let out a yelp, jumped from the chair, and exclaimed, "Don't do that!" As her hand flew to her chest and her blue eyes locked on him leaning against the door frame.

His mouth twitched as he fought a laugh. "What?" He asked innocently, pushing away from the door. His eyes watched as her breasts rose and fell under the low-cut blouse because of heavy, frightened-out-of-her-wits breathing. All thoughts of telling her what he should have weeks ago went right out of his head, replaced by his ever-present desire for her body.

"What?!" She snapped, eyes flaring. "Mason Lafayette. Don't you dare stand there and deny the fact you almost gave me heart failure!"

He shrugged. "Did I?" He walked forward until his shoes touched the fronts of her ever-present tiger faced slippers. With the tip of a finger, he trailed a light path down her face before caressing her cheek. "Do you need me to give you mouth-to-mouth, *chéri*?"

That huskily spoken endearment, combined with the gentle stroking of his fingers, worked their magic on her. She closed her eyes and pressed her cheek into his palm; her hands came up to embrace his waist. "I think so," she sighed, answering his question.

She felt his mouth-to-mouth all the way to her toes.

"How is the story going?" He inquired softly, trailing kisses down her throat until he buried his face in the curve of her neck.

"Story?" Lord, he had a way of causing her to forget everything except for his touch.

His hands worked at tugging her blouse out from her jeans. "Yes. The story." He made quick work of unbuttoning the blouse. Faster still was the speed with which he unhooked the bra that opened from the front and captured the weight of one breast, stroking the nipple with the pad of his thumb. "I need to know if Bonnie and Raymond have reconciled their differences yet." He lowered his head, replaced the thumb with his tongue, circling the dark nub, then claimed it with his mouth.

Anastasia's eyes flew open upon hearing the hero and heroin's names in her romance novel come out of his mouth. "Mason!" She screeched, pulling away. With hands on her hips, she exclaimed, "You've been reading my story!"

His grin was devilish, and he liked the way her breasts were displayed for him. He doubted she remembered her state of undress. "Would I do that, *chéri*?" He asked innocently.

She shook her finger at him. "Don't you *chéri* me, you peeping tom!" She exclaimed.

Unconsciously, Mason licked his lips as her finger shaking caused her breasts to bounce. His groin already ached to be inside her, and this juggling thing was pure torture. "Yes," he confessed, stepping toward her. "I have been reading your story at night after you have gone to sleep." At her gasp, he grinned, and it was damn near a perfect imitation of her Cheshire cat grin. "It is very good. I especially liked the first sex scene when Raymond made love to Bonnie on the winding staircase." His brows wiggled knowingly. "It seemed familiar and," his green eyes sparkled, "was it really one of the best orgasms she ever had?"

Anastasia's face turned redder than it had been in her entire life. Her eyes dropped to the black silk shirt stretched over the wide chest mere inches away, unable to meet that direct look. She never dreamed he would read that stolen idea of his, and her face burned with the memory of his making love to her on the staircase leading to the mansion's third floor. "I'm sure I don't know what you're talking about," she sing-songed, stepping back.

Mason followed Anastasia's retreat, not stopping his forward move-ment until he had her pressed against the wall and had nowhere else to go. "No?" his eyes danced with amusement. "Then, perhaps we should try something else, so you can use it to compare with that woman's ex-perience." He placed both hands on the wall, level with her face. "Any ideas?"

And she thought she'd blushed scarlet before? "No," she whispered in a voice sounding very much like a half peep. Every fiber of her being became aware of him and her throat went dry, wondering what his idea was and loving him for wanting her.

She wanted him to always want her. She wanted to be with him for-ever. But, although he treated her with gentleness, made love to her as though he worshipped her, he never told her he loved her and those un-spoken words prevented her from voicing what she felt inside. Pre-vented her from believing that he would miss her once this fairy tale was over.

"Take off your clothes, Anastasia," he whispered, bringing her out from her sad thoughts.

"Here?" her eyes snapped up and came face-to-face with that sensual smile of his that caused her to experience butterflies in her stomach.

"Here."

That one word, containing a husky promise, had her complying to the demand, though not with complete ease. Modesty had nothing to do with it and everything to do with the fact he had not stepped back enough to allow her much space. The whole thing was quite arousing to her.

Stripping under his watchful eye, forced to brush against him to remove her jeans, the leather of his skintight black pants felt cool against her heating body. His black-silk shirt seemed to grow fingers of its own when her larger than average breasts brushed against it.

Once all her clothes lay in a pile at her feet, she chanced a look at him and almost gasped at the smoldering depths watching her.

"Take your hair down," was his next command.

She had put her hair into a bun while she worked on her story to keep it out of the way, but now, for him, she removed all the hairpins securing the style in place. Once lose, it cascaded over her shoulders and lay across her breasts.

That was when Mason finally moved, and even then, he did not remove his hands from the wall but merely lowered his head to suckle her breast through the thick mass of her hair.

Anastasia groaned and wrapped her arms around his head, stroking his own long locks as she held him to her. The man definitely had a thing for her ample bosom, which was fine with her. She certainly liked the sensation his lips and tongue caused her there. She had never known how sensitive she was in that area until Mason made her aware of it, often.

"Do you want me?" He asked, moving from one breast to search out its twin.

"Yes," she told him as her breathing became labored, and her desire increased.

He reached up to capture one of her hands and forced it down between them. "Then set me free and hold me tight."

Without taking her eyes off of his, she slowly unzipped his pants and did what he asked.

When she touched him, holding his rock-hard member firmly in her palm, his hips arched forward, and he hissed, "Oh, God!"

He stepped back, grabbed her wrist, and pulled her with him to the desk he used now and then for his correspondence, and with one sweep of his hand, he pushed everything on it onto the floor. Bending her over it, he forced her legs apart, and in one solid thrust, he was inside her.

Anastasia's eyes rolled back as her hands reached out to grab ahold of the back of the desk. The sensation of him being fully clothed while she was completely naked and his large, swollen member throbbed and moved inside her, was so erotically sensual she reached her climax within moments.

When she cried out her pleasure, he pulled out, turned her around, lifted her up, and lay her down on top of it so he could watch her come the next time. But he was not finished with her yet. He brought her legs up, keeping them spread wide as he once again thrust into her.

Using his hands to wrap her legs around his waist, and without stopping his hips from continuing to pump into her, he leaned in and whispered words in her ear she did not understand because he spoke in French.

This time when she came, calling out his name, he joined her in the rapturous splendor.

And in her mind, once she could think again, she knew there was going to be a nice reconciliation between Raymond and Bonnie. Of that, there was no doubt.

Chapter Thirty

Forty-five minutes later, after they showered and dressed, Mason led her into the living room and told her the news about Danny.

"Excuse me?" Anastasia stared, disbelieving, as he moved to join her on the plush white couch setting off center in his massive living room. She did not bother hiding the confused look on her face, though she kept telling herself her ears were playing tricks on her. He could not have possibly said, "Danny has been in custody for almost four weeks?"

Mason nodded, bringing his right ankle up to rest on his left knee. "Yes," he admitted, feeling a twinge of guilt for not having told her sooner and wishing... Wishing for what? For her to tell him, she loved him? Wishing Danny was still a threat? More than anything, he wished he wouldn't lose her.

He kept trying to find the courage to tell her he loved her. However, the knowledge of her sharing with him how much she had loved Danny before he turned violent prevented him from speaking his heart. He had no reason to doubt she would run back to the man she had married. She was that sort of one-man woman he always longed for, and surely, she would want to help Danny through his recovery.

A small selfish part of him wished Hunter had killed the man. If he had, then she would not reject the words he longed to tell her.

He loved her. Loved her more than life, but there was no way he would verbalize his feelings. To say them, only to have her reject them, would devastate him to the core.

"When did you find out?" Anastasia asked, her eyes narrowing. Why had he kept this from her? Why?

"Cadman called the day after we arrived here."

She gasped. "You've known all this time, and yet you didn't tell me?!" She was more than shocked. "Then why am I still here?"

Mason winced at hearing that question, no matter how much he prepared himself for it. It still cut through him. "You… wish to go home?" His voice sounded hollow to his own ears and echoed the hollowness of his heart perfectly.

"Of course, I do!" She exclaimed, missing the pain reflected on Mason's face because she chose that moment to stand and look away from him. "I have a business to run." She kept her eyes averted, unable to face him just then. Why hadn't he told her about Danny? And why, why couldn't he love her even a little bit?

She almost broke into tears, wanting to fall on her knees and beg him to tell her to stay. God, she loved him with all her heart, more than she had ever loved Danny. But if he did not ask her to stay-

Oh, she had known what would happen to her heart if she slept with him, but she did it anyway, and now her chest felt tight and her heart broken. She wanted to confess her love but knew she would never survive if Mason's feelings for her went no farther than the fun they shared and the blissful passion that was addicting.

And yes. That made her a coward.

Sometimes she thought she caught him looking at her with tenderness in his eyes. Times when she almost believed he might love her. But he had not spoken the words she longed to hear, and that caused her to suspect she was only a distraction to him. After all, why would a man who could have any woman in the world want her? She was not famous. She had no wealth. What could she possibly bring to his life that he did not already have?

The thought of him making love to another woman with the same passion they shared twisted her heart. God. She could never look at another photo of him again without remembering this time with him and

wondering about the faceless woman who would be next in line to share his bed.

The pain in her heart was so real, it became physical. She needed to know! Needed to know if she should cling to her dreams or watch them disappear as so many others had.

"Is there any reason I should stay?" There! She asked, but how she managed to sound indifferent when the pounding of her heart was beating in her ears from this moment of truth, she would never know.

Mason felt as though a part of him just died. She asked so casually there was nothing left for him to say but, "I guess not," and knew he lost her.

Rubbing his chest, he stood. "I will phone the airport," he told her, surprised his voice had not broken. All he wanted was for her to tell him she loved him and that she wanted to stay. But she acted as though she could not care less, one way or the other, and he would not beg. He still had some pride left.

He walked from the room, damning her to hell for taking his heart and throwing it away.

Anastasia's moisture-filled eyes watched him leave the room, and she fought the urge to call him back. This had been a dream, after all. His entering her life when reality said such a thing was not possible could only end this way. She was given the chance to touch the moon, live out a fantasy, and now it was time to wake up and go forward in life.

The problem with that was, she was still a dreamer, and, like anyone else who was experiencing a wonderful fantasy, she did not want to wake up. Part of her wanted to believe her hope for a future with Mason was still possible, and maybe, just maybe, fairy tales could come true.

The idea popped into her mind, and she knew what she needed to do. Saying the words out loud was impossible, but she was a writer, after all.

Raymond and Bonnie had another scene that needed to be written before she was no longer here.

* * *

"Sweetie, are you all right?" Gale asked, sitting on the couch in Anastasia's small living room, concern evident on her face as she watched the woman sitting across from her.

"I'm fine," Anastasia turned the pages of the winter edition of the home shopping magazine Gale was so fond of.

"You don't sound fine."

Anastasia's head snapped up. "Do you want my help picking out a new dress for Christmas, Gale?" She asked, raising a brow. The season for Christmas was still over three months away, but the buy early sale the publication was having brought Gale storming into the house with all the excitement of a child making out their I want list.

Gale never heeded those warning looks in the past and didn't now. "Why don't you call him?"

"Who?" Anastasia's eyes fell back to the wish book, not wanting to think about the who Gale was talking about. If she didn't think about him, there was still a chance her plan would work. If she didn't think about it, she wouldn't have to face reality.

He hadn't called, and she did not want to acknowledge it was because he truly did not love her after all.

"You know who, young lady!" Gale tisked. "You've been back for three weeks and I'm worried about you!"

"I'm fine."

Gale threw her hands in the air as testimony to her frustration. "You keep saying that, but it's not true! You've cut back at work, and you don't talk about that novel of yours anymore..."

Once again, Anastasia's head snapped up. "Gale, you know I'm selling my salon to Nan and Tricia. Ever since the government was so kind," she said with a sneer, "to pay off all the hospital bills, that's one monkey off my back. And since they were in such a generous mood, they also gave me a tidy sum for my inconvenience," she snorted in disgust. "So there really isn't any need for me to work for a little while. And as far as my novel," she shrugged. "Maybe I've given up dreaming and became a member of the real world just like you requested so long ago." Yuck! What a bleak thought.

"Oh, really? And just how do you think you would like reality?"

Anastasia sighed willfully. "It would suck."

Gale could not prevent the laugh. "Now we're getting somewhere!" She exclaimed. "That sounds like the Stasia I know." She shifted on the sofa and noted that the calendar that once hung on the wall was no longer there but did not comment about it. "Does this mean you're going to call him?"

"No."

"No?!"

"He knows where to find me."

These brief answers of hers were wearing on Gale's nerves. "Have I told you recently that you are one of the most stubborn women I know?"

"Yep."

"Anastasia..."

"Drop the subject, Gale." This time, she did not leave any doubt that she meant it.

Had it really been three weeks since she arrived at the Bismarck airport and two government officials were waiting for her to explain what caused Danny's personality change? She wept for days after hearing that. All the heartache and pain she suffered could have been prevented

if they listened to her pleads in the beginning and Danny… She had been brokenhearted over what he was having to face now that he had undergone surgery and was in his right mind.

To say she had been stunned would be a grotesque understatement, and when she asked who she could thank for finely opening her country's eyes to the situation, they'd so conveniently swept under the rug, when she had received no response, the two men shifted uncomfortably before saying, "That's classified information, ma'am."

She suspected Hunter and his boss, Cadman Benson, had a hand in turning the tables for her. But she thanked the two men, then told them to give a message to the ones responsible for allowing Danny to endure the agony he had. She doubted the two men would have delivered the message word-for-word. In fact, she had been shocked that she knew that many foul words.

She ached for Danny. For what he went through and the long process of healing ahead of him. But that was as far as she could go. She could not bring herself to the point of visiting him at the V.A. hospital. However, she had written him a lengthy letter that told him she wished him peace and hoped he would go on with his life, as she was going on with hers. As far as wanting to hear from him, see him, she could not do it. It was too soon for that. Perhaps one day, but not anywhere in the near future.

Gale asked why she no longer talked about her novel. Well, right now, she did not feel like telling the whole truth. She wasn't working on it because she left the two disks containing her manuscript, accidentally, of course, in Mason's study, next to the computer.

Had he bothered to read any more of the story he so blatantly confessed to having been following? If so, had he understood the message? Or did he care at all?

She shook her head, telling herself to stop trying to hold on to something that obviously was not there. To put an end to this ridiculous daydreaming once and for all.

A bell sounded, interrupting her thoughts, and once she realized it was the front doorbell, she glanced at Gale. "Would you get that? I'm not in the mood for any more company." Her eyes dropped back to the wish book as Gale complied with her request.

"Stasia?" Gale said from the doorway, and when Anastasia turned her head, she was graced with a perplexed look on her friend's face. "Could you come here a minute? There's a huge package for you out here."

Anastasia's brows drew together, and she moved from the living room to the front door. "I didn't order anything," she claimed, knowing it for the truth. She stopped short upon seeing the almost seven-foot-tall crate resting on her sidewalk. "What in the world?!" She exclaimed as her eyes flew to the man standing next to Gale.

"Anastasia Sharp?" The man asked. At her bewildered nod, he extended his hand. "My name is Josh Reno," he explained, giving her hand a firm shake before releasing it. "I am the president and CEO of Country Specialties magazine."

Anastasia's eyes collided with Gale's equally confused ones. They both wondered why the president of Gale's favorite home shopping magazine would be on her doorstep. "I don't understand," Anastasia admitted, thinking that had to be the understatement of the year.

Josh smiled. "Well, a few months back, you ordered something from our summer issue."

Anastasia's gasp was nothing compared to Gale's sharp intake of breath.

"That was a joke!" Anastasia exclaimed, horrified. Her eyes snapped to the large crate. This could not be what it appeared to be. No way. They could not have possibly taken her seriously. If nothing else, they decided to play along with her little game and deliver her a male mannequin.

At least, she hoped that was all it was.

Josh chuckled and patted her arm. "Perhaps it was, but we try to satisfy our customers. I'm sorry it took longer than our average delivery time, but we had trouble filling your order. You see," he winked, "We were out of stock." He laughed at his own joke before leading her to the crate. "However, we came up with a replacement."

This is not happening, Anastasia assured herself, eyes glued to the crate as Josh moved to open it.

"Of course," the man said matter-of-fact, "our satisfaction guarantee applies." With that, he pulled a lever, and the crate door swung open on its hinges.

Anastasia's heart slammed against her chest, unable to move as her eyes focused on the crate's contents.

"*Bonjour, chéri,*" he said, stepping from the place that had hidden him from view, extending a single red rose toward her. "I hope it does not disappoint you that I am not the model you sent for." His lips turned into that sensual smile of his that always melted her to puddles.

A sob tore from her throat, and her body raced forward. "Mason!" She cried, wrapping her arms around his strong neck, clinging to him as though he were her anchor, for indeed, she felt herself drifting upon waves of unspeakable joy.

"Does this mean you are satisfied with your replacement model?" He wiggled his right hand out from between them, encircling her with his arms, and pulled her tight against his tall frame. His gaze fell to his hand, the one he had just freed. The one holding the rose and damned if the thing's delicate petals hadn't been squashed between them before he thought to rescue it.

With a smile, he tossed the stem with its crushed fragrant bulb over his shoulder and made a mental note to give up purchasing flowers for her if she was always going to damage them.

Luckily, there wasn't anyone standing in the way of the scented missile, as there had been the last time.

Anastasia laughed at the memory. "How did you find out about my crazy order?" She asked. "I never told you about that!"

Mason grinned, then confessed to having known about it since the day they first met. "And, after I read the last pages of your novel, I called Josh, and we came up with this delivery idea."

She beamed him a smile. "You understood the message?"

Mason reached up, touched her cheek with his palm. "Dear heart, I would be here, regardless of what you wrote. I love you beyond reason. I was going insane, not having you with me."

Her heart soared. "Then why did you wait so long to get here? I was beginning to think you had forgotten about me."

He brushed his lips against hers. "You, *chéri*, are unforgettable, and I waited only because I wanted to surprise you."

"And you read the last chapter?"

He chuckled. "Oh, that is not the last chapter, funny lady. Your story does not end when Raymond and Bonnie part ways because they are both too afraid to voice what is in their hearts." He placed both of his hands on either side of her face and told her, "It continues on after they become man and wife."

She searched his eyes. Did she dare hope?

"I love you, funny lady. Marry me."

Anastasia felt her heart contract. At last! Finely! Dreams did come true! "I love you too," she whispered against his lips and wept with over-flowing joy.

"Then, you will marry me?"

She brushed at her tears and smiled up at him with that Cheshire cat grin. "And give up all this luxury?" She swept a hand toward her small house.

He grinned. "It is the price you must pay if you wish to discover new things."

"New things?" She asked puzzled. But when he whispered in her ear, the kinds of discoveries he had in mind, she blushed anew. "Well," she cleared her throat, "I suppose I can endure." The swat he gave her back-side caused her to yelp and laugh. "Yes, you wonderful man. I will marry you!"

They sealed the agreement with a heated kiss, both oblivious to the two people grinning ear-to-ear behind them. Josh and Gale both doubted those two were going to be leaving New Salem anytime soon.

And they were right.

Epilogue

Bismarck, North Dakota
Two years later

A crowd jammed the Kirkwood Mall this Saturday afternoon. Events, such as this one taking place outside Gale's Dakota Land Book Store, were relatively unheard of in this part of the country. The fact that one of North Dakota's own was the cause of the unique happening brought the Capital city's population out by the droves. Everyone wanted the chance to glimpse the dreamer from New Salem who reached for the stars; her fantasies turned true. Others waited patiently in long lines, awaiting their moment to speak to the author whose last three books were still on the bestsellers list.

"We're getting closer," one woman commented, stretching her neck to see past the shoulder of the tall man in front of her.

"I can hardly wait!" Her friend exclaimed. "I've read every one of her books. She makes me laugh." Then she sighed. "And she definitely knows how to write a love scene."

"Do tell," some old guy piped up.

The two friends ignored him.

"Well," the first woman said, "with him for a husband, would you expect anything less?"

The two women sighed dreamily, lost in their own fantasies over the man whose image exclusively graced the covers of his wife's romantic tales. The only other professional shots he posed for now were the posters and yearly calendars, a percentage of the sales going to a foundation for battered women and abused children the couple was involved with. This year's poster was quite the collectors' item for fans of both

husband and wife. It featured both of them in a sweet embrace, with the husband nuzzling his wife's neck. For the first time, his face was hidden from the camera, but it made the pose even more romantic for the women who knew what he looked like.

Not only was the photo made to help fund the abuse center her husband worked with in California, having retired from his modeling career, but it was also the cover of Anastasia Lafayette's newest romance entitled, *The Dreamer*.

"I hope he shows up," a third woman spoke up. "It's his autograph I want."

A male teenager they could not see drolled, "Oh, brother."

"Personally," the tall man standing in front of them said, turning around to face the two women, "I'm here to get her autograph and," he grinned, "invite them to dine with me and my fiancé."

"Good luck with that. You're crazy if you believe they would take you up on that offer," the bolder of the two women snorted.

The man shrugged. "I was crazy for a time. But I've been given my life back, and I owe that woman and that man's friend more than I'll ever be able to repay."

The moment the guy turned away from them, the two women rolled their eyes, thinking he was still crazy, whoever he was.

At the front of the line, Gale Martin very much resembled a chicken with its head cut off. The bookstore she and her husband opened last year had never been this busy. She was almost beside herself with the overflow of people and trying to keep up with sales, and keep her eye on the very stubborn, and very pregnant woman sitting at the table in front of her store, greeting people, and signing autographs when she ought to be at home, in bed!

Anastasia signed her name to the inside cover of her newest release, handed it back to the smiling woman with a grin of her own and a

sincere "Thank you" and "Enjoy" before watching her move away. It gave her a few seconds to reach down to gently massage her large stomach, then shift in the chair, trying to ease the increasing backache and knowing she should confess what was happening, but wanting to greet as many people as possible because her fans were so important to her. She enjoyed making someone's day brighter, and the best way she had found to do that was by holding these book signing fairs.

So, she forced herself to stay put, telling herself just a few more signatures before she called it quits, and hoped Mason's flight from New York, where he was doing a public appearance of his own to speak at a convention raising money for the Children's Miracle Network, hadn't been delayed.

A murmur began in the crowd, and even before someone shouted the ever famous, there he is! Anastasia knew her husband had arrived, and she breathed a sigh of relief.

Knowing it would take a while before he could make it through the crowd, having to stop and sign his own name for the ones who were his devoted fans, she turned her attention to the next person in line and froze.

"Hi, Stasia."

She stared. "Danny!" It came out a whisper. She had not seen him since the day Hunter arrived at her home in New Salem all those years ago and prevented him from doing whatever he would have that night.

He didn't smile. He looked nervous himself. "If you're not comfortable with this", he held out his copy of The Dreamer, "Mrs. Lafayette, I'll leave."

She felt her heart squeeze. She loved this man once upon a time. Had tried to stand by and get him help when none was given. A great injustice had been done to him, to her.

She knew he was a free man. He had not had to spend time in jail because of the death of the innocent police officer because the

government took full responsibility for their part in his violent actions, declaring him innocent of the murder because he had not been in control of his actions.

But it was still a shock, seeing him standing in front of her.

Danny tucked the book back under his arm. "I understand, Anastasia," he told her softly, painfully. "I can't blame you." He turned to go.

"Danny, wait." It was the hardest thing she had ever done. "I'll... I'll sign your book."

He turned back, but there still was no smile on his face, even when he handed her the book. "I'm sorry," he whispered brokenly.

She shook her head. "Don't." God, not now. Not when there were hundreds of people around, and she could easily break into tears. He had lost all the extra weight he had gained after his discharge from the Marines and was now just as trim and handsome as he had been the night they'd first met in that bar. She was not sad because they were no longer together. Never that, for she would never give up what she shared with Mason. But the unfairness they both endured still made her angry.

He nodded stiffly. "I'm getting married," When her head snapped up from signing his copy of the book, he explained. "She was my nurse at the V.A. hospital."

Anastasia managed a smile, gladness in her heart that he was making a new life for himself. "Then, I wish you all the happiness and joy this life can bring," she told him and meant it. He deserved a second chance, too.

He took the book when she handed it back. For a long moment, he just looked at her. "I was going to invite you and your husband to dine with my fiancé and me, but I don't think we're ready for that. Maybe one day."

A sudden cramp stole her breath away momentarily. She was not sure how much longer she could continue pretending she wasn't in labor, but

if these cramps became any harder, she would spare no one's ears if she screamed.

Once the pain passed, she took a deep breath before focusing back on Danny. "Maybe," she offered. She was the last person on earth who would say something couldn't happen. After all, people used to tell her she was a dreamer, and look where it had gotten her.

"That's good enough," Danny said, then added, "Have a happy life, Stasia."

She watched him walk away. "You too," she whispered, then felt the familiar and welcome weight of Mason's hand on her shoulder. She turned to smile up at him, but that scowl on his face kept the grin at bay.

"Was that who I think it was, *chéri?*" He asked, almost cautiously.

"Yes," she managed but spoke the word as though she had sucked it in rather than out as another cramp took hold. Once it passed, she said, "He just wanted to wish me a happy life." Now she did grin, "Have I ever told you how handsome you are when you scowl like that?" It was true, but right now, she was trying to take a detour around the question she knew was coming her way.

No such luck in that department.

Mason claimed the chair next to her, oblivious to the people around him as his eyes scanned her face. "Are you all right?"

There were two meanings to that question, and she knew it. "Regarding seeing Danny, I'm fine." The next cramp caused her eyes to cross.

"*Chéri,*" his brows narrowed, and his green eyes darkened, "If you are fine, why are you gracing me with all these funny expressions?"

"To make you laugh?" She suggested.

He shook his head, not buying it. "Try again."

"Well, how would you feel about your... Son being born... right here... in front... of... Gale's store?" Mason had insisted they discover

the child's sex before the birth because he hadn't wanted any surprises, saying he had enough of them with her as his wife already.

Blasted man. He took all the fun out of it.

The dark apricot tan left his face upon hearing that question. "Tell me you are joking!"

"I wish I could." She gave him that Cheshire cat grin, warning him before she confessed. Leaning toward him, she whispered in his ear, "My water just broke."

His green eyes flew down, saw the truth to her words, and his expression turned past pale. Sickly would be close to the way he was looking right then. "Gale!" His voice boomed above the buzz of the crowd. "Call an ambulance! She is in labor!"

That announcement brought a round of applause and whistles from the crowd.

Mason's ashen face turned to his wife. "Do not do this to me, madame wife!"

She shrugged. "Don't look at me! Talk to your son. He's the one who wants to be born a mall shopper." She giggled, thinking that maybe she just might have the last laugh on him after all. No surprises, he had said, well, this was a whopper of the unexpected.

"This is not funny!"

She patted his arm sympathetically. "There, there. Don't tell me you believed for one moment that I, your *drôle de dame*, would do things the normal way?"

"I had hoped!" He exclaimed, finding absolutely nothing funny about this situation. He had not wanted her to leave California this close to her delivery date, but no. She insisted on flying here to do this promotion, saying she wanted time to visit with Gale.

Fool woman! If this was her way of getting back at him for insisting they discover the child's sex before it was born…

God! He could not believe this was happening!

* * *

The ambulance arrived just in time for paramedics to deliver the Lafayette's first child, which was the one and only thing Mason had to be thankful for. He had almost fainted when it looked as though he was going to have to do it, with Gale yelling to him instructions as she spoke to the 911 operator. But once the child, his son, arrived, he breathed easier and even forgave his displaced humor-filled wife: until the paramedics placed Anastasia on the gurney to transport mother and son to the hospital. Someone from the crowd, who helped form the human wall that had given them at least some form of privacy during the birth asked, "What are you going to name him?"

Anastasia giggled weakly and called out as loudly as her weary body would allow. "M.B.!"

Mason gaped. "We agreed upon a name months ago," he reminded her firmly.

"I changed my mind."

"Oh? And pray, tell. What does M.B. stand for?"

"My baby!" She laughed.

He shook his head. "Anastasia," he warned.

She cocked a brow. "How about Mason's boy?"

"No."

"Mall baby?"

"No!"

"Then we'll switch it around. Call him B.M. for Bismarck mall."

"No!" he exclaimed in a frustrated laugh.

The debate continued throughout the ride to one of the local hospitals. In the end, Mason won the battle, and they named their firstborn Dakota Hunter Lafayette, although Anastasia threatened to call the baby D.H. for Definitely Heaven sent.

The end

Keep reading for a sample of Eagle's Wolf.

About the author

J.R. Zimmer is Badlanders Press bestselling author of the Fisher/Lafayette Saga. The first book in the series was born from her enchantment with the historical figures Antoine-Amdée-Marie-Vincent Manca de Vallom-brosa, the Marquis de Morès, and his wife, Medora while visiting the historical town of Medora, North Dakota. You can visit her online at www.jrzimmer.com, http://facebook.com/authorjrzimmer, email: jrzimmer17@yahoo.com.

Eagle's Wolf

by J.R. Zimmer

Book seven
Fisher/Lafayette Saga

Badlanders Press

CHAPTER ONE

Rio de Janeiro
1996

His name wasn't Jack, but that's what everyone called him. He received the nickname years ago when he'd been twenty and began working for a drug cartel operating out of New York City. At first, they only required him to drop off packages at local merchants, and collect the payments owed on the delivery of whatever illegal substance he passed onto them. After that, The Family, as that's what the mob organization called itself, gave him a different job. Then another, and another, until he became one of their most trusted employees. He became known as a 'Jack-of-all trades' because he'd been willing to do anything The Family asked of him, and people began calling him Jack because of it.

That was a couple of years ago, and somehow, the name just clung to him like cheese to macaroni, regardless of the fact he didn't work for those people anymore. Now, he drifted from country to country; trying to stay hidden. Trying to stay alive. Too many people wanted him dead, and only because they thought he knew too much. But after being on the run for two years, it was becoming tiresome. And he was sick to death of continually having to watch over his shoulder, looking for whomever the New York family might have sent to silence him.

That's why he was here, in this crowded and smoke-filled bar, sitting across from the United States agents. He was making a deal with them. They would give him protection, a full pardon for all crimes he committed in the States, a new identity, and in turn, he'd spill the beans on the Lewis family.

At the moment, the FBI agents weren't saying anything. They seemed to be more interested in the commotion which began seconds ago

somewhere behind Jack than they were with the informant sitting across from them. The disturbance was of no interest to Jack. He spent enough time in these types of establishments to know - if you didn't want trouble, you kept to yourself. But when one of the two men across from him visibly paled, and the other one ducked his head and hissed, "Holy shit! What's he doing here?!" Jack threw caution to the wind and turned around.

There was no way for Jack to know if the man making his way through the crowded bar was who his companions were referring to, but that did not prevent Jack from praying the guy weaving his way through the maze of people toward this table wasn't their subject matter. Not that Jack knew the man with the face set in stone. Truth be told, he'd never seen the six-foot three-inch man, and he did not have a clue who he was. But it wasn't the height, or powerful looking build, that had Jack praying to a god he'd never believed in. It was the simple fact the guy had a look about him that said, "Danger, give me a wide berth."

It appeared everyone in the bar received the same message because they were doing exactly that. Moving away from the man long before he neared them.

The man alone wasn't the cause for the commotion going on as people moved out of his way, closing the distance to where Jack and the two agents sat. It was the large dog following close to the man's heels that was causing the bar's patrons to press up against the walls or exit the building without haste.

Jack blinked several times, thinking his eyes were deceiving him. The dog wasn't a dog, as in a house pet. It was a… wolf? A wolf?! That just couldn't be.

Suddenly, there wasn't any more time for Jack to ponder this revelation. The dog's- rather, wolf's- owner stopped walking, and stood only a foot away from the bewildered Jack.

"You, Jack?" the guy gritted out in a tone that clearly said Jack had better say yes and do it now.

Jack swallowed, thinking the family had found him after all these years, and that this was the man who was going to end his life.

One of the agents stood up and had the nerve to ask Mr. Danger, "What in the hell are you doing here, Wolf?"

That question brought a dark look from Mr. Danger, and confused Jack because, if Mr. Danger was Wolf, then what in the hell was that creature behind the man, looking at him as though he were tonight's dinner?

"You, Jack?" Mr. Danger, or Wolf, or whomever the guy was, repeated and didn't look none too pleased to have had to ask a second time. Nor did he answer the question directed at him by the United States agent.

The second negotiator stood up and said, "I don't know what in the hell you're doing here Wolf, but this is our case; not yours."

This time, Mr. Danger's dark chocolate-colored eyes never left Jack's face; though Jack wished they had. He had the misfortune of seeing those emotionless eyes turn blacker than sin, and somehow Jack just knew this was trouble with a capital T.

"Once more, then I'm through. You Jack?"

Truth or lie? Those were Jack's options, but the man did not give him time to consider what his response would be. In the blink of an eye, he found his head slammed against the table, Mr. Danger's one hand holding his head there, while his other pointed at the two pale-faced agents and said, "Don't."

Even Jack winced at hearing that single spoken word. There was enough malice in it to have frozen Satan's balls.

"Goddamn it, Hunter!" Jack heard one of the agent's bluster and wondered who in the hell the man was speaking to now. "This man has information about the Lewis family, and Uncle Sam wants it! We're making a deal with him…"

"When I'm through, feel free to continue with your bargaining." That hand on the back of Jack's head grew tighter, if that were possible. It already felt as though a vice was attached to it and was squeezing his skull into the wood.

"What do you want, mister?!" Jack yelped, trying to break free, regardless of the fact it was a useless attempt.

"Nice to know you're not deaf," Danger said.

"For God's sake, Hunter! Let the man go!"

"Neko, watch them." Danger's voice didn't raise an octave, and Jack didn't need to wonder for long who in the hell Neko was because suddenly, there was one big mass of fur, with four paws attached to it, standing on the table less than six inches from his face, and the two agents were uttering curses, but not moving a muscle otherwise. "Sit down, kids," Danger suggested, and the two sickly looking men across from him did just that. "Now, I've been nice up 'til now. And I rarely repeat myself more than once. But I'm going to give this one more try. You Jack?"

Jack didn't try to claim otherwise. "Yes!" he screamed, and suddenly, the vice holding him disappeared, and he could move his head.

Danger sat down. "Was that so hard?"

Jack slid off the table, holding his head, and found his own chair. "What in the hell do you want, mister?!"

"I'm looking for a man named Pierre Bellefeuille," Danger's voice was flat as he spoke. "He also goes by the names Jon Du Bois, and Jon Du Pree. You know him?"

Jack might have thought the two agents had looked pale, but it was nothing compared to the green coloring his face turned upon hearing those names. "I've never heard of him!" he exclaimed, terror lacing his voice.

4

One agent was foolish enough to lean forward to protest, but the snarl directed his way by the enormous wolf standing on the table sat him back in the chair real quick. "Damn it, Hunter! Call off your dog!"

Hunter didn't, but he suggested the man not move again. "Next time, he'll bite."

"This man is under our protection!" the other insisted, but he hadn't been as stupid as his partner. Not one part of him moved in any way that would send a snarl in his direction.

"Your protection?" Hunter scoffed and leaned back in the chair. "And a fine dandy job the two of you are doing!"

Both men's faces turned beet red at that sarcastic remark. If Hunter chose to, he could snap Jack's neck before they understood his intent to do so and they knew it.

Jack's head was beginning to stop throbbing, but his anger was rising. "I'm making a deal with these men, so I don't have to talk to you!"

Hunter's expression didn't change, but his eyes did. Jack hadn't known eyes could turn any darker, but what he saw in them now reflected death. His. "I'll make you a deal, Jack. You tell me what I want to know, and I won't kill you. Take it or leave it."

Jack swallowed hard and didn't doubt for a minute the man meant what he said. "I don't know the person you asked me about!" he insisted, and suddenly his face was introduced to the tabletop once more. If he wasn't experiencing this firsthand, he would have believed no one could move with the lightning speed this demon from hell did. ·

"Try again," the demon said.

"All right! All right!" Jack screamed. "Just let me go, and I'll tell you!"

That promise got his face raised high enough to be propelled back into the tabletop once more. "Tell me now, or you're going to hurt."

Going to? If the guy didn't think a broken nose was painful, obviously he'd never had one!

"The last I heard, the man you're looking for was in El Salvador!" Jack exclaimed, and from there he sang like a bird, disclosing the general location of Pierre Bellefeuille's last known stronghold, and wondered which of the two men were the most dangerous. Bellefeuille, who was involved with terrorism, illegal drug trafficking or anything else outside of the law, or this man with a wolf named Neko, and death-filled promises. "That's all I know! I swear it!"

Hunter raised the man's head, then slammed it back into the table once more, just for good measure, before letting go. "Thanks, Jack." He turned to leave.

He was halfway to the door before he called his wolf to his side, and completely gone before anyone in the bar felt safe enough to move around. And it was another five minutes after that before the three men he'd graced with his presence did anything at all.

"Who in the hell was that?!" Jack screeched, holding his nose and trying to stop the bleeding with some paper napkins.

The two agents shifted in their chairs. "You don't want to know," one of them offered. Neither one of them felt like explaining to Jack that the man was on their side. Hell, most of the time, they didn't believe it themselves.

* * *

Outside the bar, Hunter Sundance Fisher was hailing a cab and feeling a surge of adrenaline. For over six years he'd been looking for Pierre and now, finally, he was closing in on the man he promised himself and his best and only friend, Mason Lafayette, he would bring to justice, or kill. Whichever option presented itself first, although Hunter preferred the latter alternative. Mainly because Pierre was the only man who vanished from his grasp continually.

"Soon, Mason," Hunter thought to himself as he opened the taxi door, allowing his wolf in first, then climbing in beside his companion of the last two years. He told the driver to take him to the airport, then leaned back in the seat once the vehicle pulled away from the curb and headed down the road. "Soon I'll have that man, and he'll pay for what he did to your mother on the night you were conceived."

It was bittersweet, knowing Mason would not exist if Pierre hadn't kidnapped and raped Rosalinda all those years ago, impregnating her. That child became his best friend from the cradle. But it did not change the fact Pierre was a twisted monster who needed to be put down like the rabid animal he was.

There were plenty of women and young girls, starting from the age of twelve, throughout the world who had fallen victim to Pierre's perversion of mutilating, torture and rape who would dance upon his grave, and Hunter aimed to put him there if it was the last thing he did in this lifetime.

Hunter admired Rosalinda for having had the courage to give birth to the child conceived through violence, and to her husband, Charles, for loving Mason as though he were his own. And in truth, he was glad Mason had been born because Hunter doubted he would have anyone in this world to call friend.

Not that he was looking for friendships. In his line of work, he could not afford to have people in his life. They could become targets for his enemies if they were to discover anyone they could use as leverage against him. But Mason was the only person he knew who could put up with his temper and laugh about it.

However, Hunter had not seen, or contacted, Mason for over four years because of that fear he had that someone might use him as a pawn. And it was why he broke all ties with his family and had his boss erase as many records of his existence as humanly possible.

He walked away. To keep them safe.

Hunter's own parents had been hiding from Pierre for thirty-three years and Hunter was not about to lead the man to them if he were to discover Hunter's identity.

Hunter wondered what Pierre's reaction would be, if, just before he took his life, he was to tell him whose son he was. As far as Pierre knew, the hitman he hired to kill them long ago succeeded in accomplishing the job. But in truth, he failed, and it would be their son who sent Pierre to his grave.

The twist was that Pierre had been his mother's stepbrother, although when Pierre's father passed away, that unfortunate situation ceased to be a reality. Grandma Annette had not adopted Pierre when she married his father. He'd been a full-grown adult at the time and there was no need to provide for him. Even then, good ol' Uncle Pierre was neck deep in illegal activities and hiding from authorities.

It was how Hunter's parents met. His father had been a secret service agent and assigned to protect Jacqueline, Hunter's mother, and Rosalinda's best friend, from Pierre.

All ancient history now, and it was no longer about Pierre's vengeance against his parents that drove Hunter to track the man down. Nor was it because of what he did to Mason's mother. Hunter had met and spoken to enough survivors of the man's heinous acts over the years to keep the desire to see Pierre dead at the forefront of his mind.

It saddened Hunter that he had not seen his family in years, although he was kept appraised of his parents' health and his siblings' lives through the man he worked for. A man who had been a surrogate uncle to the Fisher and Lafayette children from the time of their birth.

However, Hunter missed his family. That fact was the reason he broke his resolve not to contact any of them when Cadman informed him of his sister Melissa's marriage. He called her from Somalia while on a mission to congratulate her. The connection had been horrible, but the

few times he'd been able to hear Melissa's voice helped fill the longing to see her and the rest of his family for a time.

Melissa created popular computer games. She centered one of her best sellers on him and Task Force Ghost, although she changed the name of the special ops team to something fictitious. However, she based the commander of the team on Cadman and gave him a starring role in it. And although there were choices for which team member the player wanted to control, Hunter was the major attraction for most gamers wanting to complete the mission in the make-believe world. Hell. Melissa blatantly named the game Commando Hunter, and if that telephone connection would have been better, he would have told her it touched him, her honoring him like that.

But the weather in Somalia interfered with the signal, and it was a long way from there to North Dakota.

He knew distancing himself from his parents and siblings was by his own choice.

But four years ago, when he'd gone home to North Dakota to visit his folks and take part in the annual Fisher/Lafayette reunion, gave him the realization that one of his enemies might try to get to him through them. It frightened him enough to walk away from everyone he loved. During that time, a man from the area tracked him to where everyone was staying at the lake cabin located along the shores of Sacajawea, seeking revenge against him. Fortunately, the man hadn't reached Hunter's family, but he had gotten a hold of Mason's kid sister Daniela and…

Christ! That was definitely not a memory Hunter wanted right now. Not that Danny Sharp harmed Daniela, who had been sixteen back then. Hunter arrived before harm came to the girl. But reminiscing about his friend Mason reminded him of her. Remembering her prompted him to recall the twirp followed him around during the entire reunion, declaring she was going to marry him when she turned nineteen.

Hunter had done nothing throughout the reunion to encourage her. In fact, he had been downright mean to her in the attempt to change her infatuation into contempt so she would leave him the hell alone.

Sadly, once he achieved his goal, it was far too late when he realized he hadn't wanted Daniela's hate, after all.

Well, hell. It was past that time when she told him she was going to marry him, and in all honesty, he still hated the little twirp. She caused him to feel concern for her well-being when the last thing he could afford to do was to care about anyone.

He hoped she was having a miserable life. God knew he was.

www.ingramcontent.com/pod-product-compliance
Lightning Source LLC
Chambersburg PA
CBHW060529180626
46817CB00002B/490